D0211257

DANCE
OF THE
RED DEATH

BETHANY GRIFFIN

GREENWILLOW BOOKS
An Imprint of HarperCollins*Publishers*

Dance of the Red Death

Copyright © 2013 by Bethany Griffin

www.epicreads.com

The text of this book is set in 12-point Venetian 301 BT.

Book design by Paul Zakris

Library of Congress Cataloging-in-Publication Data

Griffin, Bethany.

Dance of the Red Death / Bethany Griffin.

pages p. cm.

Sequel to: Masque of the Red Death.

"Greenwillow Books."

Summary: In this continuation of a twist on Edgar Allan Poe's gothic short story,
wealthy seventeen-year-old Araby Worth, betrayed and bereft, discovers that she will
fight for her city and the people she loves, beginning at the prince's masked ball.

ISBN 978-0-06-210782-4 (hardback)

[1. Plague—Fiction. 2. Love—Fiction. 3. Wealth—Fiction.

4. Adventure and adventurers—Fiction. 5. Balls (Parties) —Fiction.]

I. Poe, Edgar Allan, 1809–1849. II. Title.

PZ7.G881327Dan 2013 [Fic]—dc23 2013011910

13 14 15 16 17 LP/RRDH 10 9 8 7 6 5 4 3 2 1

First Edition

 GREENWILLOW BOOKS

TO MY MOM, VICKI GRIFFIN, BECAUSE SEQUELS
ARE NEARLY IMPOSSIBLE, LIKE RAISING TEENAGERS,
BUT A MOTHER'S LOVE IS UNCONDITIONAL

CHAPTER
ONE

My father is a murderer.

Above the smoldering city, the airship rocks violently. The rain stings my face and cold gusts of wind threaten to dislodge me, but I can't look away from the destruction below.

From this vantage point, the city is simplified into rectangles and squares. Burning rectangles and shattered squares. Smoke pours from windows. The cathedrals are skeletons, open to the rain.

Kent, the one who built this amazing ship, stands at the wheel, fighting the wind that threatens to blow us off course. We are escaping, to recover from the ambush that almost killed us, and from the onset of the Red Death, the horrific new plague.

"You should go inside," Kent shouts over the wind and rain. I shake my head, shielding my face with my arm, and keep my eyes on the city. The river, a ribbon of frothy blue, winds through the symmetry of the streets, everything in miniature from this height, even the destruction.

It reminds me of the model city that Father built for my brother using toothpicks. A man who would spend hours gluing tiny slivers of wood into round towers with his son couldn't be the man who would destroy all of humanity, could he? Not on purpose . . . tears start at the corners of my eyes.

"Araby?"

Elliott is right behind me. I feel him, though he doesn't touch me. Not yet. I pull myself to a standing position, unwilling to let him see how afraid I am.

"It's cold without you." His voice is ragged, and I imagine that if I turn, I might see into him for once, but the ship lurches and I can't do anything but hold on. My knuckles are bone white against the railing as the ship is blown from side to side with each gust of wind.

My hair whips around us. Elliott touches the nape of my neck. Something between us has changed, but I'm not sure what it means, not sure what I feel, besides this terrible pain at the thought of what my father may have done.

"Do you still love it?" I ask. "This city?"

"Yes."

He's looking down, but I don't think he's seeing the bodies.

"We'll save it," he continues. "The city *and* the people. But we have to save ourselves first."

Our journey should be over soon. Kent is heading for the thickest part of the forest, between the city and Prospero's palace. It's far enough to be safe, but near enough that we can return quickly. Elliott runs his hands over my hair, trying to tame it. It's an impossible task, but the repetition is soothing, and part of me likes that he is so close.

A sudden fierce gust of wind drives the ship downward, and my stomach drops at our sharp descent. Kent yells something I can't decipher as he wrestles the controls. When he has steadied us, the roofs of the tallest buildings are just below. The highest is only a grid of rectangular beams. Others have furniture and potted trees.

Boys stagger out across one of the most dilapidated rooftops, half a dozen of them, laughing and shoving. When they see the airship, they stop, staring up at us and pointing. One of them raises a bottle and salutes us, but then he stumbles and spills his drink. All of them hold muskets, and some fire aimlessly toward the street. Then several of them fire up into the clouds.

"Damn it," Elliott says. "We are far too close."

And the wind seems determined to push us closer. The airship dips again. I drag Elliott toward the stern, still clutching the railing with one hand, until we are close enough to speak to Kent.

He pushes his goggles up on top of his head, his brown hair sticking out wildly.

"Another half hour and we might have passed unnoticed," he says darkly. After the sun went down, we would have been nearly invisible. But not now. Kent's hands move quickly, trying to take the ship up, but the storm keeps pushing us down. He curses under his breath, and I steel myself for a crash. The ship careens toward the closest building.

"We have to go higher," Elliott says.

A loud shout comes from the boys on the rooftop.

Discarded bottles of wine litter the roof, as if these young men have emptied someone's wine cellar. We are close enough to see that their faces, lifted toward us, are suddenly hostile.

"We pose no threat to them," I say, even as I grip Elliott's arm tighter.

"I don't think they care," Kent says as one of the boys raises his musket and aims it right at us.

As the barrel swings my way, reality seems to waver for a moment. Or maybe it's simply the way the world looks through the cold, driving rain. How can we be shot down when we are only beginning?

"Get down," Kent yells over his shoulder, still fighting with the wheel of the ship. Gunfire cracks and Elliott throws me to the deck, wrapping his arms around me.

Will bolts out of the cabin. "What was that?"

Kent turns the wheel hard. "Not my ship," he mutters. "Not my beautiful ship."

The sky is almost completely dark now.

Lightning flashes, and the boys whoop and shout and shoot their muskets wildly into the air.

April follows Will out onto the deck, and as it lurches, she falls into me. I put my arm out to brace her. Because despite nearly falling, she's still trying to fix her hair.

"We're a hell of a target," Elliott says to Kent. "They're drunk. They won't be able to resist. If we don't get farther away, they'll shoot us out of the sky, and there's nothing we can do."

"I'm trying to turn the ship," Kent retorts, "but I only have so much control. The wind is forcing us directly over them."

They'll laugh as they fire at us, as our ship crashes and burns. If there is an explosion, they will cheer. Because who cares about life when they could die any moment from the plague? I wonder if my brother would have grown up to be like them. Thoughtless and destructive. Father used to whisper that humanity didn't deserve saving. He said it with tears in his eyes, but I never thought he meant it. I know differently now.

"April, bring me a musket," Elliott says.

"You'll have to let go of Araby." She pushes herself up and steps back into the cabin, then emerges with two guns, one in each hand.

Elliott climbs to his feet. He smiles grimly as he takes a gun from April and aims. Now that he isn't holding me, the cold is shocking.

Beyond Elliott, Will approaches the railing. His coat

is loose, and it flaps around him as the wind howls and propels us forward.

April steps up beside him and raises her own musket.

"Don't shoot to kill," Elliott says. "They're just stupid drunk boys."

I stagger to my feet. I won't hide while my friends face this danger.

One of the boys cocks his head and aims his gun directly at me. Elliott shoves me toward Will, who staggers back, as if he's afraid to touch me.

The gunman shifts, following me. "I changed my mind," Elliott says. "Kill him."

April and Elliott fire their muskets simultaneously, and then we are directly over the building and blind to whatever is happening below.

I hold my breath. The boys are shooting at us, the sound nearly lost in the storm. April and Elliott reload. Will finally moves to stand beside me, our shoulders just brushing. The gash in my back from my escape through the tunnels begins to pulse.

"We'll be out of range soon," Kent calls.

Lightning crashes again, and thunder rolls through the sky. The deck of the airship trembles with it.

As we clear the roof, I join Elliott at the rail again. Despite an odd thrill at his protectiveness, if he or April shot one of those boys . . . I steel myself, but no one looks wounded, and they seem to have lost interest in us. Instead, they have gathered in a circle.

"You didn't hit anyone?" Elliott asks April. He sounds surprised.

"Neither did you." She lifts her gun, as if determined to rectify the situation, but she doesn't shoot.

"What are they doing now?" Kent asks. The wind has shifted, blowing into his eyes. He wipes the lenses of his goggles on his shirt, but as soon as he puts them back on, the lenses are covered with condensation.

"I wish I knew," Elliott says. "Araby, go to the cabin."

I ignore him. We all shift along the rail to keep them in view as the ship moves away.

Sparks fly from the huddle of boys on the roof, frightfully bright in the gray of the storm. They back away, revealing a rocket. Sitting harmless for a moment before it shoots up, trailing flame. Headed straight for us. April aims, but before she pulls the trigger, the rocket loses momentum and spirals downward.

The boys howl with disappointment, and Elliott, pushing his hair back from his face, laughs. His cheeks are flushed. "They sound like Kent when one of his inventions doesn't work." He's still smiling when a musket shot cracks again from below.

The boy who fired stands alone at the edge of the roof.

"Impossible," April scoffs. "We're too far away." She waves her scarf at him, and he waves back, friendly enough.

"Nearly impossible," Kent says through gritted teeth. The wheel spins uncontrollably before him. "Our steering mechanism has been hit."

The ship turns.

"We're completely at the mercy of the wind." Even now, Kent's voice is steady.

"I heard shooting." Henry's high-pitched voice carries perfectly. He steps out of the cabin, pointing his finger as if it is a gun. Elise is right behind him.

I go to push them back inside, but Will is ahead of me. He takes Henry by the hand, and all three disappear into the cabin.

"Araby, you're bleeding again," April says, coming over to me. "This needs to be stitched right away."

She's right. The wound has reopened. I can feel it now, soaking through my dress. Unlike the rain, it's warm.

I'm starting to sway, and it's hard to say whether it's from the motion of the airship or the loss of blood.

Elliott lifts me off my feet, careful not to touch my wounded shoulder.

"Will we crash?" he asks Kent.

"Depends on the wind. We won't make it to the forest, though." We had planned to land there, just for a day or two, to recoup as we decided the best way to return to the city, to put things right.

"How far can we get?" The rain has plastered Elliott's fair hair back from his face.

Kent shrugs, but above his goggles his brow is creased. "We're headed straight for the swamp."

CHAPTER
TWO

MY FATHER IS A MURDERER. MY BROTHER IS DEAD, and my best friend is dying of the disease that my father may have created. It's a refrain that's repeated over and over in my mind, through feverish dreams, and even now. And yet . . . my father is the gentlest man I know. He saved us from the contagion. I put my hand to the porcelain mask covering my face—my father's greatest invention.

I blink several times because I don't want to cry, though I'm alone on the deck of the airship. The crashed airship. We're tethered between the two tall chimneys of a stately manor house. It must have been abandoned years ago, consumed by the expanding swamp.

From where I'm leaning on the railing, I can see the gatehouse where carriages would have paused before bringing guests to a ball. Only its rotting gables make the structure at all recognizable, since the rest of it is cloaked by the tentacles of swamp plants. In front of the gatehouse are two stone posts, topped with lions' heads. One has fallen and nearly disappeared into the murk. The bog ripples around the other.

Behind me, from the roof of the house, is the sound of hammering and an occasional muttered curse. We were blown far off course, and eventually Kent was able to rig the steering for long enough to land on this roof. Otherwise, we would have landed in the swamp. He and Elliott are making permanent repairs to the ship now. We've been here for two days, and I've been asleep for most of that. Will did his best, but he isn't a physician, and I can feel the burn of the gash across my back. Each movement pulls the careful stitches that he used to close the wound.

We managed to get out of the city, but getting back won't be as easy as we had thought. We're trapped atop this sinking house, a decaying man-made island in the swamp. Yesterday I could still see smoke rising from the city, but today nothing is in the distance but green water, patches of swamp grass, and a few trees. It looks calm, but that's deceptive. The swamp is filled with predators. Diseased men. Snakes. Crocodiles.

Shading my eyes with my left hand to avoid pulling at my wounded shoulder, I watch insects land on the surface of shallow pools and reptiles slither this way and that. Though by foot we're days away from civilization, Kent and Elliott aren't sure this house is safe from Malcontent and his swamp dwellers. The man who chased Will and his siblings up the airship's ladder as we launched is now our prisoner. He was one of Malcontent's soldiers, and from him we've learned more of Malcontent's nightmarish plot to spread the contagion through the city.

Now there's also the Red Death, a new disease that's sweeping the city, killing much faster than the original plague. I adjust my mask, running my thumb over the crack inside. We have to get the ship repaired, and quickly. We are in danger here, and we aren't accomplishing anything that will improve the state of the city. Since I can't do much else, I've assigned myself the task of watching for anything out of the ordinary. Anything threatening.

But this study of my surroundings isn't enough to stop the refrain in my mind. My father is a murderer. My father might be a murderer. I need to know the truth.

When I was five years old, I sat on my father's shoulders to watch a parade. Mother had kept my twin brother, Finn, at home to recover from some illness, so it was just the two of us. As Father lifted me above the crowd, I felt completely and absolutely safe. When he placed me on his shoulders, I wobbled a bit and grabbed a handful of his hair to steady myself. Though he flinched when I pulled, he kept his hands on my knees.

The parade route was lined with children, and none of us wore masks. We had no fear of the crowds, no concern that contagion would flit from person to person. In that long-ago world, I was safe because my father was with me.

People watched the city streets expectantly, pressed close, straining forward. The thought of so many exhaling bodies together now horrifies me. It seems like someone else's memory, less real than the dreams that fill the spaces when my thoughts fade . . . dark dreams of murder and death. Only one person can dispel this never-ending doubt. I have to find my father.

The hammering has stopped. I grip the railing, ignoring the burn in my shoulder and watching the swamp, listening for footsteps crossing the deck of the airship. Elliott won't like that I'm out of bed.

"Araby?" I know the look I'll see on his face, the concern, before I turn. "You're bleeding again. Let me give you something for the pain."

My father used to mix sleeping drafts. Elliott prefers injections. My arm is dotted with bruises.

The sun is directly overhead, and a bit of sweat trickles down my back. The salt stings, but the pain is much deeper, nearly unbearable. A mosquito lands on my shoulder, and I swat it away with a wince I can't repress.

Elliott whispers, "I won't let anything hurt you."

But I've already been hurt.

When the steamship exploded and I thought he was dead. When Will took me below the city and betrayed me to a maniac. When I found the pamphlet proclaiming that my father created the plague that destroyed our city.

And I survived it. Without the help of Elliott's silver syringe.

I step back, shaking my head. Now that I'm healed enough to make the decision myself, I don't want his "help" with the pain.

"At least come into the cabin and rest," he says. "You need your strength."

He's right; I do. Even standing here for this short time has worn me out, and the railing is all that's keeping me up. When we return to the city, I have to be able to fight. I have to search for my father. April has the contagion, and if anyone can save her, Father can. So, for now, I let Elliott take my hand and lead me toward the cabin.

I cast one last look over the swamp. Does something move out there? I stop, watching for even the tiniest ripple, but everything is still, and then Elliott pulls me through the door and the main cabin of the airship, to the small sleeping chamber where the prisoner was held before Will and Elliott secured him someplace within the house.

I'm still wearing my green party dress, though it's inches shorter than it was when I put it on. April cut away everything that was ruined during our escape, leaving me with something close to indecent. One of the ragged edges catches on the doorframe, and there's a rustle of paper from one of my pockets as the journal in it bumps against my leg.

Father's journal has traveled with me across the city

and out of it, through ruin and fire and flood. And I'm grateful that no one has taken it from me. Whatever revelations are in this book, I want to know them first. In private, not the middle of a crowd—the way I learned about Father and the plague. I never want to learn something so earth-shattering so publicly again. And today is the first time I've felt clear-headed enough to read it.

"Someone should watch the swamp," I say as I lie down. "Malcontent's men could be out there." Elliott pulls the blanket to my chin and pats my good shoulder. He isn't listening, but I know he isn't blind to the danger we face from the swamp. He'll have someone on watch.

I keep my eyes closed until he shuts the door, and then I pull the journal from my pocket. The pamphlet that calls my father a murderer sticks out from where I tucked it inside.

The journal's paper is wavy from water damage, and it falls open to the first passage I ever read. The ink is still clear. *Everything is my fault.* My heart stutters.

But that is near the end, and I need to start from the beginning. Some of the pages stick together. Father is careful, though, and he'd never use an ink that bled, not for his research. I turn the page.

Spent the morning showing Finn how to use the microscope. Catherine dressed the twins in ridiculous matching outfits. She wants us to have their portraits painted. It's amazing how alike they are. I don't blame her for wanting to capture this stage. Already we've seen how fast they grow and change.

She doesn't know that all of our savings have been spent. The things she wants are reasonable. But my research is expensive.

There was never enough money when we were young. Not until after the plague.

Have been hired for a new project, trying to locate a defect in local cattle. A quandary about local breeding. I've put my personal research on hold.

The next five pages detail the vagaries of cattle breeding. On the seventh page it says:

Araby dressed up in white lace and ribbons. Catherine planned to take her to visit relatives. She is a beautiful child. Finn spilled a cup of grape juice on her, and the excursion was canceled. Catherine went to bed with a headache. Entire day of research wasted.

Is that all we ever were, all I ever was? A distraction from Father's work? But I push that aside. I'm not looking for clues as to whether Father loved me. I need information about the disease that destroyed our way of life.

Pages later, my father writes about working with Prospero, before he was prince. I nearly drop the journal. I try to think. Did Father ever speak of knowing Prospero, before? I force myself to keep reading, to learn all I can about the disease. It was originally supposed to kill rats. Only rats. But it did so much more.

This is confirmation of my worst fears. Whoever wrote the horrible pamphlet was right. My father created the Weeping Sickness. The last shred of hope that he was innocent shrivels.

My best friend is dying. My brother is dead. Because of my father.

But the one thing I can hold on to is that if he created it, he could also know how to cure it. The rumors Kent heard—that Father discovered something after Finn died—could be true. So it may not be too late for April. I read on until the words begin to swim on the page.

When I wake, the room is dim. Elliott is lying beside me, though there is another bed and the one we're in is narrow. He's propped on one arm, looking down at me. His eyebrows go up as I meet his eyes. The look on his face is gentle, and I have a distinct suspicion that he was stroking my hair. For the first time since I've known him, he looks calm.

"How are you feeling?" he asks.

Crumpled. Dazed. The pain in my shoulder is a dull burn.

"Why am I so groggy?" This room is like being enclosed in a box. "Did you give me something after I fell asleep?"

He doesn't have to answer. His silver syringe is on the table, beside the makeup bag that April keeps saving and returning to me.

"You were crying out in your sleep. You needed it."

"I told you I didn't want anything." I shove away from him. How dare he? As I sit up, my hair falls against my mouth.

I put my hand to my face, hoping to touch cool porcelain, but my fingers find only skin. My mask is gone. Elliott isn't wearing his, but then he rarely does.

My father's last warning was not to take my mask off. And I know he wouldn't give idle warnings.

"Elliott, where is it?" My voice is angry.

He tries to take my hand, but I pull it back. "Don't worry, it's here." He reaches under the bed and holds up a black velvet bag with a drawstring. The same sort of bag we used to store our masks at the Debauchery Club.

I lean forward to take the bag from his him, and as I do, something rustles beneath the light coverlet. I fell asleep reading Father's journal, never expecting that I would wake to find Elliott in bed beside me.

Elliott isn't one to wait. What if he drugged me so that he could take the journal? Would he have returned it? I shift, sliding my leg over the book to keep it from rustling. I'll show it to him, but not yet. Not until I've read everything. I open the velvet bag, extracting my mask. Dirt stains the line of the ugly crack, like a scar, but it won't make the filter less functional.

Elliott stretches as I slide the mask on.

"They put us in here so that we could have some privacy," he says with a smirk.

I look away, pretending to examine the oil painting of the sea on the far wall, determined not to let Elliott know that it makes me nervous, being so near to him. Determined to ignore his innuendos. To hold on to my anger at him.

"Privacy while we recover," he adds, this time without the mocking tone. And now I do look at him. His shirt is open, and the side of his neck is pink and shiny.

I reach out but stop short of touching the painful-looking burn. "But you were working on the repairs with Kent." I had assumed he had recovered from the injuries he sustained when the ship he was on exploded.

"I did what I can. Will is helping Kent finish. I asked April to watch the swamp, since you were so worried. You and I both need to regain our strength. We have a struggle ahead."

"A struggle ahead," I repeat. Now his eyes have that fevered look, and I am drawn to it despite myself. Before I met him, I didn't know how to fight. But now I know what it feels like to have that power. And when he looks at me with the fervent expression that he usually uses for his revolution, something inside me melts.

He smells of soap, despite our flight from the burning city and our days in the swamp. When we were fleeing the city, I kissed him as if our very lives depended on it. The city was on fire below us, and I wrapped my arms around him and lost myself. The memory makes me blush.

But he drugged me, though I told him not to. Can I trust him?

He's ruthless.

But I like that about him. Perhaps my goal should be to become more like Elliott. A fighter. A revolutionary. Both of our fathers are murderers. Maybe we deserve each other. Maybe he can't trust me either.

"Araby?" Elliott is holding out a jar of salve, while fumbling to unfasten the last button on his shirt. "Since you're here . . ." His shirt falls to the floor.

Even in the dimness of the cabin, I can tell that some of his wounds are bad. Elliott's back is crisscrossed with fresh bruises and burns over the scars that have already healed. There's a long scrape where some part of the steamship must have hit him when it exploded. He's lucky to be alive. We all are.

When I dip my fingers into the ointment, they tingle immediately. Elliott gasps as I touch him, and then relaxes. I let my fingertips linger on his skin. The mocking smile has disappeared when he turns toward me. His eyes are wide, and the look in them might seem guileless if I didn't know better. In the semidarkness his hair is a dark burnished gold.

I go completely still, focused on our nearness.

My heart speeds up.

Flustered, I dip my fingers back into the salve and tear my eyes away from his face, searching for burns that need soothing. My fingers catch on a gash, and we both jump a little bit.

"You have so many scars," I say softly.

His muscles tense. I know what I've done. Once before he made me feel the scars from Prospero's torture. But I've never seen the extent of them. He was just a boy when he endured this. No wonder he hates Prospero so viciously.

"Your fists are clenched," I say, in something close to a whisper. I take one of his hands and gently pry the fingers apart, forcing him to relax, threading his fingers through my own. "I'm sorry."

He closes his eyes, and when he opens them he's back with me. Not just with me, but focused on me. His attention sends chills through me.

The air in the cabin is unnaturally still. In this moment, Elliott and I are the only people in the world.

He shifts forward, all lithe grace and strength, like a big cat. Something dangerous. But I don't feel like prey. Not exactly.

We stare at each other. I can't trust him, but for all his ulterior motives, he's never abandoned me. His free hand is at my waist, snaking around me, pulling me close, then even closer.

The door creaks open.

"Sorry to interrupt," Will says. He stays in the doorway, and his shadow is elongated by the candles in the room behind him. Will is tall, but never insubstantial, like the shadow that falls across me and Elliott. Across the bed. When Will steps into the cabin, his dark hair falls forward, but it can't hide that his cheeks are flushed, as if he is embarrassed—or upset.

I pull away from Elliott, my own face heating up. Of all the people to see me here, with Elliott, Will is by far the worst.

"For whatever reason, I've been put in charge of medical duty," Will says.

"No," I say, looking up into his eyes. His very dark eyes. "No more sleeping medicine."

Whatever Elliott gave me is finally wearing off, and I'm beginning to feel more like myself, more aware. The burning pain of my wound is growing, too, but it's a price I'm willing to pay to be alert.

Will's voice is soft. "Lie on your stomach, sweetheart. I want to get a good look at the stitches."

The throwaway endearment takes me back to the Debauchery Club. A simpler time when I didn't know dark secrets and wasn't trying to help save the world. But it doesn't wipe away his betrayal. He touches my good shoulder to try to help me, and I brush him off.

Elliott sits up, scooting down to the foot of the bed. He doesn't even try to hide his smirk from Will.

I lie down gingerly, trying to pretend that nothing hurts. I won't give either of them a reason to medicate me. My shoulder stings as Will peels the bandage from the gash. He's gentle, but my eyes still fill with tears.

"It's better," he says, sounding more genuinely relieved than a person who gave me to a madman, who left me to die, has any right to be. "The stitches are holding, and it doesn't look infected."

"Thank you," Elliott says in the voice he uses for servants.

Will's hands still for just a fraction of a second. "You're welcome, sir," he says, his tone remote. He won't let Elliott think it bothers him. But I know it does.

"I have to cook dinner now." Will rolls up the unused bandages, not looking at either of us. "No one else seems to know how. The rich have so few useful skills."

He lets the door slam behind him.

"I have some useful skills," Elliott calls.

My face burns at the suggestive tone of Elliott's comment. Here we are, sharing this narrow bed, and Elliott still hasn't put his shirt back on. But April's unmistakable laugh is the only response.

April is supposed to be watching the swamp for intruders. Why is she outside the door to this cabin?

Bedsprings squeal as I try to sit up, and I can't hold back a gasp at the sudden pain in my shoulder. Elliott reaches to help me, but my elbow hits the burn above his ribs and he groans. I grit my teeth.

"Try to hold it down, you two," April calls. "There are children on this ship."

"There's nothing to hold down," I mutter, swinging my legs over the side of the bed and standing. I leave the journal hidden under the blanket and then pick up Elliott's shirt. He hesitates, as if wanting to say something, but finally takes it.

"Promise not to drug me again," I say, looking into his very blue eyes.

"I promise," he begins, but I can tell he doesn't know how serious I am.

"I don't need it," I tell him. "I'm stronger than I was before. We have to get back to the city as soon as we can." I try to imagine what it will be like returning to a city that flooded and burned at the same time, with the Red Death striking people dead in the streets. I have to prepare myself. To be brave.

"Araby," Elliott says. "I know you're worried about your parents. Your mother . . ."

Mother. I've been so focused on Father and his secrets, but she is trapped in the prince's castle. And Elliott wouldn't have mentioned her without a reason. I narrow my eyes.

"While you were sleeping we decided not to go back."

CHAPTER
THREE

When we left the city, it was to regroup—
to pull ourselves together before returning to face
Malcontent's rebel army and the plague. To find my
father, the only man who could tell us how to stop the
death around us.

"We'll be going to Prospero's palace instead," Elliott
says. "For weapons. I know where the storeroom is.
Kent and I have discussed this for hours. We can get in
quickly, surprise the guards, load the airship, and then
rejoin my men to fight Malcontent."

"Not going back to the city?" This is wrong. We
have to go back and find Father. We have to save April.
Weapons won't cure her.

And I've been to Prospero's palace. Even with the airship,
how can we slip in and out with even a few weapons? More
likely Prospero will capture us all and torture us for fun.

I put a hand to my mask, drawing a deep breath. But Elliott isn't finished.

"We'll still be returning to the city eventually, just—" He stands, placing one foot behind him, as if he's bracing for an attack. "The way we fled, I can't go back empty-handed."

Prospero is hiding from the plague, far from the city, in the fortress where he has complete and total control. Going there is a suicide mission. Elliott and I barely made it out last time we visited.

"Elliott—"

"We had to leave the city." He cuts me off. "But we are no better off now than when we left. What can we expect to accomplish when we walk back in? We have Prospero on one side, Malcontent on the other. But Prospero doesn't care anymore, not with the Red Death raging. With his weapons—"

"Weapons that he's likely to just give us?" My voice is rising.

"He won't be expecting an attack from the air. We can land right above the armory."

"But he'll see us coming. The ship is rather conspicuous."

"Not at night. Not during one of his parties. I'll sneak into Prospero's lair to steal what I need, but I don't want to sneak back into the city. I want to return victorious."

Of course he does. We all have our fantasies. I could tell him that I want things to go back to the way they were, that I want my father to be a hero, that I want my mother to be safe, that I want my biggest decision to be what to wear to the Debauchery Club. But life isn't that simple. And I can see that he won't listen, not now, but this discussion is far from over.

I gather my shredded skirts and sweep out of the room into the main cabin. A heavy wooden table sits in the center of the room. Maps and navigational instruments have been scattered across it. April is standing at the opposite side of the room, and Kent is sitting at the table.

"There you are. I thought maybe you'd died in there," April says lightly, and then her eyes go wide, as if she's shocked herself.

It isn't like her to joke about death. April has always tried to ignore death, making her driver go out of his way to avoid the corpses in the street—but ignoring the contagion is impossible for her now. Maybe it is for me too. I suddenly realize I have an open wound, in the swamp, with two plagues raging. Sometimes I feel like the world is waiting for all of us to fall ill. For all of us to fade and die.

Despite the humidity, April is wearing long sleeves. A finger of contagion climbs the back of her neck. She sees that I am looking and shakes her hair back to cover it.

"April . . . ," I begin. We should start over.

"I'd hug you," she says. "But, you know . . ."

I nod. There are many reasons for us not to hug—her

illness, my wound—even if we were the sort of friends who usually embrace. Which we aren't.

At the table in the middle of the cabin, Kent is examining some mechanical bits and pieces that I assume are for repairing the ship. He has somehow managed to be on everyone's side at once. I first saw him with my father, but he's also friends with both Elliott and Will. And here in the cabin of the airship that he designed, April is sitting very close to him. So close that Elliott's eyebrows go up. He may be April's older brother, but he should know it's too late to worry much about her virtue. Elliott was the one who sponsored us so that we could be members of the Debauchery Club, though Kent is far from the sort of boy who she pursued there. Those were frivolous boys in velvet jackets and eye shadow. Kent is overly serious, with messy brown hair and thick spectacles.

I reach out to the shiny metal object that lies on the table in front of him.

"As soon as I can repair these parts, we can steer the ship again," he explains.

"And then we can leave this place," April says in a low voice. "Can you imagine the people who used to live here? How they must have hoped every day that the swamp would recede? They left their furniture, their clothing . . ."

"Where did they go?" I ask. "To the city?" It seems horrible when we all know how quickly the contagion swept through the more populated areas.

April shrugs. "They've been gone a long time. Everything is covered with dust or mold or falling apart. They're probably all dead."

"We should be able to leave very soon." Kent stands and walks to the doorway. "Maybe by evening. I prefer to fly the ship at night. Less attention that way."

Less attention from the people in the swamp? Or from Prospero's guards? I look over at Elliott. He's standing with his arms crossed over his chest.

"Another storm is brewing," Kent continues. "I'll stay with the ship, but everyone else needs to take shelter. Including you," he says to April, and they share a smile.

Elliott's eyebrows go even farther up.

"Where are the children?" I ask. They've barely ever been outside, and now a storm is approaching—one strong enough to blow them away.

"The children are sitting on the roof watching for intruders. I lent them my binoculars," Kent says. "They seem to enjoy being out there. Thom stays close, watching them."

Elise and Henry are so young. Is it safe for them to be watching the swamp? The willows and swamp grass surrounding the house could conceal any number of enemies. We have no shortage of them. The Reverend Malcontent wants to take over the city. He would execute me, the scientist's daughter, and he's already tried to kill Elliott once. Prospero is more devious, but I don't doubt he'd like to see all of us dead. And he'd love to have the airship that we're on.

Prospero has always been jealous of science and innovation. With something like this ship he'd have a way to take courtiers up above the city. They could hold elaborate parties. They could dance. But it would be a trap, because wherever the prince goes, there is always torture.

I cross the cabin, following Kent, and look outside. The blue-gray slate of the roof slopes gently toward the swamp. It is very quiet. I haven't once heard the high-pitched voices of the children.

"Will feeds all of us," April says. She stands at my shoulder and gestures to the thin line of smoke coming from one of the two chimneys. The one that's intact. Kent smashed into the other one when we landed. "He's been using one of the fireplaces to cook, since Kent won't let us have any sort of flame near his precious airship." She winks at Kent. He is tinkering with something and doesn't notice. "Thom took guard duty to stay out of Elliott's sight." April meets my gaze. Thom is the dis-eased boy who rescued us from drowning. And then we rescued him from the city and from Malcontent. He's covered in scabs that weep with pus. That's the best April has to look forward to, if she doesn't die. We have to find my father. How can Elliott want to waste time going to Prospero's palace?

When I glance over at Elliott, he's restless, tapping his

fingers against the table where Kent is working. Agitated.

A loud crash makes all of us jump. But it isn't an explosion. The sky is darkening. Lightning flashes, and more thunder follows.

Elliott strides past me, out the door. April and I follow him onto the deck.

From here I can smell the corruption. The encroaching swamp is taking over everything. Leaves decompose in the marsh around us, and the house itself rots underneath us. The two chimneys that the ship is tied to are part of the main section of the house. Three wings branch off to form a letter E. Except that one of the wings seems to have fallen away. Some rooms are completely open to the elements, like the dollhouse that I had as a child. Father built it, and Finn used to put lizards and frogs in the rooms. He would laugh as they knocked the carefully placed furniture about.

Elliott is at the rail. His hair gleams, and even the way he stands evokes a sense of purpose.

I walk up beside him and look straight down. The marsh water ripples dark under the green slime that floats across the surface. The long grasses move, not with the wind, but against it. Fallen trees lie in the murk, in various stages of decay. Something is moving in the swamp. Something alive and hungry.

"Crocodile." Elliott's lips quirk into an almost-smile at my shudder of revulsion. It makes a loud splash, as if to confirm Elliott's statement.

Dark clouds are massing over the swamp, and lightning strikes once more. The grasses shake. The crocodiles splash, restless.

"Kent wants us to go down into the house," April says. I jump at the sound of her voice. She's gotten quieter since she's been sick. She's biting her lip. The old April never looked so solemn. She leads us off the ship. Elliott takes my hand, but he doesn't pull me along. Only a slight gap lies between the wooden steps of the airship and the roof of the house, but he helps me down.

Henry and Elise are sitting in the shadow of one of the chimneys.

"Will won't let us play anywhere interesting," Henry complains as we approach. "There's nothing to see from here, even with binoculars."

With the crocodiles slithering through the murk, and who knows what else might be lurking out there, Will was right to make them promise to stay near the ship. I want to grab Henry and hold him close to keep him safe.

"Araby!" Elise spies me behind Elliott and leaps up. She throws her arms around me, but Elliott keeps hold of my hand. Elise's eyebrows draw together, and I know that she is frowning behind her mask.

The wind picks up, so even if I knew what to say to her, the words would be whipped away.

"Why must we always wait until the storm is actually upon us?" April asks no one in particular. This is the old

April. "We need to hurry. My hair simply cannot survive much more."

I smile, but she's right. The rain is coming—I can see it out over the swamp, moving toward us. These tiles will be slick and treacherous when it hits. I put my arm around Elise, then drop Elliott's hand to take Henry's.

"Show me how to get into the house?" I ask Elise, and she nods, pleased to help.

The breach in the roof isn't far, but it gives me pause. It's as if monstrous jaws have bitten a chunk from the top of the house. The uneven hole left is wide enough for a person to climb through.

"There was already a hole in the roof," April explains. "Kent just used a crowbar to make it bigger, so that we can climb inside." The rain pounds the roof behind us, gusting through the swamp. All of a sudden, everything is moving.

"Go ahead." I urge the children toward the wooden ladder that peeks up out of the hole. By the time April has climbed down, the storm is crashing against the house and the line of trees is doubled over.

Elliott's hair is plastered to his face, and his shirt clings to him.

"I should stay with Kent," he says. He grimaces, but I can't tell if it's from the rain or the idea of me down-stairs with Will.

I nod. He can't leave Kent to face the storm alone.

Ignoring the driving rain, I grab his arm. It doesn't

matter that I don't trust him, or that I don't agree with his plans. He can be the hero that the city needs. I'm not willing to embrace him, but I hold his arm tightly for just a few seconds longer than I should. As I'm turning away, he spins me back and kisses me fiercely. And then he's fighting the wind, back across the roof.

Not until I'm halfway down the ladder do I pause to catch my breath and push the wet hair back from my face. I lean my forehead against one of the rungs while my heart slows.

Below, the house groans, settling perhaps into its final repose. Into the swamp. I continue to climb down. The wood floor looks slick with blood, but it's just soaked with rainwater from the storm. Still, the boards seem to sag under my feet, so I move quickly to the other side of the room, where the roof above is intact.

A fire crackles in the hearth, and the glow, combined with the oil lamp, contrasts cozily with the rain that pounds through the hole and against the roof and windows.

This place reminds me of the homes of Mother's rich relations, who we used to visit when I was a child. The attic would've been a nursery, and bits of broken toys, a small desk where a child might have sat to learn to read, have been left neglected here.

Elise and Henry are nestled on a couch, and Elise makes room for me to join them. But April coughs, and I turn to her instead. She's fallen into an armchair. The diseased boy, Thom, stands behind her, holding a glass of water. If anything, his skin looks more horrible than ever, with weeping sores on his arms, as well as the one above his eye.

I can't believe April is allowing him to be this close to her. She *has* changed.

"How are you?" I ask, reaching for her hand. She pulls it away.

"I need a drink. And a hot bath. And then another drink." Thom holds the glass of water out to her. She makes a rude gesture. "Not that, a real drink." But then she smiles at Thom, a silent apology for being so abrupt. "Sorry," she says. "Wet hair is irritating, against the sores." She gestures to her neck but doesn't pull up the hair. She would rather be in pain than show what the contagion is doing to her.

She looks to Thom, as if waiting for his sympathy, and I feel a pang, knowing that this boy is the only one who understands what is happening to her.

"You can't possibly agree with Elliott," I say quietly. "You can't think that we should go to the prince's palace."

When she looks up at me, I see panic. "Everyone in the city is dying," she says. "No one can survive the Red Death. But some people can live with the contagion."

I don't argue with her. A girl died of the Red Death right in front of me. I don't doubt that conditions in the city are dire.

But April's sores are spreading, and there's no guarantee that she'll be like Thom. She's saved my life more than once. When I was suicidal over my brother's death, she did her best to distract me. She chose me to be her best friend, to take with her to the club. And now it is my fault that she is dying. When her father had us imprisoned in the tunnels, he said he could cure her of the disease. But she escaped with me instead, because he was going to kill me.

I was powerless to stop my brother from dying. But I'm not powerless anymore. I will save April, even if I have to fight her to do it.

We watch the storm through dirty windows. I eat, to keep up my strength, and tell stories to the children. Thom disappears down a spiral stairway, with a bowl of soup for Will and something for the prisoner. "The man that Elliott captured scares me," April confesses. "He reminds me of dark places under the city, and my father."

When we escaped the mob, the man followed Will and the children, clutching his musket and scaling the rope ladder. I'm afraid of him, too.

Henry and Elise, exhausted from chasing each other around the open spaces of the attic, curl up and fall asleep. April dozes in her chair, before the fireplace.

This is my chance. I'll slip away to read what I can of Father's journal before Elliott comes down. If I can find something certain about a cure, it might be enough to convince them to listen to me. I consider the spiral staircase, but that way leads to Will and Thom and the prisoner. At the far end of the attic, past the opening where we climbed down from the roof, is a hole in the floor, probably caused by water seeping down and rotting the wood.

I walk over and peer down. Below, I can see a wood floor covered with a rug. The distance is probably seven feet, eight? I sit at the edge with my legs dangling. If I can push myself away from the broken beams so I don't scrape my shoulder, I should be fine. As long as I don't twist my ankle.

I take a deep breath and drop, bracing for the pain of impact. But there is no impact.

Strong arms catch me, sliding around my waist.

Will. I would know him anywhere, even in this darkness. He still smells of the Debauchery Club, a hint of incense. The length of my body rests against his.

I can feel his heart beating. Rapidly. Unless it's mine.

He doesn't move. Maybe he's going to hold me here, against his heart, forever. Every nerve ending has come to life, making me painfully, horribly *aware*. His breath stirs my hair and his arm trembles from holding me up, but otherwise we are completely still.

"Thank you," I breathe.

"You're welcome." His voice is equally soft.

Will's dark hair has fallen over his face, hiding his eyes.

Without meaning to, I reach up and push his hair back.

That breaks his trance, and with a sigh, he finally sets me on the floor, carefully avoiding any contact with my injured shoulder.

Slowly, my eyes adjust to the dim light of the oil lamp sitting on a low table beside a faded velvet couch. The threadbare rug covers a large square of hardwood floor. It's a dilapidated sitting room in a house that is sinking into a swamp, but at this moment, as I stand beside Will, it looks warm and inviting. Even though it shouldn't.

CHAPTER
FOUR

WILL TURNS AWAY, LETTING HIS HAIR HIDE THE expression on his face. He gestures to the sofa. When I sit, it makes a terrible squealing sound.

My mother would be proud of how calm I am pretending to be. What will I do if he apologizes? My palms begin to sweat. But I wait. I won't make this easy for him.

When he faces me again, his smile is sad, but there's something in it that reminds me of the old flirtatious Will. Of a time when I spent entire days waiting to see him for a few moments as I entered the Debauchery Club.

"It was too terrible, what I did." He looks down at his hands. "You know I'm sorry, and I know it isn't enough."

It's only been days since he traded me to Malcontent in return for Henry and Elise. I understand why he did it. I would have done the same if my own brother had been taken by a madman. And that makes everything worse, because I can almost forgive him. Almost.

Tears well up from my traitorous eyes. Why couldn't he trust me to help him save the children? Why does it hurt so badly that he didn't?

He reaches out. I watch his hand, not sure whether I want to take it or slap it away. But it doesn't matter, because he pulls back. Though I try to hold back my tears, the effort makes everything worse, and suddenly I'm sobbing.

If Will held out his arms to me again, I might go into them. Afterward, I'd hate myself, but I'd let him comfort me. Instead, he looks away and lets me cry.

Minutes pass. As I struggle to compose myself, he hands me the cleanest handkerchief I've ever seen. How did he keep it so impossibly white after everything we've been through? I force my eyes away from it, but rather than look at Will, I survey the room. Something about it, the faded wallpaper, or perhaps the sloped ceiling, speaks of comfort and whispered confidences.

Will's voice is light. "I learned a few things at the club. A young lady in distress will invariably need a handkerchief. I've had plenty ruined with mascara."

I blot at my eyes, but the square is unstained. We're a long way from the Debauchery Club and the girl I was then.

Finally, I look back at him. In the partial light his tattoos are dark against his pale skin. They swirl upward, disappearing into his hair.

"You came here to be alone," he says quietly.

"So did you." I say, just to prove to myself that I can still speak. I dab at my eyes one last time.

"Our prisoner is down here, and I'm on watch until Elliott sends Thom to relieve me." His eyes move toward the corridor, and then back to the sofa, to me.

"I'm just going to sit here and read." I hold up the journal. He knows what it is. He handed it to Malcontent right after giving me over, after all.

"I'll stay close, so I know that you're safe."

I could spit out a thousand retorts to that, but I have no energy for accusations. And though I wanted to get away from everyone else, maybe I don't want to be completely alone.

He settles in a corner, nearly hidden by shadows, so I curl up at the end of the couch and open the journal. April needs answers. And maybe, while searching for information about the diseases, I can find some reassurance for myself.

I pick up reading about the years when I was very young. The city was in chaos even back then, because the swamp was rising into the lower city, contaminating the water. The Weeping Sickness was released into that madness.

I skim these pages quickly, but as I reach the second half of the book I force myself to slow down. By then, all Father wrote about was the disease.

Prospero is collecting scientists and holding them in his castle. He claims that one of his men has found a way to rid the city of the encroaching swamp. He told me over dinner, laughing to himself. He's been keeping the poor fellow in his dungeon, in chains. "Perhaps," he said, "perhaps I'll allow him to complete his life's work. It will make the city much more pleasant for your children, if they live to adulthood, don't you think?"

As always, I ate my soup without comment. "Take care of my rat problem," he said. It wasn't a request.

I told him the disease is volatile. Unpredictable.

"The city won't miss a few immigrants," he said. "More come in boats every day."

Now all the boats have rotted and fallen to bits in the harbor.

I keep going, absorbing as much as I can, until I turn to a mostly blank page inscribed with the words

My son is dead.

I lay my head against the back of the couch, trying not to think. Even with my eyes closed, I can see my twin brother. I won't think of his bloodless hand, how I let go but then lunged back and tried to grab it after we dropped him into the corpse collector's cart.

When I open my eyes, Will is watching me. He's sitting across the room, with his back against a wall of exposed brick. Once again, his hair has fallen forward, but it isn't enough to hide his concern.

The misery in this room is palpable.

I force myself back to the journal, past that terrible page.

> Prospero lied to me. He's done nothing to check the rise of the swamps, and I do not know the location of the pumping station that he promised would cleanse the water. He won't distribute masks to the people. I have only one threat left, and I don't think he believes me.

And then the last pages are about the Red Death.

> While the Weeping Sickness is passed through the air, the Red Death is contracted through both the air and the drinking water. I have nothing more to threaten Prospero with. All is lost. He's taken my wife. My son is dead. I will not be the one to save the city.

I shut the book and stare into space for a long time. What about me? Did Father think I was lost too? Was he right?

* * *

I wake to the thump of a footstep against the wood floor and sit up, clutching the journal to my heart.

The room is still shadowy, though light is streaming in through the hole in the roof and the filthy windows.

"Good morning." Elliott stands a few feet away, silhouetted by the light that's filtering in.

"Good morning," I reply, trying to hide my surprise. I dart a glance to Will's corner, but he's gone. I tuck the journal under my skirt and gesture toward the rest of the couch. "Do you want to sit?"

He collapses beside me so quickly that I'm surprised he waited for my invitation. Elliott isn't one for waiting. The skin under his eyes looks bruised. He hasn't slept.

"The storm is over?" I prompt.

He nods. "April is watching the swamp. She's the best shot, and she was feeling restless. I think she wanted to get away from the children." He gives me a sidelong look. "We'll be leaving today."

"To go back to the city?"

"Araby . . ." He reaches out, as if to embrace me, but I put out my hands to hold him back. So he twines his fingers through mine, and the way our hands fit together feels extremely personal in just the way I wanted to avoid.

"We need to talk," I say.

"Do we?" His expression is sardonic, but I ignore it. I have the right to voice my opinion.

He has to realize that if we go to the palace, everything

is lost. The echo of my father stops me before I even start.

Thom pokes his head around the corner. "Did you move the prisoner? The door is open. And he's gone."

Elliott is on his feet immediately. "Go tell Kent and April. We need to arm ourselves," he says. "He's danger-ous." Thom's eyes dart back to the corridor. He's hiding something, but Elliott doesn't see his face. He's looking at Will, who has entered the room behind the boy. Thom hurries away.

Will stops, considering Elliott, but before he can say anything, Elliott lunges at him. "You did this," he accuses. "You let him go."

Will struggles to hold him back.

"You were going to kill him." Will's voice is quiet but no less accusing.

"Yes. I was. How long ago? How long has he been gone?"

Will shrugs out of Elliott's grip and crosses his arms as he answers.

"He left during the storm. His only crime is having the disease and trying to get away from the city."

I think it's Will's nonchalance that pushes Elliott over the brink. He slams into Will, shoving him against the wall. Elliott's fist connects once, and then Will is fighting back. He hits Elliott right above the eye, and Elliott's head whips back.

Elliott wipes a thin line of blood from his eyebrow and says, "He manipulated you. His crimes were much worse than that. I recognized him—he used to work for my uncle, before he caught the contagion. And then he started doing Malcontent's dirty work. Ravaging the lower city. Killing children and feeding them to crocodiles."

Will pales. "The Hunter?"

"Ah, you've heard the stories?"

Will nods.

"He'll wait until the right moment to kill us," Elliott says. "The moment that it becomes a challenge. If I were you I'd stick close to your siblings until we get out of here." Will reacts to this like it's a threat, shoving Elliott backward.

"Why didn't you tell us who he was?" he shouts. Elliott scoffs, more than ready to fight.

I throw myself between them, facing Elliott. My arms are out to my sides, as if we are all children playing some game. But the anger in this room is far from childish.

"They want to kill us all, you know," Elliott says. "He told me about Malcontent's plan. They were told to attack, to come into contact with as many people as they can. They are going to infect everyone in the city."

Will is shaken. "He told me about his family. He couldn't live with them, because of the disease, but he was worried . . ."

"You are a fool." Elliott steps forward so my hand is pressed against his chest, and he speaks to Will over my shoulder. "We won't be safe until Kent can get us out of here, and even then, you've released a killer back into the swamp."

A bruise is forming around Elliott's eye from Will's punch, in the same spot I hit him after he dangled me over the river.

"You tortured him." Will slumps against the wall.

"I got information," Elliott says. "You heard a pack of lies. Which of us is more noble?"

I push Elliott farther from Will. "That's enough."

"Elliott," Kent calls from the room above. "We're missing a musket. We need to get out of here—"

"Did you give him a musket?" Elliott's voice is so low that it's practically a growl. "Did he tell you that he was afraid of the swamp, so you stole a gun for him?"

"No."

Will looks away from Elliott's stare. I can see by the way that his shoulders slump that he realizes the extent of his naïveté. And Elliott's anger is only building. The tension is making him practically vibrate.

Standing between them isn't enough. I take Elliott's hand. He is the one angry enough to attack. But my gesture goes deeper than that, and I know it. He looks down, and I meet his eyes. Once, I thought Will would save me. From myself. But he couldn't even do that. I pull Elliott to the ladder, and he climbs up to help Kent.

I glance back. Will knows. And he knows he doesn't deserve to feel hurt, but he does. I can see the conflict in his face before he turns and walks out of the room.

I hesitate a moment before following him. Only one door in the hallway is open, the one leading to an abandoned bedroom.

"Did you keep him locked in here?" I ask Will, but don't cross the threshold.

"In the closet," he says. "Otherwise he could have escaped." He gestures to the window. He obviously doesn't want to talk, and now that I'm here, I don't know what to say to him.

A cricket scuttles onto the toe of my right shoe. I jump back, stopping only when I hit the door across the hallway. My hand knocks against the doorknob, but it doesn't even jiggle. It's locked. If the prisoner wasn't kept in one of these rooms, why are they locked? Would a family, abandoning their home, lock doors inside it?

Curious, and seeking a reason to pause here with Will, I walk the entire corridor, trying every door. Those on the right are locked. The left are open. The crickets are everywhere now, creeping through the darkness. Spiders spin elaborate webs in the corners. I wouldn't be surprised if there are mice in the walls, and if there are mice there are probably snakes. I repress a shudder.

I push hard against one of the locked doors, but it doesn't give even slightly.

"The one at the end of the corridor is loose," Will says. He's right. The lock does wobble. But it's intact, so none of my companions must have been interested enough to break it.

I hit the door with my good side, but even so, pain radiates across my back. I gasp and lean against the wall while the pain subsides. Will just watches.

"Well," I say, "are you going to help?" I can't understand why none of them have investigated this mystery. Anything could be hidden behind a locked door.

"Araby!" April calls from upstairs. "Hurry, we're leaving!"

"Don't forget this," Will says, handing me Father's journal.

"Thank you." I straighten up and give the door one last kick. "I'll want to share it with Elliott."

Neither of us says anything more while we gather our gear and climb to the roof.

As soon as we emerge, I'm immediately covered with dew, or what passes for dew in the thick humidity of a swamp. The precipitation is visible on my arms, gleaming in the weak morning sun.

A drop runs the length of my dress and falls to the blue-gray slate tile.

April is waiting. She gives Will a quick, disgusted look, and then ignores him, leaning against me. "Thank God we're leaving. I hate the swamp."

He disappears, walking around the ship, leaving us alone.

April and I haven't had any time to talk. Part of me longs to discuss the pain of what happened with Will. Perhaps she could help me make sense of it. Perhaps she could unravel what's happening between me and Elliott, how our fake romance seems to be turning into something very real. And maybe she could tell me about that secret half smile that she can't quite hide whenever Kent is near.

She leads me to the deck of the airship and right to Kent. I'm surprised that he isn't scurrying around the ship, double-checking everything.

"How is Will?" he asks.

"His lip is bloody," I say, though I know it isn't what he's asking. Kent looks at me, and I can see that he understands. We are, both of us, throwing in our lot with Elliott. For the good of the city. And for April.

"Your father was my hero," Kent says. "*Is* my hero. Since I was a boy."

He wants me to tell him that the rumors are lies. I want him to say the same to me. Instead, neither of us says anything. We stare out over the destroyed landscape. The swamp has enveloped everything. The last remnants of a rose arbor are decaying even as I watch.

"Beautiful, isn't it?" Kent says finally.

I cast a sharp look at him, and he seems completely serious. What more does he see through his corrective lenses? April takes his hand.

"Elliott has been helping me with my inventions for years, since we met as boys. And Will is my closest friend," Kent says finally.

The way he's being pulled back and forth between his

two friends is more noble than what has happened to me. I've kissed both of them, after all.

"April is my best friend. My priority is getting her to my father. Not flirting. Or romance. That sort of thing can wait."

April is pretending she can't hear us, but I see the start of a tiny smile. She enjoys being the center of attention, even when it's because she's dying. My fear is cold and leaden in my stomach. Dying doesn't seem real to her yet; the sores are little more than a nuisance. In a few weeks, it will be much, much worse. Maybe even sooner. We do not have time to stop at Prospero's palace.

"Do you believe the rumors?" I ask. "The ones that say Father had some sort of cure? That he threw it away the night Finn died?"

"Partly. But I know he would never throw something so precious away. If he had a cure, he would have kept it. He would still have it."

Our eyes meet, and I feel a flutter of hope. Just because Father didn't write about it doesn't mean he never created it.

Kent considers me, still grasping April's hand. "In my experience, the only way to survive in this world is to find something to live for. For me, it was my inventions. For my father, it was perfecting these lenses that give me vision. For Elliott, it is power. Will hasn't found that something yet, but I think he's close."

"And what do you think it is?" My voice is harsher than it should be, given that last night I was so close to forgiving him.

"Helping people. Helping the weak."

I was weak. But I'm not anymore.

A splash from the swamp reminds us that we are all in danger. Kent turns to April. "The ship is almost ready to take off. I'll need a few moments. . . ." I leave them alone and go to find Elliott.

He's at the prow of the ship, close to the wheel, watching the swamp, gun in hand. This is my last opportunity to convince him that there's a chance for April and that she's more important than the way he looks when he returns.

Elliott knows what I'm going to say.

"What if there's nothing left?" he asks. "I've spent my life planning to save the city. What if there is nothing to save?"

I step forward, so that there is no space between us. His gun rests on the rail of the ship, but I'm touching his other side.

"What if you run away because you fear there is nothing left, and you discover later that people were waiting for you?"

He pulls away, balancing the musket with one hand and running the other through his already-mussed hair.

"The city is waiting," I push on. "You'll give them hope."

"That won't save them from the Red Death or from Malcontent."

"We'll find a way. Father didn't stand up to Prospero, but he knows things. . . ." If I'm going to throw my lot in with Elliott, if I'm going to convince him that we can save the city together, it's time to stop keeping secrets. I hold out the journal to him. "He wanted you to have this, remember? He didn't know that I had already taken it. I've read most of it, and he has insights about the Red Death." I take a deep breath and then plunge on. "He says the key is the water supply. In addition to the masks, we need clean water."

I can see Elliott's brain working. "The poorer parts of the city have almost no clean water. Their wells are tainted with rising water from the swamp. But if we could evacuate the poor areas, there is plenty of room in the upper city. . . . Do you really think that I can give them hope?"

He searches my face, and I resist the urge to look away from the intensity of it. He's nearly convinced.

"Elliott, you have to see this through."

"I never meant not to. Prospero, I had a plan for. And you were helping me with the masks. I had spies and soldiers. Even Malcontent I could handle, but the Red Death . . ."

"I know," I say softly. "But April needs my father, and we haven't got much time. You already have the plans for making masks. This is the last piece. You don't need guns."

"If we go back to the city, you'll be with me?"

A part of me wants to refuse. But if he needs me, how can I say no? The *city* needs him.

"Yes. The scientist's daughter on your arm. That's what you wanted."

His lips twist. It is what he wanted, but now that status is gone. My father has been named the greatest villain of all time.

"No, just you," he begins. "I want—" I tense at the urgency in his tone, but before he can finish his sentence, there is a high-pitched scream. A child's scream, from the direction of the swamp.

"Stay here," he says, and takes off, jumping easily from the airship to the slate roof of the manor house. Kent runs past me into the cabin, then bursts from the door carrying two muskets and follows Elliott. I try to run after Kent, but moving that quickly hurts more than I expected.

By the time I reach them, Will's there too, holding Henry, and Kent is kneeling beside Elise at the edge of a decorative stone parapet. She's pointing out over what was once a lawn, but now is just tree roots and muck.

The sun comes out from behind low, hazy clouds, and Elliott's fair hair gleams in the sudden brightness.

Beyond the parapet is a moldering staircase that was once inside the house, but is now exposed completely to the elements. The stairway turns twice, and the carved wooden banister is mostly intact.

"There's people," Henry says. He holds the binoculars out to Kent.

"Did you give him *my* binoculars?" Elliott asks.

"They're coming this way." Elise's voice is mesmerized, like she is looking at something both terrible and wondrous.

As if I am being pulled into Elise's imagination, I hear the splashing of someone running through the water. I follow the line of her shaking arm. A girl in a dress that used to be white appears through the vegetation, pulling someone behind her, barely paying attention to where she is putting her feet. The rank water is as high as her calves.

A shot cracks from the undergrowth. Elise screams again, covering her mouth with both hands. The girl in the swamp turns her head toward the sound but doesn't stop. She can't.

Will hands Henry to me, and I crouch down behind the rail of the parapet, pulling Elise with me. Thankfully, the railings are thick and ornate and haven't succumbed yet to the decay of the rest of the house. And we're four stories up. The shooter will have to get closer to pose any danger to the children.

"This way," Elliott calls to the girl, dropping to the stairwell and bounding down the stairs. April has gotten to us now too. I'm aware of her behind me, even as I watch the girl's desperate race through the marsh.

Elliott stops at the place where the stairway disappears

into the water. The girl stares at him with wild, terrified eyes. He reaches out his hand.

But she stumbles, unable to catch herself because she won't let go of her companion. The hair on the back of my neck rises. If the gunman wants to kill her, this would be the time to shoot. Elliott is moving, stepping into the muck, grabbing her. He takes the boy's arm, but then pulls back.

The boy's face lifts upward. I gasp.

Red lines run down from his eyes and stain his mask. The slight girl pulls at him, urging him to stand.

Everything goes silent. The frogs, the crickets. I'm holding my breath.

The man out there must be our former prisoner. The Hunter. He didn't kill us before, but now he's tracking these new arrivals. Stalking them like prey.

Elliott, his boots sinking into the muck, puts two fingers to the boy's throat. But the boy is dead. The Red Death takes its victims quickly.

"Let go," he tells the girl. "Take cover behind the banister." She won't release the boy's hand. In the long silence that follows, soft splashes sound below. Peering over the banister, I see the dark-green backs of great reptiles slithering toward us from every direction. Their wakes are like a starburst.

Elliott scans the line of trees and sets his jaw grimly.

The gunman fires again, shattering the window behind Elliott.

"April!" Elliott shouts, but she's already firing. My ears ring.

Elliott pries the girl from the dead boy and shoves her up onto the sagging wooden stairs. Can crocodiles climb stairs?

The girl lets out a low wail, and then Kent is there, pulling her up and handing Elliott a gun. Elliott stands tall. He raises his hand in a half salute, half wave, mocking whoever just shot at him and missed.

"I can't leave him," the girl says, her voice clear in the sudden silence.

"He's dead," Elliott says, his eyes on the swamp.

"But—" Her gaze is frozen on the dead boy's face. She's straining against Kent's grip. I know the broken look on her face all too well. April climbs down, stopping just above where Kent stands.

"Stay here," I say to the children. Ignoring the pain in my shoulder, I crawl across the last few feet of roof to where the house has fallen away.

The broken timbers form a natural ladder, so at least I can climb down, without taking a leap like Elliott did. Will is standing at the first turn of the staircase. I move to pass him, but he puts his hand on my arm.

The girl is a thin little waif, but even streaked with swamp grime, she is lovely. Though the white mask covers most of her face, her big grief-stricken eyes are visible.

"Elliott, here." I toss down my cloak, and he catches

it with one hand. "Cover his face, and then get back up here!"

He catches the cloak but doesn't indicate he heard my request or the urgency in my voice. "Show yourself!" he calls. I'm near enough to see that his eyes give lie to his calm demeanor. He's scanning every possible hiding place in the swamp. His finger caresses the trigger of the gun.

April, now halfway down the staircase, has her own poised and ready. Will's hand tightens on my arm, and Kent peers through his binoculars.

"Whoever is out there isn't stupid. He's not going to reveal himself. Araby is right. Get to the roof—move!" Kent pushes the girl up the staircase.

Elliott isn't moving. It's like he's offering himself as a target.

April lists to the side, putting most of her weight on the banister.

No one else seems to realize how weak she is. My heart pounds in my ears. I try to call out, but my voice has faded to nothing.

April's musket clatters down the stairs half a second before she collapses.

Elliott turns, and another gunshot tears across the swamp.

CHAPTER
FIVE

I FINALLY FIND MY VOICE AND SCREAM. I LUNGE forward, but Will keeps me from diving down the stairs, holding me back from both April and Elliott. I'm not even sure who I'm trying to reach first.

April is lying on the stairway in a faint, and the surprise on Elliott's face would be comical if his cheek weren't covered in blood.

"Everyone get back to the airship," Kent calls. "It just grazed him."

Elliott raises his sleeve to his face, and his eyes blaze.

Will lifts April and carries her up the stairs. How will we hoist her up onto the roof?

The girl raises her hand, perhaps to beg us not to leave her friend here for the crocodiles, but no one is paying attention. Kent climbs up, and Will hands April to him. He has Elise and Henry in tow.

"Come with me," I say to the girl. The look she gives me is far from grateful, but she obeys.

As we climb to the roof, Kent drops an ax to Elliott. He chops at the stairs, kicking the rotted wood down into the water.

Crocodiles swarm below, snapping at one another. The boy's body has already disappeared. I pull the girl away from the edge so she can't see, and then turn back in case Elliott needs help.

He kicks a last chunk of rotten wood down, onto the frenzy of crocodiles.

"I dare anyone, or anything, to try to climb up now." He passes the ax back to Kent, just as another shot rings out.

Kent screams, and the ax falls.

"My hand," he gasps.

I'm reaching for him, but Will is already there.

"It's your wrist," Will says. "It could be much worse."

Kent's face is white, and he's cradling his arm. It's the first time I've seen him upset. "I have to be able to steer the ship."

By now Elliott has pulled himself up. He inspects Kent's wrist. "Will's right. We'll clean and bandage it, and you'll get us out of here. It's going to be fine."

The sun is setting behind the two chimneys where the airship is tethered. The girl stops when she sees it, her mouth falling open.

"You aren't from here. You aren't swamp dwellers." She sounds relieved.

"Of course not," April snaps. She's sitting right inside the doorway of the cabin, fully alert now, and she waves the girl inside. "Do we look like people who live in a swamp?" Her dress is a dirty, torn mess, but the way April holds herself, no one would think she is from anywhere but the city. The upper city.

Outside, the boys prepare the ship to take off. Kent, cradling his wrist, snaps instructions that Will and Elliott hurry to follow.

"We were going to the palace," the girl says. She produces a heavy embossed invitation from some hidden pocket. "He said that we'd be safe there."

April reaches for the invitation, but then she must remember that this girl has been in contact with someone who just died of the Red Death, and she pulls her hand back.

"You're a long way from there," April says.

"We'd never left the city before," the girl says in a whisper. "We weren't even sure that it was real, the palace, and this party. . . ." The ruined dress that she is wearing was probably the finest thing she has ever owned.

"Where did you get the invitation?" April asks.

"They were being delivered in the city. People were killing each other for them . . . ." She stops speaking and looks up. Elliott stands in the doorway.

"We're taking off," he says. "As soon as Kent allows Will to bandage his wrist." The place where the bullet grazed his cheek is only a thin trickle of blood now. Turning to the girl, he asks, "When did the man start chasing you?"

"This morning. We were trying to escape the swamp. But he kept shooting near our feet, forcing us deeper and deeper into it. Finally we saw the house and decided to try to make for it. "

Elliott stays in the doorway, turned so that he can see the edges of the roof. I can hear the children's voices from the interior cabin. They've gone inside with Thom. Will pushes past Elliott to get a bandage, and April begins to stand, but I put my hand on her arm. "He's going to be fine."

"This is what comes of mercy," Elliott says, looking at Will. "The good reverend is drawing the most evil and cruel of our population to his side. It doesn't bode well for anyone if he takes the city."

It also doesn't bode well for Elliott, since Malcontent wants to kill him.

Elliott doesn't know that Malcontent is his father. I don't know why I didn't realize this before. I look down at April, but she shakes her head.

She must know that I will tell him. I have to tell him. Eventually.

His eyes fall on the girl, whose name, I realize, none of us have asked. "Is it safe to have her here?"

He's looking to me, hoping I read something useful about the Red Death in Father's journal.

"It spreads through air and fluids," I say. "Just be careful. Keep your masks on, don't drink after her. . . ." I don't really know how contagious the disease is. I hope I'm not endangering all of us.

"I guess we'll have to risk it." He doesn't sound happy. From the deck, Kent raises his hand to show Elliott that he's stopped long enough for Will to bandage his wrist, and Elliott hurries out of the cabin to help.

April moves to recline on a cot that's been brought from the sleeping cabin. The rest of us settle ourselves around the table in the center of the room.

As the ship begins to rise, Elliott and Kent stay outside, but Will stumbles into the cabin, his face pale. He busies himself folding several of the maps, and then passing around glasses and several bottles. He motions for Henry to help him, and the little boy happily retrieves a basket to help serve everyone.

The anonymous girl is staring across the cabin at Will. Henry tries to get her attention to offer her a slice of bread, but she doesn't acknowledge him. When Will glances up for a second, she blushes bright red.

I glance at April, who is also watching the girl watch Will.

"It didn't take her long to forget her boyfriend," I say under my breath. But my voice carries, and she hears.

She gives me a defiant glare. "He was my brother."

I open my mouth, prepared to apologize, but she shakes her head. Her eyes are red-rimmed, beyond tears.

I understand. I am the only one on this ship who can understand.

April leans close to me and whispers, "I know you're mad at Will . . . don't seem to be speaking to him . . . but you could have him if you want. We both know it. Even Elliott knows it. Sometimes the rest of us just need to stare at him for a few minutes."

She gives me her evil smile, and I marvel at how badly she's misjudged the situation. Will doesn't want me. Maybe he used to, but now there's too much guilt between us. And I have gained just enough self-worth not to fall for him again.

The ship lurches a few times, and then it feels like we are free of the roof. I was close to convincing Elliott to return to the city before we heard the screams. But are we headed that way now? I stand to go out on deck, but Thom comes to the doorway of the small cabin and gestures for me to join him. Henry is curled up on one of the cots, and Elise looks up when we come in but quickly loses interest in us.

"Miss April's sicker than she knows," he says without preamble. "I've seen a lot of people with the contagion. None of us know why some die and we don't. At least we didn't, until the reverend came."

His voice goes low and worshipful when he speaks of Malcontent.

"The reverend? Why did you escape with us, if you think so well of him?" I watch his face closely.

"I was afraid of the burning, the flooding. But no matter what he does, Malcontent is the only person without the disease who looks at me like he doesn't care."

As if to prove his point, the sore across his cheek begins to ooze, and I have to force myself not to look away.

"I'm telling you. You need to get Miss April back to the city." When he says her name, he blushes deep red.

"So there's nothing to be done?" I ask. "People like her would come to your settlement, and they would always die?"

"Not always," he says softly. "The reverend chose to save some. He might save her. His daughter."

Malcontent did tell April that he could cure her. But I don't trust him. Still, it's an option if my own father can't be found.

"Thank you for telling me," I say.

"She doesn't have much time, miss," he says earnestly. And I know that he is speaking the truth.

Henry follows me back into the main cabin and climbs onto my lap, pressing his face against my neck. Even in the weak light of a single lantern, I can see a new bruise at the base of April's throat. I make sure Henry's mask is secure, and then my own.

She catches me and grimaces. Shame floods through me, especially after Thom just told me how he felt about the way we look at him. But I can't help checking Henry's mask a second time.

"Does it feel terrible?" I ask.

"Yes. It itches and I look . . ." She trails off. "I look worse every day," she says finally. "You have your makeup bag. Maybe we can do something about it." She takes her small mirror from the bag and winces at her reflection. "Let's do you first. At least you're still pretty." Though I'm restless, I sit still as she pushes my hair back from my face, then gathers it in a bun at the base of my neck. "We need some feathers," she mutters. I smile despite myself.

The girl we rescued is watching us, her expression wistful. April may seem silly with her love of bright, sparkly things, but she got me through the aftermath of my own brother's death. Even now, she can make me smile. Has this girl, staring at us so intently, ever had a friend? It's hard to make them when everyone is dying.

"Where did you live?" April asks. April only knows a few areas of the city, but it's better to talk to the girl than to ignore her.

"Wherever my brother could find a place," the girl says. "Wherever we were together was home."

"What's your name?" April asks.

"Mina," she answers, before she turns toward the wall. The conversation is over. We don't say anything else to her.

Henry has fallen asleep, so I lay him on the cot, tucking a blanket over him before I walk outside.

The wind has picked up, though the sky is blessedly

free of clouds. As long as I live, I don't think I'll ever get used to flying like this.

"So, where are we going?" I ask, looking from Elliott to Kent. I hold my breath. I won't go to the prince's palace. I'll make them drop me off here, wherever we are. But I'm not sure how far I will get on my own.

"Back to the city," Elliott says. I wait for him to look at me, but instead he stares out over the wilderness beneath us. "My city needs me. My people need me."

"We can't go in during daylight." Kent smiles. He knows as well as I do that this is our best chance to save April. But then he furrows his brow. "They shot us down as we were leaving, and it was nearly dark. We'll have to bring the ship in on a night with no moon. That's five nights from now."

Five nights? April doesn't have that kind of time. "We can't wait—" I begin.

"I'm going in now," Elliott tells us. "I'm tired of waiting. Kent can set me down near the outskirts of the city. In five days, I'll have the roof of the Debauchery Club ready to conceal the ship."

Kent nods. "I can put you down half a day's walk from the city. You can be inside by lunchtime tomorrow."

"We'll have everything ready," I say.

Elliott and Kent both turn to me. "You could wait with us. With April," Kent says. "We'll be back to the city before you know it." He watches Elliott, as if looking for some sign indicating what Elliott wants me to do.

Elliott's voice is thoughtful. "It would be safer for me to go alone."

"You need me," I say.

He doesn't ask why, or what I think my presence will accomplish. Elliott won't find Father without me, but I'm not sure how to convince him of that.

And I don't have to, because he nods.

Kent presses his lips together, and I'm certain that he doesn't approve. Alone in the city for five nights with Elliott. The idea is . . . daunting. Elliott smiles at me. Not a friendly smile—a mocking, suggestive one. I'm not going back to the city simply to keep him company, and he needs to know that.

"We have to find my father quickly so he can help April. Help all of us."

"You'll find him," Kent says. He, at least, is sincere in what he says.

I look out, gripping the railing. We're no longer over the swamp. Instead, we're flying over neat squares of farmland. There are orchards and fields, farms, silos to store the grain. I point, amazed at how orderly and beautiful it is.

Elliott laughs. "Where did you think the food came from? We don't grow it in the city." Turning to Kent, he continues. "Take all of the gold. Buy whatever food you can. It must be getting scarce."

"The rising swamp threatens these farms as well,"

Kent says. "They need better ways to drain the excess water."

"It all comes down to water," Elliott muses. Then, to me, "We should give him the journal, in case something happens to us. Do you mind?"

He's asking my permission for something? Unbelievable.

"Father would want him to read it," I say. Father knows I wouldn't really understand, and he made no secret that he hates Elliott.

Kent takes it reverently. "I'll read every word. And we'll discuss when we are reunited. Elliott, find Dr. Worth and make sure he is safe. He is the key to everything."

Elliott's slightly singed eyebrows draw together. He doesn't like my father any more than my father likes him.

"We'll find him, and keep him alive, but it won't be easy. Not with these circulating." He hands Kent the pamphlet I'd picked up during our escape and tucked into the journal. "Is this Will's work?"

The wind picks up and I wish the paper would blow away, but of course Kent keeps a firm grip on it.

"No," I say, without meaning to. More than anything, I do not want that pamphlet to have anything to do with Will. He must have printed it after our friendship had begun. Another betrayal.

"Will is the only one in the city who is this good," Kent says reluctantly. His eyes shift over to me. "But, Araby, even if he printed this, it was still about survival.

He ran the printing press for money to support himself and the children."

"Perhaps," Elliott says. "Or maybe he came under the sway of a certain Reverend Malcontent. Maybe our Will had a little religious conversion?"

Below us are apple orchards, rows upon rows of beautiful trees. I try to focus on the beauty of the scene, not the reality that Will spent his spare time printing pamphlets calling for my father's death.

Will once said that science had failed. *Could* he have been working for Malcontent? If that was the case, was letting the prisoner go a mistake at all? Now it seems even more sinister.

"Will never worked for Malcontent," Kent says, with confidence that is clearly bolstered by their long friendship. But he's never had a reason to doubt Will. He gestures to some point in the distance, neatly changing the subject. "I'll set you down by that turn in the stream. You'll want to travel light."

I turn back to the cabin to grab a few things.

"I've never trusted Will," Elliott mutters as he follows me into the main cabin. "Especially not now."

In the cabin, Henry is still asleep, but Elise is awake, sitting close to April, who has carefully braided her hair.

Elliott opens a chest sitting in the corner and scoops out an assortment of coins, pouring them into several small leather pouches. "In case we get separated."

April looks back and forth between us. "Are we going

back into the city tonight?" she asks. I hate to leave her, but the way her sores are spreading, people will see that she's diseased. She wouldn't be safe on the streets. And she's not strong enough to fight back.

"We are. Not you," Elliott says. Then, to me, "It's going to be cold tonight. Grab some blankets."

While April sulks and I collect blankets, Elliott puts on a rather bulky coat, and knives disappear into random hidden pockets. Then he grabs a valise and sorts what appears to be a chemistry set. He adds several needles and vials, but then, catching my eye, he pockets a silver syringe.

I flush, remembering all the times I let him use that syringe to help me find oblivion. He sees the blush on my cheeks and smiles to himself.

"I'm going with you."

Elliott and I both turn. Will is in the doorway.

"No," Elliott says. He lifts his hand toward the bruise above his eye, and then drops it. "You are not."

"Are you sure that you can protect Araby?" Will steps closer to Elliott, and though he's not as muscular, not trained the way Elliot has been, he's tall and confident. The two of them together would make a potential attacker think twice about approaching us.

April has settled back against the wall, watching the conversation with great interest.

"Who will care for the children?" Elliott asks. "You'd abandon them?"

"Kent. He's done it before." Will's voice is steely.

"This is not your fight," Elliott says.

"Isn't the fate of the entire city in our hands?" Will asks. "I couldn't possibly stand by and do nothing."

Elliott considers Will with a half sneer on his face. "How do we know you won't turn us over to your diseased friends?" Elliott asks.

"I'll take orders from you," Will says quietly. "You don't know what you'll find there. It may be worse than any of us have imagined. Take me with you. I'll swear my allegiance to your cause. Whatever it takes."

His words are humble, but his tone and demeanor are not.

I open my mouth to intervene, but I don't know what to say. I wish, quite desperately, that April was going with us. I look to her. She's laughing to herself, but she understands my silent plea and bites her lip.

"Take him with you," she says. "Kent and I will care for the children. You'll need help, and I've heard Will is resourceful."

Elliott slings his bag over his shoulder. "Fine," he snaps, and leaves the room.

I'm surprised that he's agreed, but relieved. The city is dangerous. We need Will.

Will pushes Henry's hair back and pulls the blanket up to the sleeping child's chin.

"I'll take care of Henry." Elise puts on a brave face, but I can tell she's about to cry. She clings to me. I wish

I could think of a way to tell her that even if Will and I aren't on the best of terms, I still care about her.

April and Elise follow us out onto the deck. Elise wraps her skinny arms around Will's neck, holding him so tightly that I don't think she'll let him go. He tugs her hands away from his coat, but she presses her cheek against him.

"I have to go with Araby," Will tells her. "She needs my help." But still his sister clutches him.

Until Kent comes to the rescue. "Elise, will you help me steer the ship?" Elise sets her jaw and finally lets go.

April takes my arm. The wind blows her blond hair back, and when she tosses her head, you could almost forget she is sick. Except for the sores, oozing and deadly. Before Elliott took me into Prospero's castle, he asked if I would risk my safety to save her. My answer hasn't changed; I'll do whatever I must to help her survive. She won't die, not like Finn. Later we'll laugh about how afraid we were, about the weeks when she had the contagion, and how she beat it.

She gives me a quick hug. "Take care of Elliott," she says. And then, because she's April and can't seem to help herself, she adds with a wink, "And Will."

"The ladder is down," Kent says. He has one hand on Elise's shoulder and the other on the wooden wheel, which she is holding steady.

"Keep them safe," I say to him. "And April, too."

Elliott is already climbing down the rope ladder,

carefully balancing his bag and a musket. His sword and his walking stick—which conceals a second sword—are strung across his back. I sling my bag over my good shoulder.

"Sorry I couldn't bring the ship down. We're too close to the city," Kent says to Will, whose face is a chalky white. He's terrified of heights. When he took me up in the hot-air balloon, he could barely open his eyes.

I hesitate, wondering if I should let him go first, but he gestures for me to descend.

Kent has the ship just above tree level, and the wind whips the ladder from side to side. It's all I can do to hold on, but by the time I'm halfway down I realize that I'm enjoying the wind through my hair. The air is cool and smells of pine needles.

I feel for the next rung, and then the one beneath it. When I am close enough, Elliott grabs me and swings me down.

"We'll camp here," he says. "And enter the city in the morning."

Enter the city. It's what I fought for, but still the prospect leaves me cold with dread. I stand beside Elliott and try to watch Will descend, without drawing Elliott's attention. Elise froze when she was climbing to the airship as we escaped the city. And her terror masked Will's fear then.

The ship veers to the right, and Will drops from dangerously high but lands on his feet. He gives a little laugh, but his bravado can't disguise how pale he is.

The three of us quickly gather firewood, and Elliott hovers near me, as if he's protecting me. From whatever is out there in the dark, or from Will?

Elliott wears his sword and carries a musket. The sword looks completely natural at his side, but the gun is unwieldy.

Will starts a fire, and Elliott sets about boiling water to brew some sort of bitter tea. "I don't trust the water out here," he explains. "Of course, I don't trust the water in the city either." I imagine the bloated dead bodies that might be lying upstream.

Elliott has taken charge, which leaves me and Will with nothing to do, but somehow it's comforting that he's his old irritatingly confident self. It helps me believe that he may be able to take control of the city as well.

The forest is so different from the swamp. For one thing, the ground beneath us is reassuringly solid. The crackle of the fire can't mask the sound of the stream, or the wind whispering through the leaves. The scent of pine needles is sharp but fresh.

It was humid in the swamp, but now that the sun is going down, the chill is setting in. Tonight seems likely to be unseasonably cold, and I start to shiver and can't seem to stop.

Elliott sets a cup of tea near Will's feet, then settles down and pulls me into his arms. I should move away, but he's so warm. So I give in and rest against his chest. His legs stretch on either side of me, and after I appropriate a blanket from the stack, my shivering stops. After a few moments, when he does nothing improper, I relax as much as I can in the wilderness at night.

Our fire casts only a small circle of light, and the moon overhead doesn't penetrate the shadows beyond it. I've never slept outside. It's more frightening than sleeping alone with Finn, in the basement. Elliott senses my nervousness and pulls me closer.

"We need to keep watches through the night," he tells Will. "I'll take the first." He tosses Will a blanket.

As I turn my head slightly to watch the flight of the blanket, Elliott's lips graze my cheek. So much for propriety.

"Wake me when it's my turn." Will wraps himself in his blanket, lying with his back to us.

Elliott and I sit in silence for what seems like a very long time.

Finally he says, "You should get some sleep." His voice is intimate and low, but not a whisper. A whisper would be bereft of the actual timbre of his voice, and in the darkness, with my back pressing against him, the sound of it thrills me, despite myself.

"I've had plenty of rest, thanks to your drugs," I say, more sharply than I meant to. I'm trembling again, even though I'm no longer cold.

"You're scared," he says. "Of returning to the city? It is what you wanted."

Just because you know something is right doesn't mean it isn't terrifying. But I don't say anything. After a moment, I nod. Though it's dark, surely he can feel the movement.

"Is it your father?" he asks, but I'm not ready for that discussion.

"Can we not talk?" My voice is also low, and somehow much more intimate than I meant it to be.

"I'm not complaining," he says. "It's nice, sitting here with you. Much warmer." I shift to see if his expression is as sincere as his voice sounds, and our faces are so close. I should turn away, but I don't.

I kiss him.

An owl hoots somewhere in the trees above us. Elliott twists so that we're lying on the ground. For a brief moment, all I can think is that it's different than it's been with him before. He raises my chin with his hand, and he's frustratingly gentle, as if he wants this moment to go on and on. And it does. It's a very long time before I pull back to take a ragged breath.

"We have to find a way to get some privacy," he whispers. "Soon."

I rest my face against his chest, to keep myself from inviting more. Is privacy with Elliott what I want? How can I even think about this when my father is missing and his sister is dying? I told Kent that I wasn't interested in romance. Elliott isn't the only liar in our midst.

"Go to sleep, Araby. Tomorrow will be here before you know it."

He sits up, and I remember that he is supposed to be on first watch, protecting us from . . . whatever is out there in the night. Not kissing me.

"I can take a turn," I offer, since I'm certain I'll never fall asleep.

"It seems fairly quiet out here, and no one will be expecting our return," Elliott says, looking out into the darkness. "I'm not tired. I'm not sure I'll even need to wake Will."

"I'm awake," Will says.

CHAPTER
SIX

IN THE FRIGID DARKNESS, MY FACE HEATS UP, MY entire body flushes. Will is awake. Lying there with his back to us, but awake. The whole time.

"Well then, you can take the watch for a few hours," Elliott says. He prods the fire once, then lies down close to me. I stay very still, trying to make myself small, unnoticed.

After what seems like forever, Elliott's breathing evens out.

Will doesn't say anything. He just sits and stares into the fire. I listen to the sounds of the forest, wishing he would speak. He must know that I'm awake. The night is interminable. At dawn, Will puts more wood on the fire and begins making fresh tea.

I sit up and pull a twig from my hair, and then another.

Will holds out a cup without looking at me. "Would you like some of this . . . ?"

I take it, frowning at the contents. "Elliott has some audacity, calling this stuff tea."

"Elliott isn't lacking in audacity," Will replies.

Elliott's lips quirk just a bit. I prod him lightly with my foot. "You can open your eyes, I know you're listening."

"Of course I'm listening," he says, stretching. "It's what audacious people do." He pours himself a cup of steaming tea. "You two will have to hope we reach the city quickly. This is all the breakfast we have."

Will takes the water pail and heads for the stream. I glance at Elliott, but then I follow. I don't know what to say to Will, but after his long silence last night, I need to say something. To apologize.

He scoops a pail of water from the deepest part of the stream. "Now that we know the Red Death can spread through water, too, I wish it was flowing toward the city, rather than from it," he says. He doesn't have to mention the dead bodies that must line the streets by now.

"Because it's any better when it comes from the swamp?"

Will sighs. "We don't have any great choices here, do we?"

I could ask him if we're still talking about water sources, but I don't really want to know. And I don't have to anyway.

He sets down the pail and looks at me. "Be careful, Araby."

I raise my eyebrows and wait for him to continue.

"With Elliott."

Elliott isn't the only one with audacity. I won't have this conversation. Turning back to our campsite, I slip on a wet stone. I don't fall, but keeping my balance pulls my wounded shoulder, and I gasp.

"I should check that later," he says.

I stiffen, willing the pain to dull, but I'm glad for the change of subject.

"Thank you for stitching me up," I say.

"I seem to have a talent for it."

The comment takes me back to the warmth of his apartment. My skinned knee. The children watching from the doorway as he painstakingly removed the splinter from my hand. Perhaps he should train to be a doctor. Except that profession isn't safe—in a time of plague, doctors die faster than anyone.

"Why did you let the prisoner go?" I ask.

"I didn't," he says. "Thom did."

Now I do lose my footing, and would fall, if he didn't lunge forward to steady me. He grabs my elbow and loops an arm around my waist, but he's behind me so I can't see his expression. "Thom? Then why didn't you—"

"Because Elliott would have killed him. Elliott isn't exactly a friend to those with the disease. He was going to kill the prisoner, and he wanted a reason to kill the boy."

I'm afraid that he's right. "But you made yourself look like a traitor." I almost add "again."

"I made myself look like a fool. But the boy is alive."

He did make himself look like a fool. I glance back to the campsite. Surely Elliott is getting suspicious, wondering why it's taking us so long to get water.

"Thom's with April and the children. Is it safe? Did he know that the prisoner was the Hunter, that he was a murderer?"

"No. I don't think so. Thom wouldn't hurt April or the children. I'm sure of that."

You can never be sure. He taught me that.

"When I spoke to the Hunter, he seemed tragic, desperate," Will continues.

"Everyone in the city is desperate," I say. I'm stepping away from him.

"Have you ever seen Elliott kill someone?" He spins me around, forces me to look at him. "I have. He murdered an unarmed man with one sword stroke, wiped the blade with his handkerchief, and called for servants to get rid of the body. He smiled as he did it."

"Good thing he didn't borrow your handkerchief," I snap. "The one you keep clean in case a pretty girl needs to cry on your shoulder."

We live in a society where people die every day. I will not allow Will to pull me in with these confidences, not with the fact that he'd risk himself to save a boy's life. Not with his warnings about Elliott.

I start back to the campfire, giving Will a last glare. He shakes his head slightly but doesn't seem surprised that I'm walking away.

Elliott has put out the campfire and repacked our supplies. I wait for him to say something, but he's staring toward the city, lost in his own thoughts. I sling my pack over my shoulder, and the three of us begin to walk.

The woods thin as we near the city.

"So, we're going to the Debauchery Club?" I ask.

"Yes, but since we have four days, we're going to search the city for your father first. And for that magical pumping station that could save us from the swamp, and maybe from the Red Death."

"You think it's real?"

"Your father seemed to believe so. Do you?"

"I don't know." My father never mentioned it, and the references in his journal are unclear.

"Where do you suppose we should start our search for the venerable Dr. Worth?" Elliott asks.

"The last time we saw him was behind the science building at the university," I say. "He's comfortable in that area."

"Then that's the first place we'll look," Elliott says.

Will has been silent all morning, but now he speaks up, peering to the side of the road. "Is that a steam carriage?" Up ahead, a closed-in steam carriage appears to have crashed in the woods.

"Yes." Elliott pushes ahead of us. "A rather nice one," he observes. "I might be able to get it working—"

Will and I stop beside him. I'm the first to see the arm, peeking out from under the ornate scrollwork, draped by a lacy shawl.

"Party finery," I say. "They must've been going—"

"To my uncle's ball." Elliott readjusts his mask. "But how did they die? The contagion or the Red Death?"

"Red Death," Will says. "If they were invited to the party, they had masks."

"It doesn't matter." I put my hand on his arm. "Either way, they are contagious. We can't risk it, Elliott. Standing over an infected body is still dangerous. We need to get out of here."

Elliott looks at the carriage wistfully. "What a shame. It's lovely."

"Beautiful sentiment," Will scoffs. "I'm sure the owners were very proud of their carriage. Care to step away from it? I'd rather not catch the Red Death."

As we continue, my bag feels heavier and heavier. Elliott keeps one hand on his sword, as if he can fight off the disease.

The road turns, and the river blocks our path. We have to cross a low bridge to enter the city from this direction. It's built of white stone; cool to the touch, I learn when I reach out for the railing. The water is about a foot lower than usual. It ripples over knees and elbows and faces with the same cheerful sound it makes when flowing over the smooth stones that line the bank.

I break our prolonged silence to ask, "Do either of you . . . smell something?"

"It's death," Elliott says. "Or, more precisely, the city."

I look away, to the buildings that line the shore: a simple white church that is, astoundingly, unscathed by vandalism; some apartment buildings; a house with a corpse hanging from a balcony. He has a sign pinned to his shirt, and I strain to make out the writing. Did he hang himself, or was he a victim of violence? Did he pin the sign to his shirt before tying the noose and jumping from the balcony, or was it attached to him later?

"Araby?" Elliott breaks my trance. "Come on. We need to find an inn. I'm starving."

I am too. Despite the death and decay around us, despite the stench of corpses decomposing in the city streets, I am ravenous.

We pass to the other side of the bridge, like so many others who have come and gone in this dying city, and there's no one to notice. The streets are mostly deserted, but I see faces watching us from behind sheer curtains. Men lounge in doorways.

A man in uniform, a courier perhaps, hurries toward the market. He has a gun but moves nervously.

Red scythes have been painted on the sides of many buildings. One on a warehouse has a staff that is nearly two stories tall. Elliott frowns. A few blocks away, near an inn, is a heap of something white. Bones?

"Masks," Elliott says when we get closer, prodding them with his foot. A nearly intact one falls over the toe of his boot.

From the corner of my eye, I catch sight of a man with a dark robe. Could Malcontent's men have found us already? He slides something from his pocket, coming straight toward us. I open my mouth to scream, but Elliott shoves me through the door of an inn. I turn back, but Will puts his hand on my shoulder. Elliott is blocking the door, sword in hand.

I push Will away, but before I get any farther, Elliott turns, sheathing his blade. "Coward," Elliott mutters. "He ran when he saw I was armed."

I release the breath that I was holding, relieved that we haven't come to violence in our first few moments back. But Elliott slams his fist down on a wooden table, as angry as I've ever seen him.

"Malcontent's men don't have to come close enough to fight. They can sidle up to unarmed people and infect them." His face is red. "I know how to fight a tyrant. I don't know how to fight a disease."

I struggle for the right words. My father's life was spent fighting a disease, but of course, he knew more about it than anyone suspected. Except Prospero.

The inn is crowded, but conversation is muffled. The patrons look tattered, dirty. Will threads his way through and claims a table. We stow our packs underneath.

When the innkeeper comes over, he's surprised that we want food. "Most people just want to drink," he says. "To forget." He gives us the menu for the day, finishing with a dark "It will cost you."

"That won't be a problem." Elliott drops a piece of gold onto the table. The innkeeper picks it up to examine it, and when he sees Elliott's sign on the coin, his demeanor changes. He hurries to the kitchen and brings back a tray, then hovers over Elliott, answering questions about the availability of food. Supplies are low, but people with money are not starving. Most people do not have money.

"In many areas, the streets are impassable," the innkeeper adds. "Bodies are everywhere." I stop eating, but he continues. "No one is sure what happened to the corpse collectors. Some say that the prince stopped paying them." He looks quickly to Elliott, as if he might have the answer, but Elliott shrugs. "Personally, I think they're all dead themselves." He shudders. "Doesn't matter who they are—if someone can remove the dead from the streets, the city will be theirs."

"And once the streets have been cleared of the dead, we'll have a way to bring in food," Elliott suggests.

"Exactly," the innkeeper beams.

"Araby, you need to eat," Will says softly from across the table. His expression reminds me of the way my mother used to watch me. I am free while Mother is a prisoner. I have plenty of food while other people are starving. The guilt makes me feel even less like eating.

"People are ready for some good news," the innkeeper intones, looking around the common room. So many are drinking though it isn't even midday yet, and the air is one of gloom, not the boisterous one of freely flowing wine.

"I hope that my return to the city is good news," Elliott says. "I have plans." He drops his voice, and Will chooses this moment to scold me once again.

"Araby," he says in the voice he uses with Elise and Henry. "Eat some bread." He slides the basket across the table at me. I take it angrily, and when I do, the sleeve of my dress tears loudly enough to draw Elliott's attention.

"You need something new," he says. The innkeeper takes the hint and hurries away.

It's heartening that Elliott has found support here, at the first establishment we've visited. Perhaps people are still capable of hope. I hope that I will have the same success on my mission of finding Father.

Moments later, the innkeeper's wife brings a dress to the table for my inspection. It's overly large, demure, and has a busy flowered print. I start to say that no, I would never wear this, but then the innkeeper speaks from behind his wife.

"It belonged to my daughter. She's been dead for two years now."

"Will it do?" Elliott asks.

I take the dress. It's even more shapeless than I expected, faded from multiple washings. It looks like a dress sewn for a twelve-year-old. A large twelve-year-old. The innkeeper's wife has tears in her eyes.

"Lovely," I say, wondering if I can repair the damage to my own dress instead. Elliott counts out a few extra coins, but the man won't take his money.

"We are glad that you've returned," he says. "My brother was one of Prospero's former guards. When he defected to your cause, the rebellion gave him something to live for."

Elliott nods slowly. "Spread the word. We'll need a meeting place. . . ."

"Some of the men have already been gathering here."

"Excellent. I'll return tomorrow, around noon, to rendezvous with whomever you can contact."

The innkeeper beams, but his wife looks more skeptical. She has lost her daughter. Nothing Elliott does will change that.

The innkeeper arranges for one of his workers to drive us across town in an illicit steam carriage. "I would give it to you," he tells Elliott, "but we use it to fetch supplies, and without transportation . . ."

"I won't ask that of you." Elliott claps the man on the shoulder, seeming for all the world like a ruler already. But I see the way he looks at the carriage when we go outside. It isn't fancy like April's, or modified for speed like his old one, but it's transportation in a city where movement is limited. He won't take it today, but he doesn't have to. We've all seen that the innkeeper hides it in an abandoned building behind his establishment. He sends a driver and a guard with us. The guard has two guns and stands in the back, on a platform similar to what April's guards used to occupy.

"Drive along the river," Elliott requests. "I want to have a look at the factories."

A corpse blocks the street, so the guard gets out and moves it, carefully using a wooden beam that he seems to keep on hand for this exact purpose.

"Not many carriages for hire, it seems," Elliott remarks, watching with an air of longing as the driver works the controls.

"Prince Prospero has been commandeering them," the man says. "His men take them at gunpoint."

"Yet another challenge to moving enough food into the city," Elliott says.

We are driving past an entire city block that has burned. Some walls are still intact, even a blackened window. In a partial wall a brick fireplace stands alone, charred and abandoned.

"Have Prospero's soldiers tried to take this carriage?" Elliott asks. He's scanning the buildings that line the river.

"More than once," the driver says. "We know a few hiding spots."

Elliott grins his approval. "I like a man who can avoid Prospero's traps," he says. The taciturn driver nods.

"Turn ahead," Elliott says. "We'll want to approach the university from the upper city."

We've been gone for less than a week, but I'm seeing the city through fresh eyes. I glance at Will. Once he tried to make me see the beauty of this place, but there is so little left. Everything is dirty, crumbling, gray. A sickly sweet smell pervades everything, and I try not to gag.

Abandoned objects litter the road. A child's hair bow, a wooden soldier, a fine silver flask that someone must have treasured.

Instead of dwelling on these things, I focus my attention on the buildings. So many are simply shells and ruins, but the city doesn't feel emptier. Behind a collapsed apartment building we see more tenements, an exposed cellar, as if the layers of the city have been peeled back, revealing more and more. The hole that was once a cellar is now filled with greenish water.

Elliott pays the driver and salutes both the guard and driver before sending them back across town. We're on the main avenue, and while stately trees still stand, the stately buildings have collapsed into piles of white rubble behind cracked marble columns.

Several are completely gutted. Elliott set his old apartment on fire before we left. Perhaps it caught other buildings on fire, too. Windows are smashed and glass gleams from both grassy areas and the streets. The walls of the science building are chipped from gunfire.

I hear the stream gurgling before we reach it. The sound of running water is soothing amid all the destruction, but the bank is empty. I hadn't expected Father to just sit here, waiting for me to return. Still, I'm disappointed. Above the stream, where Father used to come feed the fish, is a hand-painted sign. DOWN WITH SCIENCE. THE SCIENTISTS ARE MURDERERS.

"The scientist *is* a murderer," Elliott agrees, but he shuts his mouth when he sees the expression on my face. Will doesn't say anything.

"Let's look inside," Elliott says, leading us around to the side of the science building. He tests a door, and the lock is broken, so it swings wide. The smell in the hallway is overpowering. I put my hand to my mask, and my eyes begin to water.

"Is anyone here?" Elliott calls.

"No one who was even half alive would stay here." Will chokes out the words. A body is sprawled across the hallway.

Elliott takes my arm and attempts to pull me outside. "Will can check. He'd recognize—"

"No." I won't allow them to protect me.

"Let her look," Will says. "She needs to know."

"Besides," I say, once we've stepped over the body and I can think a bit more clearly, "whatever bodies we find . . . Father won't have died of the Red Death."

Will's dark eyebrows go up. He doesn't know about the tiny vial that Father gave me, which may, perhaps, save me from the Red Death. If we can find him, maybe he can provide the same medicine for the children. And Will and Elliott.

We pass several large lecture rooms strewn with blankets and discarded clothing, but everything seems to be abandoned now. Some of the rooms have charts on the walls, with Latin terms that Father would understand, but I don't.

Under a chart are some other notices, messages for the people who stayed here. Times and places for meetings. I reach out to touch the scrip about a rendezvous that happened sometime last winter.

We search all of the rooms. Nothing.

Elliott sees how disappointed I am. "It was our best place to begin," he says. "The university is huge, Araby. Hundreds of rental rooms in dormitories. We'll keep searching, and I know a man who can help us. We'll check the Akkadian Towers as soon as we can."

"We have four days until April returns." Will's tone is reassuring. "Plenty of time."

We leave the building through the wide double doors of the front entrance. Above them are the words EXPERIMENT ON THE SCIENTIST. SHOW HIM HOW IT FEELS.

I stare at the words for a long time. Father may not be susceptible to the Red Death, but that doesn't mean he's safe. He'll be doing everything he can to stay hidden from people like the ones who wrote that. He could be anywhere. We might never find him.

But what if he could find me?

"Where could I get paint?" I ask.

"I'm sure Will can find some." Elliott gives Will a challenging look, perhaps reminding him of his promise to follow orders.

"I'm good at finding things," Will agrees. "You want something dark to put your own message on the walls?"

He can read me too well. I nod.

"We'll split up," Elliott says. "It's growing late. My acquaintance won't answer his door after dark. Meet us on the steps of the library in an hour." Elliott walks away. I don't like the way he assumes that I will follow. If I go with Will, it might communicate something to Elliott. But I know what Will is doing. Elliott's visit to this person—who he does not refer to as a friend—is more mysterious.

I don't have to hurry to catch up with Elliott. He's only taken three steps around the corner and stopped. Our way is blocked by a pile of freshly dead bodies.

CHAPTER
SEVEN

I'VE SEEN DEAD BODIES NEARLY EVERY DAY SINCE the first plague started, but never so many at once. They are heaped together, lying all intertwined. I gag like Will did in the science building and force myself not to be sick. The carefully tended lawn, once so vibrant and green, is totally obscured. Most of the bodies are in shrouds, but some untended corpses lie around the periphery. Red tears stain their cheeks. One is holding a bouquet of wilting flowers. Did she bring her loved ones here, and then die herself?

This disease leaves you little time to mourn. Little time to live with guilt and loneliness. People are dying so quickly.

I want to shield myself from the awfulness, but I can't stop looking. Puddles surround the corpses. Soon this rainwater will mix with the groundwater, spreading further contamination. The innkeeper was right—whoever can rid the city of these bodies will be a hero. It is the first step in saving the city.

"Step away," Elliott says, even as he goes closer. He doesn't check to see if I've obeyed, and I don't. Taking a vial of liquid from his pocket, he pours something over the nearest victim and then lights a match. As he drops it, he takes a quick step backward. Despite the recent rain, the corpse catches fire immediately. The blaze is very hot, hotter than any fire I've ever encountered, and the smell is terrible. Elliott's face is illuminated by the blaze. He looks radiant.

"If I can mix enough of this compound, find enough men, I can begin to clear some of the streets."

He empties two more vials over the heap, lights another match, and soon most of the bodies are burning.

What he's doing is terrible in its own way. Cremation is better than leaving the bodies here, it must be. But one of the women who died here was blonde, and when her hair begins to burn, all I can see is April's face. I crumple to my knees, tears streaming down my cheeks. We have to find a way to save her. I won't let her end up like this.

Elliott doesn't comment, and I'm glad. I collect myself and stand. "Where next?"

"This way."

We walk, gingerly, around the burning bodies, to a main avenue lined with tall, cramped buildings where students used to live. Rows of identical doors face a paved courtyard. Elliott's gaze darts everywhere, searching all of the alleys and shadowy nooks. A wise precaution, since men in dark robes seem to appear wherever we are. I watch over my shoulder as Elliott raps on a door.

"The man who lives here knows a good deal about the university and what is happening here. He also garners information from throughout the city."

"If Father has been seen . . ."

"He'll know."

"What should I do?" I ask.

"Listen. This man . . . doesn't have much reason to like me."

He pounds on the door again, harder. When we hear slow footsteps from inside, Elliott shifts from one foot to the other. A completely unexpected emotion crosses his face. He's nervous.

The door begins to open, and for a moment I see my father standing on the threshold. But of course the person inside the apartment isn't my father, just an older gentleman with a white beard.

"The prince's nephew," the man says, sounding neither surprised nor pleased. But Elliott braces himself, throwing his shoulders back before he pushes me into the room and closes the door behind us.

The room is sparsely furnished with a cheap desk, a couple of rickety chairs, and a doorway leading to what might be a bedroom, or possibly a kitchen.

I study the occupant's lined face, but he hardly seems

threatening. What makes Elliott so nervous?

"So you're following your uncle's footsteps, taking over cities?" he asks.

Elliott nods. This is the first time since we've reentered the city that he hasn't seemed proud of his role.

"Have you abandoned your writing? I'd always hoped to read your account of the day you and I met. But then I heard you'd burned everything you left."

"As usual, you heard correctly. I'm . . . fighting for the city. Things will be better when I'm in control." His usual arrogance is starting to seep back in.

"Your uncle did train you to continue his work."

"We both know what my uncle did," Elliott says. "Let's go downstairs."

"The girl stays up here." The man eyes me with distrust.

"I go where he goes," I say.

I expect an argument, but the man just turns and leads us downstairs. Elliott looks pained, as if the man's rapid acquiescence hurts him.

"You will have to unlock the door to the workshop," the man says, and he turns to Elliott and holds up his hands. My gasp is loud in this small subterranean antechamber. His hands are not really hands at all—rather a formless mass, as if he doesn't have any bones beneath the scarred flesh.

Elliott jerks away as though he's been punched. In fact, he looks worse than when Will actually did hit him yesterday. When he finds his voice, he gets out only a strangled "Of course."

Elliott turns a series of locks and opens the door gingerly. The man leads us across his cellar to another, narrower doorway with the muffled noises of movement on the other side. When he opens the door, the cellar floods with light from rows upon rows of gas bulbs in the room beyond. It is lined with clocks, and there are tables covered with cogs and gears of all sizes and shades of shiny metal. The clocks are ticking and their parts are turning. As we step in, I realize with amazement that they are all set to the exact same time, that the thousands of parts are all moving together. It's astounding.

"I make clocks," the man says with a half smile. "Or he does." A boy sits at a low table, putting gears together with nimble fingers.

A wide table sits against the wall opposite the clocks, with an assortment of mismatched chairs. This would have been a wonderful place for students to congregate before the plague.

"The domain of artists, scholars, and poets." Elliott sounds wistful.

"They still meet here. The group that you started," the clockmaker says.

But we have no time for nostalgia. The clocks tick, and it's getting late. We told Will we'd be back in an hour.

"Have you heard anything about Dr. Phineas Worth?"

I ask, since it's the point of our visit. "The scientist who invented the masks?"

"I've heard many things about him," the clockmaker replies, and I feel ill, waiting for him to tell me whether my father is dead.

"But nothing recent. The last I heard he was chased off campus about a week ago by Prospero's soldiers."

Elliott and I exchange a look. That was the last time we saw my father. Elliott called off the soldiers, but one was loyal to his uncle and shot at Father anyway.

"Dr. Worth is in hiding. I need you to organize a few spies to scour the campus. They will be compensated for their efforts, rewarded if they find the man." Elliott picks up one of the gears from a table and toys with it.

The clockmaker inclines his head. "I'll arrange a full-fledged search. If he's on campus, we'll find him." The boy looks up at us, drawing his master's attention. "The others will search. You need to keep working," he says, and then to Elliott, "He's my only trained apprentice, and we have a large commission. From your uncle."

The gear falls from Elliott's hand, hitting the wooden table with a loud *thunk*.

"The prince wants a great clock. The biggest I've ever built. And he wants it soon." The clockmaker gestures to the wooden body of what will be an enormous ebony grandfather clock. It's beautifully crafted, but the dark wood and austere lines are imposing.

"Why?"

"Prince Prospero doesn't deign to tell a clockmaker why he wants a clock," the man answers.

"Is it for his party?" Elliott asks. "Does it do anything besides mark the hour?" He walks over to the clock and puts his hands on the wood of the casing. "Are there weapons inside? Does it dispense poisonous gas?"

"If he wants to install instruments of torture, he'll have to do that himself. I only design the clockwork."

"My uncle loves oddities," Elliott murmurs. "But a huge clock?" He looks over the cabinet one last time. "I thought you swore never to make anything for him again."

"The boy is making it."

I clear my throat. This cryptic conversation isn't going to find my father.

The clockmaker turns to me. His eyes are piercing. He studies me while asking Elliott, "Does she love you?" Even after the audacity of the question, he doesn't look back at Elliott. My face burns at the personal question, and my anger builds at being discussed this way. Still, I wait to hear Elliott's answer.

"Not yet," Elliott says. "But she will. Araby's used to loving people who've done terrible things."

I frown. "I wouldn't count on it," I say quietly, and I don't bother to look at Elliott either. If all he can do is ignore me or talk for me, he doesn't deserve any better.

The clockmaker smiles, as if my words amuse him. "Shall we test her?" he asks. Without waiting for an answer, he holds up his mangled hands. "Elliott did this," he says.

The shock of it is like the time Finn jumped on my chest and knocked the air out of me.

"He wasn't much older than my apprentice," the clockmaker says. "Though his hands were less steady. This boy is well trained."

"So was I." Elliott's face is drained of color, and his voice is hoarse.

Many emotions cross the clockmaker's face. Hatred for Elliott, remorse, worry.

"My wife and my children died of the plague very early," he says. "The prince never had an opportunity to hurt them. Be careful, my dear."

"I'm through being careful," I say. I'm sorry for his pain, and I'm sorry for Elliott's guilt. But none of this is helping me save April. I step back toward the corridor and notice a small, nearly concealed door.

"How is Prospero paying you?" Elliott asks the clockmaker.

"Clockwork parts. Scrap metal from his storerooms. And this." The clockmaker goes to a cabinet and pushes the door open with his wrist. He has just enough movement in his thumb that he can clumsily pick up a thick envelope. It's an invitation to the prince's ball.

"Why would you ever want to return to the palace?" Elliott asks.

While they are occupied, I take a few steps closer to

the small door. When I lived with Father and Finn in the cellar, there was a door like this in the room Father adopted as his laboratory. He always kept it blocked with heavy boxes and a wardrobe.

"I never thought I would, but if things get worse here, I may seek sanctuary there."

"Sanctuary?" Elliott's eyebrows shoot up, truly surprised.

"The invitation is for two. I could save the boy. Better for him to live among evil men than die of the Red Death."

I reach out to the door and turn a green-tinged brass knob. Neither Elliott nor the clockmaker notice my movement, though the little apprentice looks up for a moment.

"You won't have to go," Elliott says. "I'm working to make the city safe."

"We'll see."

Elliott starts to say something and then stops, shaking his head. "I have something else to ask, and it's important."

I'm edging closer to the little door, but the urgency in his voice makes me pause.

"Tell me about the device that is supposed to hold back the swamp."

The clockmaker's gaze shoots up. "People have talked about it for years. The commonly accepted belief is that it never existed."

"But you don't believe that."

The clockmaker smiles. "No. I don't. I know that it existed, because I made parts for it."

Elliott strides forward. The clockmaker falls back, nearly cowering. But Elliott doesn't apologize, not now. "Where?" he demands. "Where is it?"

"That is the mystery. I never saw it assembled. The scientists who built it have either died or disappeared into your uncle's dungeons. All I can tell you is that there are two keys. They look like watch keys, but bigger. To begin the machine, both keys have to be turned simultaneously."

"And where are these keys?"

"They're in Prospero's throne room," I hear myself say. Both Elliott and the clockmaker spin to face me. I remember seeing them during the terrible visit Elliott and I paid to the castle only a few weeks ago. They were on a table under a green glass window. Two gold keys among the instruments of torture that covered the table.

"Which means that Prospero must have found the device and destroyed it. He enjoys destruction." The clockmaker stares at his hands. "The minutes are ticking away, and I do have a clock to design."

I nearly reach out to Elliott, he looks so stricken, but I'm not close enough. Instead, I try to lessen the tension between the two of them. "Where does this lead?" I gesture to the small door, and as if the movement of my hand is magical, it creaks opens just a hair. I push it the rest of the way and peer into the darkness. A rough stone stairway leads down into the murk.

"It's a passage into a network of earthen tunnels." Elliott has crossed the room and is directly behind me. "Many of the older buildings have access to them."

"The tunnels Malcontent has taken over?"

"They all connect." Elliott turns to the clockmaker. "Does this one come up someplace near?"

"Yes, if you go down, and then to the left. You will come out near the library."

"Perfect," Elliott says.

I take two steps down, running my fingers over the crumbling masonry. Bits of red brick rain down to the grimy floor. Then I turn, waiting for Elliott. The clockmaker hands him a candle on a metal holder.

"I'm sure you have something to light it with."

In answer, Elliott strikes a match against the wall. Then he makes a formal bow. "As always, I am sorry."

If the clockmaker makes any reply, I don't wait to hear it.

At the bottom of the staircase the tunnel widens, though not quite wide enough for us to walk side by side. The floor here is made of packed earth. It's not muddy, but it is damp. Malcontent's flooding must have swept through here, too.

"I can walk in front if you'd like," Elliott offers.

I shake my head. I'm tired of following him around. "No."

"Don't blame me if you walk into a spiderweb," he mutters. "Here, take the candle." The darkness beyond my candle is absolute.

"I didn't think he would tell you," Elliott says, "About what I did."

The horror of it overwhelms me.

"He wanted to punish you. You'd visited him before?"

"After I left the palace, I visited him often. I made sure he had enough food. He never seemed to appreciate it."

"It's hard to blame him. . . . Your visits probably reminded him of what he had lost." We walk on in silence. "Did you check on all of the people your uncle made you hurt?" I like that he cared enough to do this.

"Only those who are still alive." And the conversation seems to be over. We move slowly, fumbling through the passage. Every few feet there is an arched area made of brick. The mortar crumbles down on us as we walk along.

"I can still remember the way my hands shook, holding the hammer. I was thirteen years old." His voice is steady, neither confession nor bragging. Just simple fact. I don't know how to respond. But even with this new insight, I can still believe that Will saw Elliott kill a man while smiling. "My uncle doesn't always kill the people who anger him. Sometimes he does worse."

"Did you have nightmares?"

"Yes." He is silent for a time. "Eventually I found ways to deal with them."

The first time I met Elliott I asked for oblivion, and he brought out his silver syringe. "That night in the Debauchery Club, you said that you rarely shared . . ." My voice is soft.

He puts his hands on my waist, pulling me back and spinning me around. "I know all about the need for oblivion," he says. His mask hangs down around his neck. He lets his pack fall to the earthen floor of the tunnel.

We are very much alike, Elliott and I. He takes the candle in its bent metal holder from me and sets it on a rough rock ledge. It flickers, casting weak shadows around us.

"But I haven't needed it since I met you," he tells me. And then he pulls my mask away from my face and kisses me.

This time he's not gentle. He's rough, and my head snaps back, hitting the wall. Bits of stone to fall all around us. I kiss him back, just as hard.

My hair catches on the rough stone of the wall as he lifts me, so I'm pressed against him. I wrap my legs around him. What's left of my dress bunches up around me. The bandage on my shoulder shifts and the wound stings, but we don't stop. My arms are around his neck.

I've been looking for oblivion in all the wrong ways.

I pull back for a moment, and in the flickering candle-light he's so handsome. His eyes are just slightly open, and I want to memorize all of him in this instant.

Elliott sets me down.

"I'm sorry," he says. He lifts one hand to smooth the mortar and dirt from my hair. "We shouldn't be . . . this is not a suitable place. . . ." I can't pull my eyes away, fascinated and confused as his sudden regret is replaced by wariness. His eyes narrow. "It's been a long time since I lost control like that, even for a few moments."

I retrieve the candle, readjust the shreds of my dress. My heart is racing, and yet I feel ashamed that we stopped here to kiss when so much is at stake.

Eventually I start walking again. Leading the way back to Will.

Ahead of us is a ladder leading upward, much like the one that April and I climbed to escape when the tunnels were flooding. A draft from above blows the candle out.

"Elliott?"

"Yes?"

"Do you think there are crocodiles in these tunnels?"

He laughs. "No. Why do you ask?"

I caress the tender area to the left of the wound on my shoulder. "No reason." I reach up, and Elliott gives me a boost. His hands linger at my waist, and for a brief moment I think that he may try to rekindle whatever just happened between us. I pull away, ready to see sunlight again.

"Wouldn't want to keep Will waiting, would we?" he remarks.

But we have. I've lost track of time, but it must have

been more than an hour. It feels like we've been underground for a very long time.

At the top of the ladder is a heavy metal cover. Instead of asking Elliott for help raising it, I push with all my might, relying on my left hand, and the metal circle clanks to the side. I like being in the lead. I feel like everywhere I've gone, I've been following April, or Elliott, occasionally even Will. I'm ready for someone to follow me.

Once we're out, I let Elliott put it back in place.

Will is lounging on the third step of a columned building that must be the library. A small bottle and a brush sit between his feet. His left boot is untied, and the laces are muddy. His eyes travel up my body, from my own muddy shoes, to what's left of my dress. When he gets to my face, I inadvertently put my hand to my mask, as if he can see through it. As if he can tell how my lips are still throbbing.

"Your paint." He holds a bottle out to me.

"Maybe it's stupid, to try to leave a message," I falter, but then I catch sight of a wall unmarred by graffiti, and my resolve returns.

I uncork the paint and test my brush strokes. They are messy and the surface of the building is uneven, but it will do.

FIND ME, I write. IF YOU REMEMBER FINN.

CHAPTER

EIGHT

I HATE WRITING MY BROTHER'S NAME. IN ALL these years, it was never said aloud in our home. But if Father sees this, he'll know it's from me.

"How can I tell him we'll be at the club?"

Elliott grabs my wrist to stop me from writing. "We don't want to announce that. Not yet." He takes the paintbrush and draws an eye.

"I'm not sure Father knows about your—" I begin.

"He will," Elliott says. The meeting with the clockmaker certainly didn't affect his arrogance for long.

I scrawl messages wherever there is room, desecrating every wall with any proximity to the science building. Elliott paces, checking alleys and scanning balconies. Whenever I need more paint, Will is next to me, holding the bottle.

"He's manipulating you," Will says finally, in an undertone, eyeing Elliott.

I answer him while still painting my message. "From the stories April tells me, and from my only experience . . ." I flash him a look. "That's what guys do."

"You deserve better." His hand hovers near the side of my skirt, where the seams are nearly destroyed and the green satin is stained from my time in the tunnel with Elliott.

We've circled behind the building once more. Evening has fallen, and the quiet of this area has become ominous. Once the university had the most well-preserved buildings in the city. Now it feels haunted.

"Time to go," Elliott says, surveying the area. "We need information. The best way to collect it is to buy some drinks, and to listen."

Will and I fall into line behind him as he winds his way off the university campus. Dropping beside me, he opens his pack and removes the terrible flowered dress that the innkeeper's wife gave me.

"You should change. Yours is in extremely poor condition, and we're trying to avoid undue attention." As if he has any right to complain about the condition of my dress. Especially when his hand strokes down my side, lingering where my skin shows.

"This *was* a nice dress," I mutter, taking the cotton one from him. Elliott leads us into a narrow alley, thankfully free of corpses, through a back door, and into a dimly lit room.

Low tables, sofas, and chairs are scattered through a

series of interconnected rooms. A makeshift bar has been set up on a table, with an array of bottles and glasses. Though I can't see into the darkest corners, I think I see a door opened to a bedroom or sleeping chamber of some kind.

"This place was popular with university students," Elliott says, "when the university was still open." He points to the back. "The washroom is back there."

I can already tell this is not the sort of place where one wants to linger in the washroom. And I'm right. Though a mural has been painted on the wall, an alfresco painting of flowers and a scene that I think is supposed to be Venice, the room smells of mold and something even worse. A wide mirror is flanked by several candles, so at least there is some light as I attempt to make myself presentable.

I pull off my dress and fold it, then hold the new one in front of my body. It has a wide lace collar, and the hem falls almost to my ankles. Once I slip it over my head, I no longer look like a girl who spends her evenings at the Debauchery Club. I look sallow and lumpy in places where I am not. I know it's silly to care—at least I am alive—but . . .

At least by candlelight my hair still looks lustrous. April always said that candlelight was flattering to almost anyone.

I step out of the washroom and retrace my steps to where Elliott leans against the bar. Will stands next to him.

"You're good at this," Elliott is saying to him. "People talk to you. Circulate and listen. We need any rumor, no matter how ridiculous, about Araby's father. Everything people are saying about our enemies."

"I'll keep my ears open." As Will disappears into the shadows of an adjoining room, the way he walks takes me back to the days before I knew his name, when he was just the tattooed guy who worked in the Debauchery Club. The one whose voice made shivers run up and down my spine.

Elliott gestures to the barmaid, who shakes her head. "You can't afford the price," she says, taking in his muddy shoes and the poor condition of his clothing.

"You're new here." He throws several coins on the bar. Within moments she's brought us a chilled bottle and two glasses.

"We won't be drinking the water in the city," he says. "So this will have to do."

Elliott strikes up a conversation with her and several men sitting around us. I listen closely but don't say anything. Voices rise and fall. The anger and fear are practically palpable. This place is dangerous, but I suppose it's no more so than the city itself.

The people gathered at the tables are near our age, a few older, some younger. They are dirty and patched and ragged, and are constantly gesturing. They drink hard liquor. Mostly they are boys and young men, though there are a few girls who are as loud and vehement as anyone.

Everyone knows about Prospero's ball. They hate him for it. They despise him for his indifference while people are dying. Malcontent, however, is a more immediate threat. People speak of him in hushed voices. They speculate about what he looks like, whether any of them have walked past him on the street. Whether he could be here in this room.

They don't seem to know about the scar, where Prospero slit his throat while Elliott and April hid behind the curtains. They don't know who he truly is. I can't keep this to myself much longer.

Malcontent's people have been seen in the streets, but not en masse, the way we saw them, their feet pounding in unison through the tunnels beneath the city, the night that we escaped. They show up in groups of two or three, telling people their weird beliefs about the plague being sent from God.

Hours pass, and the clientele changes from the creative types who still gravitate to the university grounds to workers with lined faces and suspicious eyes.

The serving girl disappears into a back room, and I notice that the other girls have left the establishment, along with most of the younger men. A fellow at the bar looks me up and down. He elbows the man beside him and says something. They both laugh.

I lean in to Elliott. "I think it's time for me to leave."

He surveys the room. "It's not safe to travel after nightfall, but I'll rent a room. You didn't get much sleep last night. I'll stay here a bit longer and listen."

I nod. Ever since our trip through the tunnels this afternoon, I've been thinking about the book of maps I stole for Elliott from the Debauchery Club. He wouldn't have left that behind, so it must be in his pack. I need to find it and study it. This is as good an opportunity as I'm likely to get, if Elliott plans to leave me alone for a while.

He summons the bartender, and they speak quietly for a few moments. As we make our way across the crowded room to retrieve our packs, a bulky man snags my puffed sleeve and pulls me toward him.

Elliott reacts so fast that I can barely follow. He yanks the man from his barstool and holds him for a moment by the lapels of his coat, then throws him to the floor, hard. I expect the man to bolt to his feet, angry and ready to fight, but Elliott stands over him, hands clenched. The man stays where he is.

The bar is quiet for a moment, and then erupts into loud conversation, applause, vulgar suggestions. The ruckus draws Will. He eyes the man, who is slowly climbing back to his feet.

"That was impressive," Will says.

"Quick reflexes." Elliott gives Will a pointed look, directed at his slightly swollen lip. Was it just yesterday that Elliott hit him?

"You'll keep her safe?" Will asks.

"I'm fine," I say. "And I'll be fine."

"Tomorrow, then." Will picks up his pack.

And then Elliott sweeps me up two flights of stairs to a sleeping chamber. This establishment is as much a makeshift inn as a makeshift tavern.

"Bar the door behind me," Elliott says. "I don't know how long I'll be. The conversation was just beginning to get interesting."

Once he's gone, I hoist his bag onto one of the beds and search every part of it, even the tiny pockets sewn on the inside. I remove each of his weapons, laying the knives side by side on the coverlet. Ammunition. Gold coins that I let fall through my fingers. I ignore the silver coins and pennies and carefully unfold and refold a perfectly clean change of clothing, complete with a vest. In one of the smallest of the bag's pockets, I feel something hard and cold and sharp. I know what it is even before pulling my hand out to look at it. The facets of the diamond ring Elliott gave me gleam and glitter in the candlelight. I drop it back into the pocket and then replace everything except the book of maps, which was the very last thing at the bottom of the case.

I'm determined not to be dependent on Elliott's knowledge of the city. If we can't find my father, I'll have to go to Malcontent for the cure. I won't go blindly.

Memorization is a skill that my father taught both

me and Finn, making us recite nursery rhymes, poems, lists of scientific words, and finally graphs and illustrations. Finn was always better at it, but at least when I close my eyes, I can picture bits and pieces of the maps that I'm studying.

Once I've put the largest thoroughfares to memory, I focus on the tunnels. It isn't safe for a girl to move through the city. Even before the Red Death I was attacked and nearly lost Henry's mask. The danger has only increased now that Malcontent and his men haunt the streets. They also haunt the tunnels, but the risks may be less than on the streets.

Too soon, Elliott taps at the door, and I slip the maps back into his pack before unbarring it to let him in.

He's carrying a bottle of wine. He sets it on the table between the beds, and then stares at it as if he's never seen it before. His hair is messier than usual, and he's smiling to himself.

"People are talking about me," he says. "They didn't realize that I was among them, but they know that I've returned." He pulls back his coverlet and practically falls into bed.

As I lie down in my own, I realize that I won't be able to sleep in this dress. The fabric is rough, and it bunches up under me and scratches my arms.

Elliott is facing the other way, so I step out of the dress and hang it across a chair before sliding beneath the coverlet.

Without that discomfort, I fall asleep immediately and don't even dream.

When I wake to sunlight streaming through the window, Elliott is sitting in the chair beside my bed, sharpening one of his knives. Leaning back against my dress. I stop myself from bolting upright just in time.

"Good morning," he says. He looks at me curiously. "Are you naked under that blanket?"

"I'm wearing undergarments," I say through gritted teeth.

He raises his eyebrows, as if he doesn't believe me. I'm not going to prove it to him, if that's what he's expecting. I clutch the blanket around myself and glare at him. "Please hand me my dress."

"Oh, dear," he says, standing and lifting it with exaggerated care. "I thought it was a floor-length, flowered seat cover."

"It's better as a seat cover than a dress, but it's all I have now." I don't look at him when he hands me the dress. "Turn around while I put this on."

"I'd rather not."

"Elliott," I say in a low voice. When he doesn't move, I try a lighter tone. "You bought it for me. I suggest, if you don't want to look at it, purchase another dress."

"I will," he says. "I suppose for now you'll have to wear it."

He makes an exaggerated show of turning away, and I

pull the dress over my head. The collar flaps into place. I try to adjust the sleeves, wondering how the dress can be too big, but the sleeves too small.

When I tell Elliott he can look, he shifts back into his original position, tossing the knife on his bed, and begins cleaning his sword.

"Will you give me another lesson?" I ask, nodding toward the weapon.

He cocks his head to the side. "I don't think so." He retrieves the knife and hands it to me. "That is what I'm going to teach you to fight with. I should have from the beginning. Knives are easier; you have the element of surprise."

I pass the knife from hand to hand. Unlike the ivory-handled one that he gave me when we fled the university, after the last time I saw my father, this one has a handle of polished wood. The blade is wider.

"I've used a knife," I say.

"Yes, but not well. Come here, and I'll teach you a few tricks."

Who taught him all these tricks? His father? His uncle? A weapons master?

He takes my hand in his and shows me how to grip the wooden handle. Then he guides me in making controlled motions.

"Be sure your movements mean something. Don't just wave it around."

"It doesn't seem that hard," I say.

He laughs. "The hard thing is actually sticking the blade in someone." He slides back onto the unmade bed and pulls me with him. His back is against the headboard, and I'm practically on his lap, facing him. "Pushing a knife into someone's flesh is difficult. At first. If you have to do it, don't think. Just stab. You probably won't get a second chance, so make it count. Put the knife down, and I'll show you the places where you can do serious damage."

I set the knife beside us on the bed.

He takes my wrist and places my palm against his chest. "You can turn the knife and stab between the ribs," he says. And then he pulls my hand down to his stomach. "Or, if you want to kill him, aim here."

How much harm I could bring myself to inflict? Do I want to know how best to do it?

He's watching me closely. "Do you think you could kill someone?"

"If I had to," I say.

"It gets easier over time."

He releases my wrist, but I leave my hand resting right above the third button of his shirt. He's no longer giving me matter-of-fact instruction on how to kill a man, but the way he's looking at me is unsettling.

He closes his eyes and leans in to me. I slide my hand up to his shoulder and push him back.

He opens his eyes and frowns. "Why is it that we never kiss unless we've almost died?"

I shift sideways so that my shoulder is against his chest. He has a point. "It's easier, after we've been in danger, for us to let go of our distrust of each other."

After a moment, he puts his arm around me. "I don't suppose I trust anyone," he says finally. "Not fully."

Hearing him admit it is sad. For him, and for us. But I don't blame him.

I have never trusted Elliott. Not completely. And he never wanted me to. But our experiences have not been so different.

I hear a voice from the hallway, and then another, a conversation beginning. The establishment is waking up.

"Sun's up," I observe, grabbing the knife as I slide to the side of the bed. "Time to look for my father."

"The clockmaker is sending out his scavengers to search."

"It isn't enough." Being in the city makes me realize the difficulty of finding one man who does not wish to be found.

"I'm not going to spend the entire day walking the streets and calling your father's name," he says. "The only way we'll stumble over your father is if he's dead."

"That isn't funny."

If Father is dead, he can't answer to me for his lies and his crimes. He won't be able to save April.

"I wasn't trying to be funny." Elliott's strapping on his sword, readjusting his pack. "I'm being practical. We won't find him by wandering around. Today I will mobilize my men, begin the takeover of the city. Once my soldiers are patrolling, they can look for your father, too."

He's only reaffirming my fear that the city is too big and has too many hiding places.

"I sent Will out on some errands last night. He'll meet us at the tavern where we ate yesterday. I may need to put their steam carriage to use." He opens the door to the room and gestures for me to exit.

The sun is shining outside. Mornings in the city are often foggy, but the sky is clear today.

It seems strange, walking with Elliott without Will on my other side.

"What sort of errands did you send him on?" I ask.

He raises his eyebrows. "He took messages to some of my men."

"This morning? Or last night? Traveling at night is dangerous."

"He knew that coming with us would be dangerous."

"Try not to get him killed," I say. Elliott makes a show of scanning the street ahead of us, his hand on the hilt of his sword.

"I wasn't trying to get him killed," he says finally. "His ideals are misguided, but I don't wish for him to die."

"What would it take for you to trust him?" I ask. Because we need to somehow trust one another.

"What would it take for *you* to trust him?" he counters.

I would have to forget how he betrayed me.

"At least in a few nights the children will be in the city. If he falls out of line— well, we know his weakness."

"I would never threaten Henry or Elise."

"Then I know your weakness, too." I wait for him indicate that he's not serious, but his attention has shifted to the city around us.

Smoke rises from the next city street. At first I think another building is burning, but instead it seems to be coming from a series of contained campfires.

A village of dismal burlap tents has sprung up across what must have once been a park, and it spills over to cover the cracked foundations of a warehouse. Clotheslines are stretched between some of the tents, and a few brave vegetables are growing in pots. A dog barks at us from inside the perimeter.

"Can't they find buildings to live in?" I ask. The city has always had enough empty buildings that most people can find at least partial shelter.

"Perhaps they think the buildings are contaminated in some way," Elliott says, and I remember how the corpse collectors used to paint black scythes on doors. What happens when all the doors have been marked? Perhaps people will just abandon the city, whisper that it's haunted, and live in tents.

"At least they are trying," Elliott continues, "instead of just squatting in their ruined buildings with the dead. I can work with people who have the initiative to make their lives better."

I don't know how it happened, but I'm holding Elliott's hand. Not clinging to it or allowing him to pull me along—my hand just somehow found its way into his.

We pass the burned shell of an apartment building. A paper is nailed to the charred remains of a door. I stop to reach for it with my free hand. The ink is red and ran in a bloody trail down the parchment.

DOWN WITH SCIENCE. KILL THE SCIENTIST.

I drop the paper. The tip of my finger is stained red. I wipe it inside the sleeve of my dress, where a stain is less likely to show, but the ink has soaked into my skin.

"They want to kill my father."

"Do you blame them?"

I don't answer him.

"I find it ironic . . . when I asked your father for information about the masks, he scorned my help. Your mother may have told him things that I'd done as a boy, and he judged me, but at the same time, he was never truly the hero he pretended to be. Was he?"

"He was to me," I say quietly. "And I'm not going to stop thinking that until he looks me in the eye and tells me that when he made the virus"—this is the first time I've admitted aloud that I know he did it—"that it wasn't an accident, that he wasn't forced to—"

"Why does that matter? Thousands of people died either way."

"I just need to know," I say. "Wouldn't you want . . . ?"

I trail off. Elliott isn't aware of the truth about his own father. I throw him a sidelong look and brace myself to tell him, but he doesn't give me the chance.

"*Your* father is a hypocritical murderer whose only thought was the sake of discovery. Not the safety of the people."

The words are ugly. And they could be true.

If I tell him about his own father now, it will seem as if I am simply retaliating.

We walk in silence for a long time. I try to get my bearings, to connect the maze of streets and buildings to the grids and squares that I memorized last night.

Looking up at a wrought-iron rail that surrounds a low balcony, I gasp. A dead man's head, streaked with red, is in the window box, as if he was crawling out the window of his apartment and died before he made it.

We pass a series of scythes painted in the same garish red as the pamphlet calling for Father's death. The same red as my fingertip. Malcontent's sign.

Elliott scans the buildings that line our route very carefully. A pile of broken masks lies beside a charred brick wall. "Malcontent," Elliott mutters. "If he has his way, only his faithful will survive."

He stops and reaches into his pack. "Before we reach the tavern, I want to give you this." If he gives back the diamond ring, I'm not sure what I will do. The first time he gave it to me, our relationship was fake. Now, I'm not sure what it is.

But instead of the ring, he pulls out a small handgun. A gun that can be concealed, like this one, is very rare and very expensive.

"Thank you." I'm able to exclaim over the little gun more effusively than I ever could over the ring. The ivory handle matches the knife I keep in the top of my boot.

"It only holds two bullets. So shoot to kill and don't miss."

I nod, amazed that he bought me such a gift. That he's thinking of my safety.

"You may be wondering where it was hidden, since it wasn't in my pack last night."

I look up. What gave away that I'd rummaged through his things? And is he truly laughing about it?

We really do deserve each other, Elliott and I.

"Keep it close," he says. And we continue on.

Our footsteps echo against the paving stones. It seems this entire area has been emptied. I only see one corpse lying in a dilapidated doorway. But the marching of many feet resounds from nearby. The last time I heard that sound was from Malcontent's men in the tunnels. Can Elliott and I hold off a whole troop of soldiers and live?

Elliott pulls me into a doorway and stands in front of me. The pounding feet draw closer. I grip my gun tightly, ready to fire.

A group of men turn the corner, and Elliott lets out a

breath. He leaves our hiding place. "Don't worry. These men are mine."

I count twenty, in makeshift uniforms.

"Elliott, sir," the one in the lead says. "We were heading to meet you at the tavern."

"Let's move." Elliott motions the men forward, and I step out from the doorway. "I don't want to linger in this area."

"She'll be going with us?" The soldier glances at me.

"Yes," I say, holding his gaze.

Elliott smiles. "Araby isn't afraid of less than reputable establishments."

I don't like the way he said my name, possessively, informally, as if his men should all know it. But I follow them down the street. As I turn the corner, I nearly run into the soldier in front of me, because everyone has abruptly halted.

Before us is a uniformed soldier, his gun drawn, the tip pressed to the head of a child.

CHAPTER
NINE

THE BOY CAN'T BE OLDER THAN ELISE. SORES mar his forehead and left cheek. He's obviously infected with the contagion. The soldier has his gun pressed so hard to the boy's forehead—if he took it away, it would leave a mark.

Tears stream down the soldier's face. He doesn't look away from the child, even as Elliott speaks.

"What is the meaning of this?" His voice is calm.

"Tell him," the soldier growls. His hand is beginning to tremble.

The boy's eyes move to Elliott. "The reverend commands us to walk through the upper city, speaking to everyone. Touching them if possible."

"You're spreading the contagion."

"Yes." The child collapses to the sidewalk.

"This is what we are up against." Elliott casts his voice

so that all of the men behind can hear him. "Malcontent wants the city, even if that means infecting each and every one of us. Those who live with it, like his soldiers, can remain. The rest will die."

I kneel down beside the boy. "Leave the city. Don't ever come back."

"I can't," the boy says. "He'll send the Hunter for me."

"Araby, he can't be allowed to continue," Elliott says.

He is not rational on this topic. Elliott is terrified of the spread of disease. It's the one thing he's never been able to plan ahead for, and he is enraged by the way Malcontent is using it. I don't blame him. Malcontent's intentions are horrible. His use of this child is vile. But fear and anger are not a good combination.

The soldier, sensing approval in Elliott's words, refocuses on the boy, prepared to shoot.

"Put your gun down," I say. "Please."

He looks to Elliott. Elliott's eyebrows go up. And they don't go down, even when I add the "please." He doesn't like me commanding his soldiers any better than he likes me telling him what to do. But I can't let them hurt this child. The way the man's arm is shaking, I'm terrified that the gun will go off.

"Please, Elliott." My voice rings out in the alley. "Think of April—"

"If we let him go, he'll return tomorrow. Who knows how many people he's already infected?" Elliott grabs me and crushes my face into his immaculate white shirt.

The gun fires.

I shove Elliott as hard as I can.

But the soldier shot wide. The gun falls to the ground with a clatter beside the boy, who looks up at us, eyes wide. Tears stream down the soldier's face. But I'm afraid if the soldier couldn't do it, Elliott will kill the boy himself.

"Take him back to the swamp," I insist, standing between Elliott and the boy.

"We have to send a message to Malcontent that we won't let his people attack us."

"If everyone had masks, there wouldn't be a reason to fear them." I don't move, even as Elliott steps toward us. "We should be saving people, not killing them."

The soldiers shift, and the boy seems so small and lost, crouched beside the gun that was meant to kill him.

"Take him out of the city," Elliott says finally. "We won't stoop to Malcontent's level, using children. But if any of you hear word of him, I want to know immediately."

Across the street, someone opens their shutters and peers out. What do they make of so many men standing over a shaking child?

"If Malcontent's followers are willing to leave the city, escort them to the periphery. Otherwise, shoot to kill. Burn the bodies. And if any of our men do not have functional masks, send them to me."

A soldier prods the boy with the barrel of his gun.

"Come along," he says. Two of the soldiers fall in line behind them. The rest follow us.

As we approach the tavern from the opposite side, I look for Will, searching the shadows where the cloaked man was hiding yesterday. All I see are more of Elliott's soldiers. They seem to be everywhere, standing in doorways, talking, smoking. Elliott nods to them, lifting one hand in a half wave before we enter the common room of the inn.

Inside it's dark, and I stand beside Elliott, blinking while my eyes adjust. Every table is filled, and men line the walls. Some of them are in uniform, others in ragged street clothes, but they all come to attention when they spot us.

Elliott surveys the room, and then gives a little half bow. The men at the tables raise their mugs and cheer. The room may be dim, but it can't hide the startling whiteness of Elliott's teeth as he grins.

At the back of the room there's a table on a platform, so it sits a little higher than the rest. We make our way toward it. I'm surprised to see Will sitting there, and even more so when he slides a stack of papers down to me and hands another to Elliott.

Elliott places the pamphlets on the table and pulls out a chair for me. Once I sit, he stays behind me, both hands gripping the back of the chair, and clears his throat.

"Thank you," he calls. "Today we begin the takeover of this city." All eyes are fixed upon him, and his hands are trembling hard enough that I can feel it through my chair.

"But we must work strategically," he continues, his voice steadily growing stronger. "First we will take up residency in the Debauchery District. You can find me in the Debauchery Club when I'm not on the streets fighting by your side. Starting tomorrow we'll move families into the empty buildings. We will find workers for the distillery to make our water safe to drink. We will work together to kill the coward who calls himself Malcontent, who hides in the shadows and plans to kill us all."

The men raise their tankards and cheer. Some are stomping their feet, some clapping, and the room reverberates with their enthusiasm. One after the other they rise to their feet, saluting Elliott.

Did Elliott have this plan all along, or did the sea of tents we encountered this morning give him the idea?

Will also stands, but the way he's clapping, I'm quite sure that no sound comes from the meeting of his hands. He isn't mocking Elliott, not openly, but I can tell he's questioning Elliott's intentions.

I reach for the stacks of papers that he gave to us when we arrived. One stack outlines Elliott's plan. A plan that he shared with Will, obviously, but not with me.

Not only does everyone who wishes to have Elliott's protection move to the Debauchery District—Elliott has promised to find them clean water and food. How can he and the men in this room guarantee that?

The other stack, the one that Will gave me, is twice as tall. It is my message to Father, printed in bold letters.

IF YOU REMEMBER FINN, FIND ME. With Elliott's symbol printed beneath.

When I look up, Will has disappeared. His spot at the table has been taken by three men, pushing forward, ready to follow Elliott to the ends of the earth.

The innkeeper, also beaming, brings us plates filled with food and some sort of distilled beverage. Men circulate through the room. Some of them slap Elliott on the back. Others want to shake my hand, which is awkward, since for once I'm trying to eat.

Elliott is not eating, but he takes his seat beside me and rests his hand on my thigh. Possessively.

A group of older men enters the inn from the street and approaches our table.

"I like your ideas," one says. He stands awkwardly, holding one of Will's papers. I lean forward to get a better look at him, and our eyes lock. He stops speaking, his lip curling. He recognizes me. And I recognize him. He was one of Father's guards.

Elliott takes his hand from my leg, and I think for a moment that he's repudiating me in the face of this man's distaste, but instead he pulls my chair closer to his and drapes one arm over my shoulders.

"You were saying?" he asks. The man continues his

praise for Elliott's plans, still trying not to look at me. Other men begin to whisper.

Not only do these men hate Father, they hate me. Even though they've never met me, they eye me with disgust. The mood in the room has shifted from friendly camaraderie to something dark and menacing.

"Scientist's daughter," I hear someone hiss.

The scientist. It used to be the name of their hero. Now it is a curse. Their disillusionment with my father mirrors my own. And yet I don't deserve their hostility.

"Elliott?" These are his men. I cannot allow myself to get angry, not yet. He touches my jaw with his thumb, caressing my face.

A soldier with an eye patch pipes up. "How many of us have lost our children, our wives? It would serve the scientist right—"

It's too much. Some of these men, these fighters who have come at Elliott's call, would hurt me to punish my father. I stand, ready to condemn their hypocrisy.

"I am the scientist's daughter." But my voice comes out low, and I doubt anyone who isn't at this particular table can hear. I take a deep breath and continue. "I'm also a sister. I lost my brother to the plague, and my mother to the prince." My voice breaks.

The room is silent. Elliott puts down his tankard.

"Yes," he says, pushing back his chair and standing beside me. "And she's here *with me*. I want her father found, and I want him *alive*."

The soldiers look at one another and slowly nod. Elliott sweeps his gaze over the rest of the room and then sits down. He gestures to my chair, but sitting feels weak. Though the aggression has dissipated, I don't want to stay here. This room is crowded now, claustrophobic. I search for Will, but he's nowhere to be found.

"I'm going outside," I say to Elliott. "To get some air."

He prepares to stand to go with me, but I don't want him. I need a few moments alone. I never cared much for my celebrity status as the scientist's daughter. But I'd grown accustomed to it. I knew that he was no longer a hero, not even in my own mind. But seeing the hatred, the violence here, is shocking. I clench my hands into fists to keep them from shaking.

As I walk out of the inn I try to meet as many soldiers' eyes as I can. I don't want them to think that I'm running away.

The inn is close to the river, and I can hear running water. I force myself to picture it flowing over creek stones rather than the rib cages of the dead. Some of Elliott's men are outside, standing in small groups. They seem very relaxed, and though several of them glance at me, sneering a little, they don't say anything. Why are they standing around drinking? They should be acting. Elliott should be doing something. Anything.

I scan the street and spot Will on the front steps of a building across the street. He sees me at the same time and leaps up. I hadn't noticed before, but he's dressed like he used to be at the club: fitted pants and a black shirt.

"Elliott let you come out here alone?" He's a bit short of breath as he approaches.

"He didn't *let* me. I told him I was leaving."

He leads me back across the street to the vague shelter of a partially intact brick wall, scuffing his boot in the dirt.

"I shouldn't have left you in there."

"I'm not your responsibility either," I snap.

He leans against the wall, crossing his arms over his chest. His dark eyes bore into me.

"I'm here to help you. I can't make up for what I did, but since we're both here now, I'm going to aid you in any way I can." He looks tired. His eyes are framed with beautiful thick lashes, but there are dark circles beneath them.

"Just don't get in my way, trying to protect me."

"I wouldn't dream of it. If you wanted to be coddled, you wouldn't be here."

"Walk with me," I say, because I need to move. Getting away from the tavern, the hostile glances, makes me feel lighter, less weighted by guilt and worry. I smile, and Will smiles back at me. We pause in late-afternoon sunshine for several long moments.

"Come," I say, and take off with renewed energy.

The buildings on this street merge into one another,

rectangular windows, square, white stone ledges. A small face gazes down from a window. How often did Henry and Elise watch passersby from the window of Will's apartment? I miss the children. The days I spent there with them.

As we move from one alley to the next, oily smoke obscures the sunlight. The wood frame of an apartment building is smoldering. I run my foot over the gritty paving stones, and the movement reveals a carving in one of them. A flower. This city was once beautiful.

"Let's hang some of these flyers," Will says. "Elliott wants me to hang his, anyway."

"Is it hopeless?" I ask, looking up at him. Yesterday, walking through the city, I was overwhelmed by the odds of finding Father, particularly with the mob also hunting him.

Will shakes his hair out of his face. "There's always hope," he says quietly.

He digs in a bag he's carrying for a light hammer and some nails before taking one of the flyers from my hand. As he affixes it to the charred door of an apartment building, the cuff of his shirt slips back, revealing a tendril of dark tattoo around his left wrist.

It's thinner than the rest of the tattoos, and I never noticed it before. He reaches out for another flyer. But my hand is empty. I touch the tattoo for a moment before pulling my hand back.

"Sorry," I mumble, and shuffle for another flyer.

"Might as well give me one of Elliott's also," he says.

"Why did you agree to work for him?" I slide one of Elliott's papers into his hand, careful not to touch him again.

"I'd rather be useful than not." Will attaches it to a wooden door with a thin nail. "As long as Elliott is keeping his side of the bargain and keeping you safe." He sets a small stack of papers on a stoop outside an apartment building. "Though if you're outside alone in that crowd, then maybe he's not."

"His men are loyal. They won't hurt me. The way they . . . looked at me didn't hurt me." My voice shakes a little at the end of the sentence, negating everything I just said.

Will reaches for another paper, and once again I am very careful not to let our hands touch. Careful not to look up into his eyes. I don't want to see the concern there. Can't let the quaver in my voice turn into full-blown weakness.

"It's difficult to be hated after being loved," I say quickly. "For Father to become a villain overnight. I'll get used to it."

"I hope you don't have to."

"If I stay with Elliott—"

Will freezes. Is he upset because I suggested my relationship with Elliott might be permanent, or was his stillness in response to the word "if," suggesting that it might not?

I study the flyer in my hand, unwilling to look at Will. I don't want to see his surprise, his hope, whatever emotion he is struggling with.

"This building is just a shell," he says. "Let's get out of this alley."

The air is fresher out of the shadow of half-burned buildings with their charred timbers exposed. We're now several streets away from Elliott and the tavern.

These must be the oldest buildings in the city. The masonry on the ornate doorways and around the arched windows is crumbling. Does anyone even live here anymore? Could Father be in one of these desolate homes? We pause in the shadow of a cathedral.

"If I remember correctly, there are steam-powered bathhouses on this street," Will says. "Kent used to drag me here to look at the mechanisms. And I just wanted to hang out in the Debauchery District. Now I see how important it is to learn about the world around us. Now, and the world before the plague."

I nod, enjoying the sound of his voice.

"I could have learned so many things from my father."

He knew more than anyone in the city, and I never even questioned him. All I experienced was what I could see from April's fancy steam carriage. Will knows this, but he has the decency not to say anything.

We walk along together, stopping occasionally to hang more flyers. The shadows are lengthening, and as always, the city looks increasingly sinister as darkness falls.

"We should get back," I say. "We've come a long way."

"That we have." Will stares out across the street for a moment, and then he turns to me, his eyes crinkled in a smile above the white of his mask. He hangs one more flyer. His hands are as deft as they ever were in the Debauchery Club, taking my blood. "I'll get these up as widely as possible," he offers. "I know a lot of places, and I can operate on very little sleep. You never know where your father might be hiding. He could be someplace you would never expect."

I used to think that Father was predictable, with his thoughtful but fumbling way of speaking, his vagueness. "Parents are supposed to be boring," I say bitterly, hating myself for a burst of anger that feels childish. Useless.

"He's smart enough to find a hiding place where the mob won't find him." Will's voice is neutral.

But I don't respond, because something brushes against my ankle. I look down at a hand thrust through rotten wood at the base of the building. It grips my ankle and pulls hard, knocking me sideways into Will. The flyers scatter around us.

I scream once, and then the hidden assailant pulls my feet completely out from under me. I try to scramble backward through the dirt, but the hands don't let go, and now a whole arm is exposed. A man's arm, marred with weeping sores, reaching from some unseen cellar. The wood splinters at the base of the building.

Papers fly everywhere in the wind.

As the man pulls me forward, my left leg twists under my body. I claw at the knife in that boot, feeling a brief chill as the blade slides against my hand, a flash of pain. Then, finally, it's free. I thrust it forward, aiming for the area between his thumb and forefinger, the fattest part of the man's grimy, infected hand.

Will's shadow falls over me. He stomps down hard, and his boot crushes the man's grubby wrist. Then he lunges forward, grabbing the diseased man by both of his arms and pulling him up. He dashes the attacker's head violently against the building wall. When he lets go, the man falls away from us, into the cellar, as if he has no bones to support himself.

I'm sprawled in the street, and Will is half over me. We don't move for several breaths.

A bloody stain drips down the wall. I lean forward and peer into the cellar. It's full of low tables and bodies. I gasp and almost scramble away. But . . . there is no sudden stench. No sickly sweet smell of rotting corpses. No sign of movement. Perhaps the black shapes aren't victims, but simply heaps of dark cloaks.

Is this some sort of hideout or storehouse for Malcontent's men? How many of them are down there?

A crash from inside the cellar makes me jump, and Will wraps his arms around me, yanking me away from the opening.

"Come on," he says. "If someone is down there . . . we need to run."

My first step lands on a flyer and I slip, but Will catches me. Then we are running, my hand in his, threading through streets and alleys to the tavern where Elliott's men come to attention as they see us wildly dashing toward them.

We burst through the front doors, gasping for breath. Will explains quickly, and Elliott takes off in the direction we came from. His men follow, pouring around me as if I am some sort of blockade in their path.

But I won't be left behind.

Will tries to hold me back, but I pull away, so he follows. By the time we return, Elliott and his men have pushed through the wooden door. Others are involved in knocking away the rotten wood at the base between the foundation stones and the upper part of the building.

A soldier carries out a heap of ragged homespun robes.

"Don't touch anything if you don't have a mask." Elliott's voice is not exactly afraid, but concerned. I see him jump from the top of the cellar stairs, all movement and excitement. He's at his best, commanding his men. "We'll burn everything except the weapons." But then his demeanor changes. "Out," he yells, just as I cross the threshold, his voice higher than usual. "Everyone out. This man died of the Red Death."

The soldiers flee the building. But Elliott won't join them. He won't risk his men, but he isn't afraid of risking himself.

And he has no protection from the Red Death. I

offered him whatever was in that tiny vial that Father gave me, but he put the glass to my lips and made me drink it instead. If anyone is protected from the Red Death, it's me.

Slowly, ignoring the twinge in my ankle, I enter.

The last sunlight has faded outside, and it is fully dark inside. In his deliberate way, Elliott strikes a match against the wall, watches it for half an instant, and then drops it onto the pile of robes. "This will provide a little light," he says as they ignite. "But also smoke. We only have a few moments to discover what this place was."

It seems to be something of a storeroom. Several bottles of liquor stand on a table, as well as a loaf of bread and some dark lumps that must be rotting vegetables.

"Look for a door," Elliott says.

I spot it before he does and move forward across the uneven floor. The body of the man Will killed is close enough that I could touch it if I wanted to. But I try not to look at it. The door is small, like the one we saw in the clockmaker's basement workshop. Elliott pushes against it, but it won't budge.

"Sir?" One of the soldiers asks from outside.

Elliott throws his weight against the door, but still nothing happens.

"It's locked from the other side," he says. The cellar is filling with smoke. We're out of time—my eyes are watering and my throat is closing. I start back, but I trip over the body, and even in the inferno I see it clearly. Two blood tears stain the cheeks.

"Come." Elliott guides me back to the street, and then turns to help the men. Will pulls me around the bend in the alley, where none of the soldiers or bystanders can see us.

His face is set. Calm.

"You killed him, before the Red Death did," I say softly.

He shrugs. "If he wanted to live, he shouldn't have grabbed you."

The light of the moon is faint, but it shines on a tiny jagged scar just above his eyebrow. There's disgust on his face, but no remorse.

Without meaning to, I reach up and touch the scar. "How did you get that?"

"That one is from a girl in the Debauchery Club. I was trying to get her to the door. She lashed out. Her fingernail caught me there."

He's calm about the memory, and about what he just did, but I know how he loathes violence.

"I'm sure you saw many . . . interesting things at the club."

He laughs. "I'm not sure 'interesting' is the right word. But yes, I saw things." Before I can ask him to elaborate, Elliott is there with us.

CHAPTER
TEN

ELLIOTT OFFERS ME HIS COAT, BUT I DON'T NEED IT.

The crack in my mask seems to have gotten worse, probably in the fight, and it's sharp against my lips.

"Are we going to the Debauchery Club?" I ask as one of Elliott's men quietly hands him our packs. He must have sent him back to retrieve them.

"That's what I told everyone," Elliott says. He looks to Will. "Did you prepare for our arrival?"

"Yes."

"Good. We'll arrive early tomorrow. Tonight, I'd rather no one know where we are sleeping." He gives the smoldering cellar a last look, as if the man's attack is tied to his caution.

Behind us, the entire building that housed Malcontent's supply cellar is burning. A few families from the upper floors stumble down the stairs and to the street.

"Make sure they find someplace safe to stay," Elliott tells one of his soldiers, and then he's leading us away, though my legs feel rubbery and weak.

"I'll want to continue our search for my father tomorrow," I tell Elliott.

"Of course." He nods but shifts from one foot to the other. Today he got a taste of leadership, and while I'm happy for him and I support his quest to take over the city, I won't let him forget his sister.

I walk by Elliott's side through the frightful streets and alleys, always aware of Will two steps behind us. Shadows creep in around us, full of the threat of Malcontent's malice. We killed one of his men today, but how many hundreds does he have? Do we have any chance fighting both them and the plagues?

Elliott stops before a wrought-iron gate. The building it guards is set back from the street. Elliott leads us through the gate to a shadowed stairway that winds around the side of the house and then down beneath.

The entrance isn't like the one that led to the cellar where I lived with my father and Finn. This house is much nicer, the neighborhood grander. But something, the angle of the stairs, the brick on the side of the building, takes me back. All of a sudden I am ten years old, staring down the cellar stairs that led to years of exile. Years in the dark with Finn. Mother slinking away, out of the corner of my eye. I know now that she didn't choose to leave us, didn't want to go, but the memory still stings. And Finn died in that cellar.

"We'll be safe here," Elliott claims. But I feel anything but safe. "We shouldn't be where we are expected to be, not yet. Not with so much riding on me. On us."

It makes sense, but I shake my head. My nightmares, the ones that forced Father to sedate me, always occurred in a cellar.

I look away from the entrance, and I focus on the empty street. The leaves rasp against the sidewalk. The moon is unnaturally bright. Footsteps echo from the street beyond. Heavy footsteps.

Both Will and Elliott are waiting for me to continue, to descend into this new cellar, but I don't move.

"We need to get inside, Araby." Elliott's voice is cool, calm.

"No," I say.

But he ignores me, walking carefully down the stairs and opening the door into darkness. I tremble.

I feel Will come up behind me. He's standing very close but doesn't touch me. "You can do this." Then he takes my hand.

He eases forward, waiting for me to take the first step. I draw a deep breath—I've done things that were harder than this—and follow Will into the darkness, through a door and into a dimly lit room. Luckily this cellar didn't get any overflow from the flooded tunnels, so it's not wet, just stuffy. I imagine spiders in the corners and other insects under the faded rug.

A bed is pushed against a far wall of the room, and a chest sits beside it. There are also several low tables and oil lamps. Elliott has already lit some, and Will lets go of my hand to take care of the rest.

A large wardrobe stands against the back wall.

"Is anyone thirsty?" Elliott pulls a bottle of wine from his pack and pours it into a few short glasses. He passes one to me, and I drink deeply, trying to force myself to be calm. This cellar is safe, secret, and nothing like the one where Finn died.

"You take the bed, Araby," Elliott says. He wraps himself in his own blankets and settles in a corner.

I set one of the lamps on the chest beside the bed. The quilt thrown over the mattress has a dark stain— not unlike the blanket we wrapped my brother in. But I will the panic away, taking a blanket from my pack and spreading it on the floor. Neither of the boys says anything or moves to claim the bed. Will sits at the table. Both he and Elliott seem lost in their own thoughts.

I carefully position myself near the center of the room, away from corners where spiders might nest. I wrap myself tightly in the blanket so that nothing can crawl in and touch me. Sleep doesn't come easily, but eventually, lying very still, I nod off.

My dreams are dark. Men descend the stairs with knives. A familiar armchair sits where Finn and I used to read. In my dream, the men carry bloody knives. They have killed Finn. April is next. Someone grabs me. I throw myself to the side . . . and that's when I wake, my throat tight, my shoulder throbbing. And I can't move. I thrash for a moment until I realize that I'm wrapped in Will's arms and I'm holding on to him as if he will save me from my memories.

It's like the first time I woke beside him, the night he took me home from the club. I shift carefully, propping myself on one arm just enough so that I can see him. Two buttons are undone on his shirt. Were they like that earlier, or did it happen as we moved together and intertwined? His hair is so dark against his collar.

As if he feels me looking, he opens his eyes. I start to pull away, embarrassed to be caught like this, looking down at him.

But then he reaches up to touch my cheek.

"Araby, go back to sleep. Otherwise you'll hate yourself in the morning."

"I already hate myself." I should pull away, but instead I settle back against him and pretend that this isn't a cellar. That Elliott isn't sleeping only a few feet away.

In the darkness, my eyes find the single lamp that the boys left lit. The floorboards are hard and unforgiving. I think I hear something from behind the wardrobe, a soft tapping that reminds me of a frightening story that Finn used to tell me when Father worked late in the laboratory and the two of us were alone in the dark. If I got too afraid, he would hold me, like Will is now.

And just like it used to, it keeps the nightmares at bay.

The next morning I wake lying alone, and the three of us walk across the city to the Debauchery Club. It takes hours, so by the time we approach the club it's afternoon.

The day we fled the city, Malcontent's soldiers were climbing up from the sewers, swarming through the district. They chased us up three flights of stairs at the Morgue, and the Debauchery Club was not left unharmed either. The door leans against the frame, the hinges twisted and broken.

Elliott lifts it from the entrance and props it far enough aside that we can enter. Once we do, Will puts it back into place as well as he can.

"Who's there?" a voice calls. We all jump, and a serving boy peers around the corner. "Oh, it's you," he says to Will, relief in his voice. "And you, sir." He gives Elliott a long, unfriendly look. "I prepared rooms," he tells Will. "We expected you last night."

The paneling in the hallway is slightly charred from fire, but otherwise this area seems fine. The lights in the floor are still glowing. I run my foot over them, relieved at the familiarity.

"My old rooms?" Elliott asks.

The boy nods. "They weren't damaged, much. The young lady's room is across the hall."

Elliott's eyebrows shoot up. Will smiles to himself.

"Excellent," I say to the boy. Regardless of Will and Elliott's power plays, I'll enjoy having a room to myself tonight.

"I'll check everything," Will says. And then he's gone, following the boy to the servant's quarters.

When he's gone, I immediately feel less secure. Even though that's preposterous. I'm safe with Elliott.

"I'm going to go examine my steam carriage," Elliott says. "You can go upstairs if you'd like."

But it's worthwhile to see where his carriage is housed, so I follow him to the stables. A few saddles hang from hooks on the walls, as well as strips of metal that I think were used for guiding horses, but the stalls have been removed.

Elliott's steam carriage is in the center of the stable. Even in the dingy surroundings, it gleams. He runs his hands over the metalwork.

"No more walking," he murmurs.

"They say your uncle is requisitioning carriages," I remind him. "We have to be cautious."

"He can only take it if he can catch us. With the modifications I've made to this one, it can outrun any other carriage in the city."

That won't help if someone ambushes us, like Malcontent tried to do before, stretching ropes across the street to stop us. But Elliott won't be careless with one of the last steam carriages in the city. Will he?

In the doorway to the stable, we look up at the

mishmash of buildings that form the Debauchery Club. Three buildings interconnected around a courtyard.

"What is our plan for the rest of the day?" I ask. I haven't prompted him to look for Father today, but yesterday passed too quickly. I know we need a permanent place to stay, where Father can find me if he gets my messages. Still, I'm ready to begin the search again.

"I asked Will to compose a rough map of the building and all of its entrances." Elliott says. "He already compiled a list of the current residents. Servants. Aristocrats who never went home after the last attacks. Anyone who could be lurking around the building."

"And when will we search for Father?"

"Soon," he says. "And don't worry. I have people searching."

Yes. I heard him say that he wanted Father taken alive.

We enter through a side door that is still on its hinges, the very door that Will led me through when we fled the club for the one next door, the Morgue.

"Are his men on the third floor still here?" I ask, meaning Prospero's old henchmen who used to watch us from the shadows of the club.

"They're still here," Elliott says darkly. "As always, avoid them."

In this quiet passage of the Debauchery Club, it feels like the outside world can't touch us, and yet we have enemies, even here.

As we pass the door that leads to the kitchens, Elliott

says, "If you are ever in the cellars, watch for trapdoors. Secret rooms. I want to know where that printing press is located."

"Why don't you ask Will?"

"Because, my dear Araby, he won't tell me," Elliott says. "And I think you would object if I suggested torturing him."

He's testing me. But I'm not sure what he is trying to determine. Whether I care about Will? Whether I'm completely dedicated to his cause?

"I would never let you torture any of our friends." I smile at him, but his response is completely serious.

"I doubt I'll need to resort to it. The printing press is large, it can't be that cleverly hidden. We'll find it."

"Unless we're going to search for it now, I suppose we'd better move on," I tell him.

"Come upstairs." He offers me his arm, and after a moment, I take it. "You'll need something to wear," he says. "We need to eat, to regroup with the men and whoever's left here. And your dress reeks of smoke."

His rooms are exactly as I remember them, except for the state of his bookcase. The leather volumes are shoved haphazardly on the shelves, some even upside down. Elliott leads me through the sitting room to his sleeping chamber. I pause at the threshold, but he continues to the dressing room.

"Here," Elliott brings out a dress and tosses it to me. "This should do. I'll wait out here."

Once I'm alone I scrub my hands quickly in his wash-basin, wincing at the state of my fingernails. I take off the flowery dress and kick it to the side. The new dress is a soft silvery-gray silk, shot through with threads that are almost white.

It fits perfectly, and when I open the door of the dressing chamber, Elliott has changed too. Waiting for me. He's wearing black, with a gray vest of the same fabric as my dress. He takes out a matching silver pocket watch and considers it.

"This dress is lovely," I say. "I'd have expected something brighter from April's spares."

Silence stretches out between us. His posture is stiff and uninviting. I touch the fabric of my sleeve. He never said the dress belonged to April. I am a fool. The green one he gave me for the steamship's christening was probably not April's either. Elliott's life didn't begin when he met me. I never assumed it did. But the way the vest and the dress match—that had to be intentional.

Before I can find the words to question him, he snaps the pocket watch closed. "Let's go to the dining room," he says. Elliott takes my arm, and as we pass by a mirror I can't help admiring the picture we make.

As we enter I search the room for Will, but the table holds six chairs and he isn't in one. All of the men are older. The frightening one, with the face of a lizard, the one who tried to keep me from taking the book of maps, is flanked by two other villainous-looking fellows.

Between them sits a slumped man with wild hair and sad eyes. He is the only person in the room who doesn't have a mask, so perhaps that is why he looks so out of place. Or maybe it's his obvious nervousness.

Elliott's step falters as he sees the man, but he recovers immediately.

"Dr. Winston," Elliott says smoothly. "When did you leave my uncle's palace?"

Dr. Winston nearly falls out of his chair when Elliott greets him. "Just days ago. I . . . used the tunnels."

"We're lucky a man of your knowledge grew tired of my uncle's hospitality, then." Elliott draws out a chair for me, then takes one himself.

A servant enters the room from the opposite side with a great tray, and I look up too quickly, some part of me expecting it to be Will. But it's the boy from earlier, staggering under his heavy burden.

Like the dining room at Prospero's palace, the one here is decorated with polished mahogany and dragon statuettes. Our rather frugal meal is served on antique imported china.

We eat our soup in near silence. Then Elliott says, "So tell us, gentlemen, what is the news in the Debauchery District?"

"We understand that a certain young man has been inviting people to our territory, to our building, no less," Prospero's former henchman says. "Men in uniform have been arriving all day."

Elliott smiles. "You can keep your rooms for as long as you need them. I know you have nowhere else to go." His words are low and loaded with threat. I watch the scientist. He's eating steadily, but he eyes Elliott the way you watch a serpent.

"How did you get away?" I ask the scientist, unwilling to play along with Elliott's pretense that he was Prospero's invited guest.

"Someone left the doors of the dungeon open. All of us escaped." He puts down his soup spoon and smiles at me. "Someone very courageous . . ."

When he glances at me, my heart stops. My mother is with the prince, in his palace. "Someone who has a soft spot for scientists?" I ask.

He nods.

And now I'm both proud of Mother and worried about how the prince will punish her.

"Why did you come *here*?" Elliott interjects. He isn't even pretending to eat now, just interrogating the man.

"The other men went to the swamp." The scientist's voice drops. "They were looking for something. A rumor." He looks up quickly at the men who are listening, and then back to his soup. "But I have a grandson. I plan to search the city for him."

"I'll assign a soldier to help you search," Elliott offers. "If there's anything else—"

"Thank you." His consideration of Elliott has softened a bit.

"Dr. Winston has been telling us fascinating rumors," the old man across the table says. "He says that both Prospero and Dr. Worth knew that there was a way to protect against the plague, and they chose to suppress the information."

"Those rumors aren't new. They start up every few months," I say. And who can blame people for being suspicious, when Prospero kept control of the masks and Father never fought him on it?

"The prince never cared about anything except control," Elliott says. "Now he's focused on his masquerade balls. Those, he can control."

Elliott doesn't seem surprised that rumors are circulating. He knows something that he isn't saying.

"I suppose you would know the prince better than any of us," the old man says. Looking at Elliott, he says, "Your familial connections are quite . . . surprising."

Elliott ignores him, but I meet his hooded eyes. What does he know?

I'm glad when Elliott pushes back his chair and places his napkin on the table. I can't stand being in this room any longer.

"We'll talk soon," he tells Dr. Winston. I follow him out of the dining room, where he pauses to speak to the guard on duty. After assigning a man to Winston, he walks me upstairs.

"Will picked this room for you." We've stopped at a door, and Elliott hands me a key. "I think you would be safer in my room. I'm not sleeping on the floor again, though."

"This will be fine," I say. "I don't wish to sleep on your floor either."

He pulls the book of maps from an interior pocket.

"You've spent more time reading this than I have. I need to know which passages are near, which ones may connect with the cellars. Whether Malcontent can attack us from below."

I take the book from him, and in the same movement grab his wrist.

It's time to tell him who Malcontent is.

I never meant to keep this secret from him. Never wished to know more than he did about the enemy who foiled all of his carefully laid plans.

"Come inside with me," I say.

He arches his eyebrows and follows me.

This room has two upholstered chairs, a tapestry depicting a tree with white leaves, and a doorway that must lead to a bedchamber. "Sit." I gesture to the chairs. "I need to tell you something."

"You adore me and are having trouble keeping your hands to yourself?" he suggests.

"No." But my seriousness is lost on him.

He sits and pulls me close. "I'm having trouble keeping my hands to myself." The look on his face is completely earnest. I don't pull away. It's better that we are touching.

The silk of my dress billows as he draws me into his lap. Removing his mask, he kisses the side of my face, and slides my mask off. I turn to meet his eyes, but I don't kiss him.

"Elliott." We are so close I can see his pupils contrasting with the pale blue of his eyes. "Your father isn't dead."

CHAPTER
ELEVEN

HIS HANDS DROP, AND HE STARES AT ME.

I plow on. "The corpse collectors took him, but he was alive. He survived. He stayed in the swamp. The diseased men took him in and worshiped him because he seems to be immune to the contagion. They consider him some sort of saint, a miracle."

"Malcontent," he says slowly. "You're saying that my father, who I watched my uncle murder when I was a boy . . . is alive . . . is Malcontent?"

I grip his shoulders tightly, waiting for the knowledge to sink in. He shifts, and I slide from his lap, hitting the floor hard. He doesn't seem to notice. He sits very straight, staring ahead.

I expected him to curse. I expected indignation, but he surprises me.

"Does he know who I am?" He's gripping the arms

of the chair, his knuckles white.

"Yes. He knew what he was doing when he blew up the steamship."

The confident, arrogant Elliott that I've come to appreciate is gone. He slumps in his chair. I don't blame him. His father—not an unknown madman—tried to kill him.

I don't reach out to him or speak.

I kneel beside him. It isn't the most dignified of poses, but I don't care. My mother might have adopted the same position to comfort me as a child. I know how it feels to have your world crash down on you.

"Are you sure?" Elliott's eyes are haunted.

"Yes."

He starts to say something else.

"Elliott," I say gently, "April was with me."

A clock in the corner ticks away the minutes.

Elliott is so pale I'd be afraid he might pass out, if he was the sort of person prone to fainting. I reach to touch him, and then pull back.

"If anyone finds out, you must hide how you feel. Let them think you don't care."

"Like you, Araby? Nonchalant? Uncaring about your own father's sins?" He's getting angry now, defensive. That's the Elliott I know.

"I don't suppose I was very good at hiding my feelings when I learned about Father. But you have to be."

"Your father didn't try to kill you."

I used to like to see Elliott with his guard down, saw it as a chance to peer past the walls that he's constructed. But now that I know him, it makes me uneasy to see him so unsure. Even when he doesn't know the right course of action, the Elliott I know is always ready to fake certainty.

"No," I say. "My father tried to kill everyone in the world because I wasn't happy."

Elliott puts his hands on either side of my face. He looks into my eyes. I don't look away. For once, I don't try to hide the guilt. The pain.

"You told your father you couldn't find happiness?"

"The world is bleak," I say.

Then his arms are around me. It's an embrace, but not a passionate one. He bows his head. I put my own forehead against his cheek. And we don't move. Even when there are footsteps in the hall, and they stop in the doorway.

"Sir?" It's one of Elliott's men, blushing furiously at whatever he thinks he interrupted.

"Our meeting." Elliott groans. "Of course. Araby, I'll be back for you in an hour. We'll make plans." He looks pointedly at the book of maps.

Elliott releases me and strides across the room. He hesitates in the doorway, but I don't say anything, don't ask to go with him. The regret is setting in. I shouldn't have been so open, shouldn't have revealed so much about my father and my feelings.

So he goes.

I walk over to lock the door behind him, and suddenly Elliott reappears in the doorway, alone.

"I'd like to give you a reason to live." He tosses something to me, and I catch it without thinking. And then he's gone again, and I'm holding a diamond ring in my fist.

Is this some sort of diversion? Is he trying to keep me from the overwhelming guilt? Was he afraid for my sanity? Or was it more?

It seems so long ago that Elliott asked me to wear the ring, to pretend I was madly in love with him in front of his uncle. Since then I've come to understand him, and on some level I think he understands me. I slip the ring into my pocket.

While I appreciate the sentiment, I don't need him to be my reason to live. And I don't plan to wait around for him to come back for me.

As I reach the stairway, I see Will slipping down a side corridor. And I follow him.

At first I mean to call out to him. But he's moving furtively, and every time he passes a corridor, he looks down it quickly. He's sneaking off, and I want to know where.

He grabs a candle and starts down a flight of stairs. I wait until he's passed through the door at the bottom before I follow him. In the darkness on the other side of the door, I can't tell where he went. As I turn, while my eyes adjust, a hand reaches from the shadows and grabs my arm. I stifle a scream.

"Did Elliott ask you to follow me?" Will asks.

I shove him. "Did you really think I'd spy on you for Elliott?" I cross my arms over my chest, furious.

He grins at me. "So you're following me because you want to."

My anger is replaced by confusion. I'm following him because I wanted to see where he was going. That's all.

"He didn't ask me to follow you." I try to steer the conversation back to Elliott. "But he does want to know where your printing press is."

"He'll figure it out soon enough. And then he'll have someone take over the machine and print whatever lies he wants."

"And you only print truth?" Somehow the darkness makes it easier to ask the question.

"I don't always *know* the truth. But I don't print things I know are lies." His voice is quiet and thoughtful. "Give me your scarf."

"Why?" I ask as I unravel it.

Will sets the candle on the floor, and then his hands are on me. He puts the soft fabric of the scarf over my eyes.

"You're blindfolding me?" My anger is returning. Does he trust me so little?

"Araby—"

"I trusted *you*. Despite—" I clear my throat. I won't

throw his betrayal in his face. "I don't spy for Elliott."

"I know you can keep secrets. You've kept plenty of them. But he has ways—"

I'm blushing. Will is careful not to pull my hair as he ties the blindfold. He can probably feel the heat coming off my cheeks.

"I didn't mean—" From his voice, I guess that he is blushing too. "I was thinking of torture," he says finally. "Not anything improper." But then his voice becomes bitter. "Not that I have any say over what you and Elliott . . . the way your relationship—"

I turn toward him, though I can't see him through the fabric. I trip over my own feet, and Will steadies me. "You already warned me about Elliott," I say.

"I did."

"That's really all you can do." Because even though I'm sure that my relationship with Elliott isn't what he thinks it is, or will be, it's my problem to fix.

"I know," he says. And then, changing the subject, "We'll be going down another flight of stairs. I'll tell you when we reach them." We walk to the end of the corridor, through a creaky door, over a place where the floor is uneven.

The stairs are torture. Even with Will's guidance I have to feel to find my footing, and it's distracting having him so near. Finally we reach the bottom. And then he leads me across a floor that gives under my feet . . . wood planks? And through another room.

"Stop," Will says, and I hear him fumbling with a key. Then "Come into my lair." Something in his voice makes my heart speed dangerously. I try to hide my discomfort by taking my time removing the scarf from my eyes and then smoothing my hair.

We are in an underground room, lit by gaslights. The printing press takes up most of the space. The mechanism looks complicated; it's wooden with a series of knobs and handles, as well as a huge wheel, where it appears the paper is fed through.

"How did you learn how to work it?"

He picks up several pieces of lead type, arranges them to spell my name. And then, as if embarrassed, knocks them away with the side of his hand. "I found some books in one of the libraries and studied. In the beginning I just printed messages to take home for the children. Eventually I learned to print more sophisticated jobs."

"Did you come down here often? Every night?" I ask.

"Probably once a week." He sets to work, consulting a sheet of paper covered with Elliott's bold handwriting.

Wooden crates line the walls. At first I think they are filled with extra printing paper, but they are actually yellowing newspapers.

I step toward them. "Where did you get these?"

"Kent and I rescued them from the same cellar where we found the printing press," he says. He doesn't even look up from arranging the type with deft fingers.

I pick up a delicate paper, holding it ever so carefully. Even with the gaslights, it's difficult to read the newspapers. I'd like to take them upstairs and comb through them for days. It's like a glimpse of life when the world was normal. Before the plague.

They feel precious.

I flip to a society page with a picture of a girl in a fancy wedding dress with a veil. April would love something like that, and with the contagion spreading she could use a veil. I set the paper down.

"What are you printing?" I ask.

"Warnings, from Elliott. A list of symptoms of the Red Death."

"By the time you have the symptoms, it's a bit too late, isn't it?"

"I don't question my orders, but I don't think he means the diagnosis to help the victim. I think he means for the other citizens to avoid those who are infected. It makes it easier to kill them. Or exile them."

He's judging Elliott. And maybe Elliott deserves it. The print on one of the flyers he's already made reminds me of the one about my father. I steel myself to ask him about it.

"Did people find the one you wrote about my father helpful?"

Will flinches. But he can't ignore this question. He abandons the press and looks at me.

"Araby—"

"Did Malcontent pay you to say those things? To make my father a villain?" My fists are clenched, my nails digging into my palms.

"I wasn't paid. I chose to do it."

"I wish you hadn't." My voice is small, and I hate myself for it, but at least I said it.

"The people who approached me felt that the knowledge should be out there. We've been living with this, with the aftermath, for our entire lives. It seemed better for people just to know."

"Did you think of me when you printed it?" The audacity of the question makes me feel sick. But when he stands there like that, his hands shoved into his pockets, his face so young and yet so world-weary, I want to touch him, to wipe the pained expression from his face. And that makes the betrayal rush back, more overwhelming than ever.

"I always thought about you. From the night I took you home, I never really stopped thinking about you."

I won't let myself dwell on this answer, or the pain of what could have been. I won't let myself reach out and brush aside the hair that's fallen over his face.

"Did you discuss me with Malcontent? Tell him that you could bring me to him?"

Anger feels better than fathomless grief. For years I simply wanted to hide from the world and all the pain. Now I want to fight. At this moment I want to fight Will.

"I never—" He steps away from me, pivoting, and

then pacing across the room. "It wasn't like that. I didn't make offers to him."

He crosses the room in two strides. With the low ceilings, he seems even taller than before. He towers over me. I can see his agitation in the movement of his hands. The look in his eyes.

"I never met Malcontent before that night. He didn't know anything about me, or the club, or the printing press. He just knew that you had been in my apartment. His men followed you the night you skinned your knee. The night you brought Henry the mask."

I reach for my own mask now, thinking of that night. Of the terror, and the dark cloaked men creeping out of the alley. Of Will removing the splinter from my finger when I was safe.

"He took my neighbor, you know. I couldn't save her."

I feel my anger dissipating. "What . . . did he do with your neighbor?"

"I don't know. She disappeared at the same time as Henry and Elise, only he never let her go. Her mask was left broken in her apartment. It was my fault for drawing his attention."

"Or my fault, for coming to your apartment."

"I suppose we could spend all evening assigning blame. You are who you are, and all the villains want you." I wonder if he includes Elliott among the villains. "It's why I returned to the city. To do what I can to protect you."

"As long as you don't get in my way," I say with more bravado than I feel.

"I won't." He goes back to the press, arranging sheets of paper on the machine, turning knobs. "I told you yesterday, I'm here to support you. And I'll honor my agreement to help Elliott as long as he doesn't become as much a tyrant as the others."

"He won't," I insist. "Elliott is nothing like Prospero or Malcontent."

"Not yet. But he isn't in power yet. I've studied how the government worked, before the plague. Eventually, we'll need elections. Real elections."

Elliott is not likely to approve of such an idea. Or agree to it.

"I can finish this later," he says. "You don't want to stay down here with me."

Yet I do. This room feels safe, but I have too much to accomplish and we can't linger here.

Will picks up my scarf. If I let myself, I could enjoy his touch as he wraps the fabric around my eyes, as he takes my hand to lead me outside. But I will not allow myself to feel such things. Not when I've agreed to be by Elliott's side.

I don't let on that the blindfold is loose, that I can see enough to be able to retrace my steps. It seems to take him forever to remove the blindfold. I stand, my chin tilted upward, as he unties the knot. We're standing in front of a window. Will looks out.

"The moon is covered by clouds tonight. Let's check the roof to be sure everything is ready for when Kent and the others arrive."

We climb multiple stairways until we finally come to the roof. Outside it is fully and completely dark. Nervousness wells up from the pit of my stomach. April and the children and Kent will be coming in on the airship. We were shot down once before; it could happen again.

Elliott is on the roof, smoking a cigarette. He grimaces but doesn't say anything. Not about me arriving with Will. Nor about my absence from my room, if he went back to retrieve me.

The sky is filled with hazy clouds, and I suspect it will rain before dawn.

"I wanted to make sure everything was ready," Will says.

"I had the same idea." Elliott stubs out his cigarette and moves to help Will.

They prepare lengths of rope and the huge piece of canvas that was used to hide the ship when it was on the roof of the Morgue. I stand to the side and watch the sky.

Elliott pauses beside me. Being on the roof reminds me of the fireworks, the celebration in the bay. "Just think how beautiful the ship would look, if it were illuminated."

"Kent would never risk that," Elliott says.

"But imagine a world where it wasn't a risk. I'd like to live in that world."

"I'd like to create it for you."

His gaze is too intense; I can't hold it. Glancing over, I see that Will is checking the great iron rings that will hold the ship down once it is in place. The wind is blowing the clouds, and as I watch I think I see something. The prow of the ship. I point upward.

"They shouldn't be here for two more nights," Elliott says.

"Unless something happened. It's cloudy. If Kent was desperate . . ."

"Kent doesn't get desperate," Elliott says. But Will has gone very still. Finally he looks at me.

"It's why I wanted to have everything ready. He told me he might bring the ship in early, if things weren't going well . . ." He pauses. "With April."

CHAPTER
TWELVE

I can't breathe. Something has happened
to April, and in the days we've been in the city, I've come
no closer to finding Father. We don't even know if he's
alive. I watch the progress of the ship. What if April is
dead?

"So you've been checking the roof?" Elliott asks Will.

"On and off. Tonight is the first night I thought their
arrival might be a possibility."

There's nothing we can do but wait. Half an hour
passes. We don't speak. We don't assure one another that
nothing is wrong. We simply wait, the three of us, standing together, but not close enough that I could reach out
to either of them.

The ship is mostly obscured by clouds, but when it
emerges from cloud cover, it's magical. Like something
from a children's story.

Kent guides the ship in, and Will and Elliott begin tying it down as Kent leaps to the roof to help them.

The wooden stairs lower, and even as the boys work to secure the ship, Henry and Elise descend, hugging me and inadvertently pulling my hair. Something sticky smears from my cheek to my forehead. Before I can wipe it away, Mina is approaching.

"April's gotten worse," she begins. But she doesn't have to say anything. April is right behind her. I gasp. She looks awful. Exhausted, her skin deathly pale and her eyes sunken. I'm careful not to be too obvious about adjusting my mask before I reach to embrace her, but then Elliott is there, picking her up in his arms.

"I'll take her downstairs," he says. Kent follows.

The balloon is deflating, and they've completely covered the ship with gray fabric. Unless you were standing on the roof looking for it, I doubt you would pay it any attention.

Will stops in front of me. "Elliott has asked me to take something across town for him tonight," he says. "Some message for one of his officers. Could the children sleep in your room?"

I rub at whatever sticky residue Henry smeared across the side of my face. "Of course," I say. "I've missed them."

In the light of a lantern, Will's smile is sudden and radiant.

"Where is Thom?" I ask, turning to Kent.

"He didn't want to come in this far. Not with his very obvious illness. We set him down on the outskirts of the lower city."

April's room is in the same corridor as mine and Elliott's. Kent tucks her into bed; Mina goes to a cot in her dressing room. After I'm sure April is comfortable, I retire to my room. Elliott grimaces when he sees the children following me.

But I'm relieved. There can be no repeat of what happened this afternoon. I never wanted to share anything like that with Elliott. I've always known better.

I lie awake for a long time. I can't even toss and turn because Henry is curled up on one side, Elise on the other. I can't get the image of April, and her pallor, from my mind. If I can't find my father very soon, then I must go to hers, as Thom suggested.

And as I consider giving myself to Malcontent, I realize that if the children on either side of me were in danger, that I would do exactly what Will did. That I can't hold his betrayal against him any longer.

I forgive him. And with that, I fall asleep.

The next morning, sun is streaming through the window. Henry reaches over me to pinch Elise, and she slaps his hand away. I push both of them back to their own sides of the bed and sit up so I can look down at them. "I haven't seen you in days," I say. "Did you have many adventures while we were apart?"

"We saw animals in the forest," Henry says. "Cougars

and wild dogs. Kent said that maybe we could tame a rabbit, so that I could have a pet."

Finn and I had a cat when we were young. She disappeared soon after we moved with Father to the cellar.

Henry is working up some excitement for telling me what he saw in the woods. "And then we saw a large animal that I thought might be a horse, but it had horns—"

"Antlers," Elise corrects, shaking her head at her small brother. "Is there something to eat?"

"We'll have to get dressed and go downstairs," I say. I show them to the closet. "Take anything you want.

Before I know it, Henry is wearing a coat that nearly drags on the floor, with the sleeves carefully rolled up, and a woman's hat with two feathers in it.

It isn't exactly what I expected when I told him to take what he wanted, but Elise starts to giggle and can't stop, and her laughter is infectious. We are all laughing when we are interrupted by a light knock at the chamber door.

"Good morning." It's Will. My heart speeds up at the sound of his voice, and I'm not sure how I should feel about that. Everything has changed, and nothing. I can't just blurt out that I forgive him, and he's not likely to see it on my masked face.

"Look how pretty Araby is," Elise announces loudly. "She hasn't even washed her face yet, and she's still pretty."

"Actually, I have washed my face," I say, and feel myself blushing.

"She smells good," Henry adds.

"I'm thrilled that you could spend your evening with such a pretty and fine-smelling young lady," Will says. He hasn't really looked at me, and his face is drawn.

"What's happened?" I ask.

"More cases of the Red Death. Some areas are over-run with it." He starts to say something else, but he looks to the children and closes his mouth.

"Do you want me to take them to get something to eat?"

"I've asked one of the servants to deliver breakfast to my rooms." He smiles. "It's like I'm a patron here, instead of a glorified servant." He yawns.

"Go, get some rest," I say. "I should check on April."

"It doesn't look good, Araby," he says softly. And then, as we all walk into the hallway together, "Don't take off your mask."

He leads the children, smiling quietly as they chatter, and I stop at April's suite. A servant is outside with a tray. "I'm not going in there," she says. "No matter what Mr. Elliott says."

So the servants know already. I don't blame her for not going in. She has a mask, but no one trusts the masks completely.

"I'll take it." I lift the tray from her hands, and she looks at me with suspicion, as if I might have the plague too.

I push the door open, but April is sleeping. I put my

hand to her forehead. She's feverish but breathing well. The best thing she can do is sleep. I set the tray beside her bed and tiptoe out.

Down in the dining room, Elliott's at a big table, talking to several of his officers.

"I'm going out," I announce.

He raises his blond eyebrows.

"We haven't done anything since we arrived. I don't know where my father is, but he isn't here. I have to do something. April—"

"I'll go with you," he says. "I want to get a feel for the streets around the club. As long as you don't mind stopping to burn bodies."

"It's how I long to spend all my days," I say. "Burning the dead."

He nods to his man, and then we exit the building to midmorning sunshine. Elliott toys with a match that he's taken from his pocket and doesn't say anything.

"What shall we do?" I ask. "Have you heard from the clockmaker? We're a day overdue in searching the Akkadian Towers."

"The clockmaker promised to contact me if he discovered anything. To get to the Towers, we'll need a steam carriage."

"Then we should go back and get it." Did he not see how deathly sick April was? Kent risked his ship to bring her home early. But Elliott does not seem to be in any sort of rush.

"It's too dangerous to take the steam carriage out during the day," he says. "But I'll take you this evening. I promise. And I'll send someone to question the clock-maker. Be sure he's doing what he said he would."

He stops to burn some bodies in a courtyard behind the Morgue. To his credit, he doesn't tell me not to look. To my own, I do not avert my eyes. At the same time, I don't think about who they once were. Elliott says something under his breath, what seems to be a sort of benediction for the dead. Then he drops the match.

"This is likely to be unpleasant," he says.

It's worse than unpleasant. The metallic-sweet smell of death is inescapable, and ashes fly up into the air. If I didn't have my mask on, I'd be choking on death.

"Will says that the Red Death is getting worse," I say.

"It is. Two of my soldiers died yesterday. And another was killed. We think he was ambushed by some of Malcontent's zealots. They're using the tunnels to reach more people. Climbing into houses through cellars and basements."

We've stepped back, away from the burning remains.

"We need to find a way to use the tunnels against them. Perhaps block them off," he says. "Do you want to have a look? I'm open to suggestions."

Exploring tunnels seems better than standing here, choking on ashes. And if our search for Father is as fruitless tonight as it's been since our return, then I'll need to use the tunnels to find Malcontent.

We climb down into earthy-smelling tunnels, much like the ones that we entered from the clockmaker's basement.

"Who built these?" I ask.

"No one knows. They're ancient. My father"—he grimaces—"was a student of history, and he said that city after city has been built on this site because of the harbor. He used to fund excavations, and I'd go watch the men dig, waiting to see what they would uncover. My uncle thought it was foolish, but when they uncovered something shiny or valuable, he was the first person on hand."

"Was he always so ruthless?"

"Yes. Father didn't see it. He was a good man . . . then. Easily led, I suppose, but a good man."

"So was my father."

I wait for Elliott to argue, but he's stopped, examining a skull embedded in the wall. A pile of ancient bones lies in the tunnel. After the diseased corpses we just burned, these brittle bones have an antique sort of elegance.

Eventually we come to an intersection that looks more frequently used than the one we've been traveling.

"This is the path his men are taking," Elliott says in a hushed voice. "I can't spare enough men to waylay them, but perhaps Kent could devise some sort of trap. At least to keep them out of this area."

I memorize the route that brought us here, paying

special attention to the last few twists and turns. If I need to reach Malcontent, this is my best path. And with April in such poor shape, I suspect I will be using the tunnels before Kent sets up any traps. At least I hope so.

"I could use some fresh air. Let's go back to the club. I'll dispatch a soldier to check in with the clockmaker," Elliott promises. "We will find your father."

We backtrack to the nearest ladder and climb up to the street.

The streets we traverse in the Debauchery District seem in relatively good repair. Only one small building looks burned out; a few have broken windows. The streets are relatively free of debris, though I nearly trip over a broken jug. Was it dropped as someone fled from the Red Death, or used as a makeshift weapon?

We turn a corner and see dozens of people carrying luggage, looking up at the buildings with hopeful expressions. The first of Elliott's settlers.

A soldier leads the group.

"The Morgue is nearly filled, sir," he says to Elliott. "I've sent men to search the surrounding buildings. We've been sending those from the upper city to the Debauchery Club."

"Be sure you leave room in the club for some officers," Elliott says. "Consult the list of safe buildings."

"We've cleared three city blocks so far," the soldier says.

One of the women falls to her knees before Elliott

and tries to kiss his hand. He pulls back, his cheeks flushing.

"Thank you so much, sir," she says. "We've been afraid to go outside."

"You're welcome," he says gravely.

"We're going to need more food," the soldier says. "And something for them to drink, since we've been telling them the water isn't safe."

Elliott nods, and the group plods away.

"I should check in with Kent," Elliott says. "He's in the brew house, working on the water problem. We need more of everything."

"Yes." We're back in sight of the Debauchery Club. Elliott makes a move to walk with me, but his attention isn't on me anymore.

"Go to Kent," I tell him. "I can walk down the street by myself."

He doesn't argue, so I set off. After a few moments, I hear footsteps behind me, and I turn to tell him that I'm not completely dependent on him to protect me. But the street is empty.

I speed up. Malcontent's people could grab me from the street and sweep me into a tunnel deep underground.

And . . . maybe that's what I want. To make contact with Malcontent. But not before trying the Akkadian Towers. And on my own terms, not as a prisoner. I'm close enough to the club that Elliott's guards will hear me if I scream. So instead of being afraid, I find myself annoyed that someone is following me. I turn, waiting for the person to emerge. It's a man in a dark hood.

Before he can react to me waiting for him rather than running away, I reach up and push his hood back. I don't recognize his face, but his skin is unblemished.

"Who are you, and what do you want?" I ask.

"Are you the scientist's daughter?" the man asks.

"Yes."

"I want to know if there is still a reward for information about Dr. Phineas Worth."

"Yes." My voice quavers, and I put a hand to the lamppost beside me to steady myself. "Yes, of course there is." I have gold to reward him for his information, but it's in Elliott's room, in his pack. "What of my father?" I ask.

The man steps away from me. "I want to see my payment first."

I reach into my pocket. The diamond ring is there. Can I trade it to this man for his information? I can't take him to my chamber, and if I go up to retrieve the gold, he might well disappear.

"Take this," I say.

The man stares at the ring, and unexpectedly, his eyes fill with tears. A long-lost memory of some other diamond ring? I don't know, or care. "What do you know of my father?"

"He's dead," the man says. I can't tell if he's happy or sad. His voice is weary. Emotionless. I study his face for some sign that he's lying, but he meets my eyes.

He believes what he's just said. The world wavers for a moment, and I have to grab the rough wall of the building beside me to keep from falling.

"How do you know this?"

"He used to feed the fish in the stream behind the science building, at the university, yes?"

Father always saved bits of bread for the fish, in the same way that he saved food for hungry children. That stream is the place Elliott and I last saw him.

"Some of the students realized who he was. They went after him. Killed him and threw his body in the river. It's better, I think, throwing them in the river, than leaving them in the streets."

It's this detail about the fish that convinces me.

Could he be dead? A wave of dizziness and nausea sweeps over me, but I force it down. My father, who took me to parades. Who comforted me when I was hurt. Who made me sleeping drafts and kissed my forehead as I drifted to sleep.

"Did you see it happen?" I ask. "Or simply hear about it?" Either way, his story rings painfully true.

He reaches into his robe. I step back, expecting some weapon, but instead he pulls out my father's spectacles. I put out my hand, and the man drops them onto my trembling palm.

They are lighter than I would have expected. But they are his. The left earpiece is twisted. I'd recognize them anywhere.

My legs refuse to hold me up, and I collapse there in the street.

"I'm sorry," the man says. And this time I can hear the regret in his voice. He steps to the mouth of the alley, calls to the guards at the club. They come running, helping me to my feet. The man is gone. Along with Elliott's diamond ring, and my hopes for repairing my world.

Without my father and his elusive antidote, there is only one person who can save April. Malcontent. He claimed that he had a cure. If it isn't too late for that. If he isn't too angry that she allowed me to escape. Would he forgive her transgression if I turned myself over to him? I need to prepare myself to find out.

CHAPTER
THIRTEEN

As I approach April's room, I'm expecting the worst. But she is sitting up, dressed in a bright gown.

"You keep leaving this," she says, instead of "hello" like a normal person. She's holding my makeup bag.

I throw myself into her arms and hug her. "How do you feel?" I start to ask, but she puts her hand to my mask, shushing me.

"Let's not talk about that. We're back in the Debauchery Club." I stare at her, at a loss, and then she laughs. "Let's dye your hair."

She pulls bottles and vials from her own bag. I want to laugh with her, but I'm afraid if I do, something inside me might break. The most I can summon is a smile.

"This is the first time I've seen you smile in a long time," she says softly.

"There hasn't been much to smile about." My father can't be dead; April can't be dying.

But I know better than that. I held my twin brother while the life bled out of him. Bad things happen every day. Unspeakable things.

"You aren't even going to recognize yourself," she says, and it takes me a moment to realize that she's talking about my hair.

The first time she dyed it was so that I wouldn't see Finn when I looked in the mirror. Whether or not the color had anything to do with it, I rarely see him now. For weeks, since Malcontent's attack, I've barely thought about him. But the memories are still there. With Father dead, and if Malcontent kills me, then only Mother will be left to remember Finn.

Preserving his memory is important. But he'd still want me to fight for April. Even if it means losing everything. Including him.

"You told Elliott about our father," April says, pouring water into a basin. "I can tell by the way he looks at me. Halfway pitying, half angry."

April's room is more opulent than mine. Hangings cover the walls and carved furniture looms over us, dressing tables and mirrored chests and armoires. A dressing room stands open, and a variety of dresses are strewn about. The tray from this morning with the remains of breakfast is still on the bedside table. The servants haven't come back for it, too afraid of catching the contagion.

"He needed to know."

April turns me so that she's behind me. Her hands are in my hair, massaging in the herb mixture that will change the color.

"Does he deserve to know that you're in love with Will?" she asks softly.

Even though she's working with my hair, I move to face her. Her blond hair is lustrous, falling in waves over her shoulders. But a sore oozes over her left eyebrow, and she isn't wearing eye makeup because of it. Her eyes look naked.

"I'm not in love with him," I say.

"You're angry at him. That doesn't mean you don't love him."

"I'm not angry anymore. I understand what Will did. The decision he made. And I won't pretend I'm not attracted to him. But I'm not in love with him. I'm not in love with anyone."

"Is this the same speech you gave Kent?" she asks, spinning me back around and smearing something that smells of lavender into my hair. "'April is more important than kissing boys,'" she mimics. "He believed you. I don't."

This is what girls are supposed to do with their best friends. Gossip about boys. My lack of interest in it has always been a sore spot with April. And now . . . the weight of the world seems to be on my shoulders. I can't forget that Father is dead, that April is sick. That

I shouldn't be sitting here—I should be devising some plan, no matter how crazy, to save her.

She wraps my hair in a towel and drops into a matching chair, so close that our knees touch.

"Who is a better kisser?" she whispers. And then her nose wrinkles. "If it's Elliott, I don't want to know details. *Is it Elliott?*"

"I'm not going to tell you details," I say, indignant. But then, because she's my best friend, and because she's waited a long time for this sort of discussion, taking me to the club two or three times a week . . . I sigh. "Elliott is insistent. Intense. With Will, it's like I forget that anything else exists." I feel my face burning. "I don't know," I say quietly. "They are both important to me. Without kissing."

"But kissing makes everything better," she says. Her eyes meet mine, and I laugh. A real, true laugh.

I reach out and take her hands. "What can we do for you?" I ask, though I know that this change in subject will kill the laughter.

"Nothing. Kent has tried everything. If there were any cure, he'd know. He lost his mother to the plague, and he knows everyone who's been experimenting and inventing. He's smarter than anyone I've ever met." She glows a little when she says this.

"What about your father? He said that he could cure you." This is as close as I will come to revealing my desperate plan.

"Don't believe him, Araby. I've thought about it, wondered if I should've stayed." She gives me a sad smile. "Not because I regret saving you. That was the good part." She runs a comb through my hair, untangling it. And then she rinses it with water from a small pitcher.

My heart sinks. If Malcontent can't save her, then she's doomed.

"Why shouldn't we believe him?" I ask.

"Because he's a liar," she says. "And he's crazy. If he could cure the contagion, wouldn't he cure all those men who are following him?"

But I'm not so sure. It's convenient that Malcontent has never gotten the disease. His men believe he is a saint. But we know better. He must have some cure that we aren't aware of. He's my last chance to save April.

She's running her hands through my hair, though surely the tangles are all out by now. I lean into her, comforted by her touch.

"Will took me up in the hot-air balloon, the one that used to be tethered on the roof of the Morgue," I say. Because I've not told anyone. I've not let myself think of it. But lately Will is slipping back into my thoughts.

"What? Why didn't you mention this before? Tell me everything!" She's animated suddenly, spinning me around to look at her.

"He showed me the city and said that I had to believe in good things." This is where my heart drops. "Because he was getting ready to betray me."

Tears well up, and I force them down. April squeezes my shoulder, then busies herself by lining up the leftover vials of hair dye on the bureau across the room.

"You're pale. We need more of that sparkly eye shadow," she says.

"Yes," I agree. "We do."

"I left some in Elliott's room, before we left the city. I'll call for Mina to fetch it." Her new protégé seems happy to do April's errands.

April helped me through my darkest moments, and now she's doing the same for this delicate girl. When she comes back into the room, April has finished with my hair.

"It's beautiful," Mina says.

"Sit down," April commands. "I'll put makeup on you, too." The girl smiles, but her expression is sad. She's still in mourning for her brother, when every bit of happiness is followed by guilt. Mina pulls up a chair and April carefully lays out a selection of makeup brushes on a silver tray. "Close your eyes," she tells Mina, and smears something over her eyelids.

"Tell me about your brother," I say.

Mina's eyes fly open, and April tsks. Mina closes them again immediately. The silence stretches so long that I think she isn't going to say anything, that she's still mad at me, but finally she answers.

"He had a crooked smile," she says. "He kept me out of the orphanage. Made sure that I was always cared for."

"My brother liked to play pranks," I say. "I hated it every time he put a spider in my bed or jumped out from behind something. But I miss his laugh."

"At least he had a sense of humor," April says. "Elliott was always too serious for pranks. Too *intense*." She arches an eyebrow at me.

"Elliott's eyes scare me," Mina says. "I think he sees everything. That he can see through people. But Will's eyes are dreamy."

"Will's eyes *are* dreamy," April agrees, giving me another knowing look.

April reaches over to examine the color of my drying hair. Her fingers, as she brushes my forehead, feel warmer than they should. I raise my hand to her cheek. She's still feverish.

"Close your eyes, Araby," April says. "We didn't get all this glittery stuff for nothing." And then the brush is moving over my eyelids, feather soft, and I'm transported for a moment to the simplicity of getting ready for our evenings at the Debauchery Club. "Perfect." April turns me toward the mirror.

Mina claps her hands. "Oh, I love it." I glance over to see if she is sincere or if she is mocking me. Her eyes are shining. She claps once more, as if to emphasize how much she loves it.

I stare at myself. April has done it again. Last time she dyed my hair violet. This time, she's colored half of it a dark midnight blue that shimmers in the candlelight.

I look like someone new. Not the scientist's daughter. Not Finn's twin sister. Just Araby.

"Thank you," I say.

April smiles.

Footsteps in the hallway distract me. Has Elliott returned? April doesn't seem at all surprised when I excuse myself, hurrying to Elliott's rooms. But he isn't there.

Back in my chamber across the hall, I find quill and ink and carefully pen a message to Malcontent. I tell him that I will trade myself for April's life and where to find me. Even if that man was wrong and somehow Father is still alive, I don't have time to waste searching for him. April doesn't have time.

Pushing the letter deep into a pocket, I open the door to my chamber, prepared to go down to the cellar, to try to find a passage that connects to the ones Malcontent is using. But Will is coming down the hallway, pulling Henry along with him, and I can tell immediately that something is wrong. Anger and distress radiate from him. His hair is wild, and his brow is furrowed.

He shoves Henry at me.

"Elise is gone. She went outside for a moment and Malcontent's men snatched her."

I fall back against the paneled wall. "Oh, no," I breathe. "How do you know it was Malcontent?"

"Henry said they had dark robes. I have to go try to find her, and I can't take him. I know I have no right to ask, but will you keep him safe?"

Henry's eyes are huge in his face. I wrap my arms around his too-thin shoulders. "You're scaring him."

"He needs to be. In a world where someone grabs . . ." His voice breaks. "I kept her inside for years. I kept her safe. I'll do anything to get her back." He turns away.

"Will, wait." I lift Henry to my hip and block Will's path. "You don't know where to go, you don't know—"

"I know that Malcontent is stealing little girls. I'm going underground. To the place where I took you when he had the children before. The tunnels by the pier. If she isn't there, I'll keep looking."

"Do you need me . . ." I start to ask. "You could take me again . . ."

I hold Henry close and look directly into Will's eyes. Without breaking our gaze, he grips Henry's shoulder in a way that must be painful, but the little boy doesn't complain.

"It's amazing, how right your boyfriend was. Prophetic, really."

"He's not—" I begin, but then I shake my head. "Right about what?"

"The dangers of caring for too many people." The flash in his eyes makes my heart stop for a moment. And then he releases Henry and walks around me.

Henry and I watch him until he turns a corner, and then listen to his footsteps get farther and farther away. "Let's go downstairs and find you something to eat," I finally say to Henry. His face is white and drawn, and he buries it in my shoulder. Before we reach the kitchens, a servant stops us.

"You have a visitor," he says. "An old servant of your family?"

Our old courier stands in the hallway. I'm so glad to see him alive and well that I would embrace him, if I wasn't already holding Henry.

He rushes up to me and grabs my arm. His fingers are shaking, and his eyes are sunken in, as if from some terrible pain or worry. "Miss Araby! Thank God I found you. Prospero's men took my daughter."

"*Prospero's* men?"

"Yes. They say they are rescuing them, but the people in the lower city know better."

"Are you sure it wasn't Malcontent?"

"It's Prospero," he insists. "You must have heard of his orphanages, where he trains his servants and his . . . entertainers. He's planning some last entertainment for his great masked ball."

I look at Henry. I swore to protect him, but Will is after the wrong man. Elise and who knows how many other girls are in danger.

"Do you know where this orphanage is?"

"No. People whisper about it, but . . ."

"Come upstairs." I set Henry down and lead him and the courier back to April's room.

April is in bed, propped on pillows. The tray of food still sits ignored on her vanity table. I push Henry toward the food and gesture for the courier to help himself, too; he's grown gaunt in the weeks since I've seen him.

"I was planning to eat that," April says as Henry discovers a pudding and spoons it into his mouth with such intense concentration that I think his eyes have crossed.

"I'll ask the servants to send more," I say. "Where's Mina?" Even as I ask, the girl pops her head in from April's dressing room. I wave her into the room. "The orphanages. You said your brother protected you from them. Can you tell me where they are?"

"The building is near the last place we lived. It's one reason my brother wanted to get me out of the city, why we ran away. . . ."

I take out my book of maps and lay it on the table, gesturing for her to show me where to look. After a moment her forehead wrinkles. She doesn't understand the maps.

"I could take you there," she says finally, "but these . . . I'm sorry."

"We have to find Elise," I say. "And this man's daughter. If you can't read the maps, will you lead us?"

Mina nods, though her eyes are larger than usual. Terrified. My estimation of her goes way up.

"I'm going with you," April says, swinging her legs over the side of the bed. "Where are my shoes?"

"You can't," I say. "You need to rest. And I need you to watch Henry."

"I've been resting all day," she counters.

CHAPTER
FOURTEEN

HENRY AND I STAND IN APRIL'S DOORWAY FOR A moment. I can't think how to force April to stay, other than locking her in her room. Which never really works in the Debauchery Club, at least not in my experience.

"Wait!" I call, running to my room for the small gun that Elliott gave me. I catch up to them at a closet where April is handing out cloaks. Unlike those that Malcontent's men wear, these are made of velvet and lined with satin. But they are heavy enough to hide our shapes a bit. Someone will have to approach us to tell that we are three girls alone with one man and a child.

I have no idea how we will save Elise and the other kidnapped girls. My mind races, trying to form some sort of plan.

We exit through a side door and down an alley. I hold Henry tight, and as we reach the street, he moves closer to me. Like Elise, he was never allowed to go outside. I squeeze his shoulder.

The streets are busy today. Groups, families—or what's left of them—with luggage, some moving toward Elliott's safe zone, and others in finery, hoping to beg or bribe their way into Prospero's ball. Twice we hear crying. Discreet sniffling through an open window, and then wailing from a courtyard. I doubt Elise and the courier's daughter are the only girls who have been stolen away.

As we turn the corner, my attention is caught by a man looming over a woman holding a grubby child. Her suitcase is open, spilling into the dirt of the street. I keep my eye on them, even as our small group crosses the street, hurrying toward our destination. The man empties the suitcase, and then knocks the child from the woman's arms.

"Henry, hold Miss April's hand," I say under my breath.

People walk past, ignoring the scene, but I can't tear my eyes away. I have to do something.

The man pulls himself up to his full height and reaches back for a weapon that's strapped to his back. He's discovered this woman doesn't have anything worth stealing, but he hasn't moved on.

I stride across the street even as the woman throws herself over the boy.

I hold my gun in front of my body. I don't even

remember pulling it from my pocket.

My gun only has two shots, so I must be careful.

He's holding a wooden club. It's an ugly weapon, rusty nails protruding through the wood.

He arcs his arm, ready to take a swing at the woman.

"Step away." My voice escalates on the second word.

The man raises his head and sneers, until he spots the gun in my hand. He spits into the scattered belongings. I see the disdain in his small, mean eyes. He doesn't think I'll shoot. I want to prove him wrong. Because if I don't, he'll terrorize other women and other children.

But I only have two shots, and I may need both of them to save Elise. I wait.

Very deliberately, the man gathers himself and spits again, not into the clothing, but at me. It hits just below my hairline, hot and disgusting, and slides down behind my mask. I hold the gun as steady as I can, forcing my fingers not to pull the trigger, because he's retreating. The man saunters away as if he hasn't a care in the world. My hand shakes a little, wanting to hurt him. But I don't.

I keep the gun trained on the man until he disappears down a side street, out of sight. The woman pulls herself up and clutches her child. I lower the gun and force myself not to pull the mask away. Not to wipe at the sticky residue that has pooled below my cheekbone. Even if no one else is infected, there's still April, only a few steps behind me now. I must keep the mask on.

"Thank you," the woman says quietly.

I don't look closely at the child she is holding. He hasn't cried out once, not even when the man knocked him from his mother's arms. If he's badly hurt, I don't want to know. I can't do anything about it.

"The Debauchery District is in that direction," I say, pointing. "Take the child and get inside. One of the soldiers will find you medical help if you ask."

"Araby?" Mina has my arm and is pulling me away. "We have to keep moving. He might come back. With friends."

The woman heeds the warning and starts moving, scooping a few of her belongings into the battered case.

But I'm rooted in the middle of the street with my gun in hand.

"Araby!" It takes Henry's small voice to bring me back to reality. I slide the gun back into my pocket.

"Let's go," I say.

"It's near the river," Mina says. "In the lower city. We have to hurry. Don't stop again."

She leads us to the abandoned industrial district. The buildings are massive enough to block out the sun. They loom on every side of us. The streets themselves often disappear as if they've been consumed by the factories.

We walk up one street, and then down another. There are hardly any people here, but I watch for the dark cloaks of Malcontent's men.

As we pass a tent set up in the shadow of a blown-out

factory, a girl stumbles into the street, scratching at her bleeding eyes. Henry screams, and all of us step back. The girl falls to her knees, and before I can let out the breath I'm holding, a man runs out of the tent. He sees us watching and grimaces as he throws a rough blanket over her. I lead our small band away. I'm not sure if she was already dead, but it's just a matter of time.

We reach the stench of the river soon.

"There," Mina says eventually, pointing.

The orphanage is a squat one-story building surrounded by hulking factories. All of the windows are barred.

"So here we are," April says. "Now what?"

"First, we find a cellar with access to the underground tunnels," I say, trying the closest door. It is locked.

"Araby, last time we were in the tunnels—" April begins.

"We need a way to escape out of sight once we find the girls." I cut her off. "Look for a tunnel entrance. Prospero's men won't want to follow us into Malcontent's domain."

"They came into Elliott's domain to take Elise," April mutters.

"If you have a better plan, you can tell me. Otherwise, we find a tunnel entrance. You and Henry wait there, ready to help the girls to safety if we get them out. I'll go up to the orphanage and knock on the door."

"Are you going to tell them you want to adopt a few

little girls?" April's expression is almost identical to one that Elliott makes.

I lead them down the street that passes in front of the orphanage.

Studying the paving stones, I find the mark of an open eye. Before it was Elliott's symbol, it was the symbol used by a secret society to mark entrances to the tunnels. I kneel and press the stone until it slides back to reveal a gentle slope leading into a narrow passage.

"All of you stay here in the shadows. I'll knock on the door and try to find out how many guards are in there. I doubt Prospero has many people in the city. But if there are lots of guards, then we'll have to think of some way to sneak into the building. Look for a back door or a tunnel entrance."

If the sun wasn't fading, I'd look for a way to sneak into the orphanage first. But it's already late afternoon, and I do not want to be out at night with a pack of young girls. Whatever happens now, we have to do it quickly.

I approach the door, and rap heavily. A guard answers. He looks tired and unhappy.

"I'm looking for someone," I say. "A guard. He's very handsome. . . ." I try to make my voice wistful, like a girl in love.

The guard frowns. Clearly this isn't what he was expecting.

"You need to move on," he says. "This isn't a safe place."

"He said he would meet me last night," I say in a rush. "And I couldn't make it." I hope that the frightened flush on my cheeks looks like a blush.

"Sorry, miss," he repeats. "I'm the only one here. The boss has pulled the others—"

My gun is out and pointed at the center of his chest. If he's the only guard, then my two bullets will be more than enough.

"Where are the girls?" I demand, waving across the street with my left hand. April and the others leave the doorway across the alley.

"Inside," he says. "Believe me, I want nothing to do with this."

Looking into his exhausted eyes, I believe him. "You should've joined the rebellion. They won't make you kidnap children."

"My family is at the palace, under Prospero's . . . protection," he admits.

He means his family is held hostage.

"I'm sorry for that," I say. "Some of these girls are under my protection."

"Keep the gun on him," April commands. "I'm going to go in and bring them out. We don't want to be trapped inside if more guards show up."

The soldier's eyes shift from me to April, and she grabs his lapel. "Is that what you hope to happen? Are more guards on their way?"

"Hurry," I tell her. "Get them out."

April and Mina disappear into the building. Henry stays near me. I keep my gun trained on the guard. He sits down on the step, seeming resigned. Mina appears in the doorway with five chubby toddler girls, all dressed in frilly white outfits. Elise is not with them.

I stare at the girls. "What're they supposed to be?"

"Swans," the guard says.

I look at him, but he just shrugs. "That's what they are calling them. Prospero's little swans." Then he adds in a low voice, "Crocodiles eat swans."

My heart sinks. I don't trust Prospero, and I know his entertainment is often depraved, but surely . . . I study the girls' tear-streaked faces. While my attention is on them, the guard lashes out, kicking my legs from under me. I land hard, the air knocked out of my body, just as his boot connects with my ribs. My mask has been pushed askew. Shrill voices are screaming.

But I'm still gripping the ivory handle of the gun. The guard aims another brutal kick at my chest, and I pull the trigger.

He falls beside me, clutching his own chest, and I scramble away, afraid it's a feint, but blood trickles through his hands. As I stagger to my feet, I realize that I can't quite catch my breath. I think he bruised one of my ribs.

The courier leads the bigger girls out, and Elise runs toward me, wearing the same ludicrous swan costume as the others.

"Don't hug me," I gasp, forcing a smile so she isn't frightened.

Her face pales anyway. "Araby?"

"Henry's waiting for you," I say, nodding toward him and trying not to wince. Elise puts her arm around him protectively, as though he's the one being rescued. Some of the girls bounce up and down on their toes, the lace and feathers of their outfits spinning around them.

"We need to go," I call. Mina is carrying a girl who's little more than a baby, and April is right behind her.

And I walk away from the man I shot. The first person I've ever killed.

The children squirm. Several girls sit on the steps, and one of them lies down in the dirt, staining her white costume. In the near silence, we hear the sound of wheels against paving stones.

Nearly all of the carriages that are left belong to Prospero. These girls were collected in his name. His men are coming. We have to go now.

April shouts, "Everyone grab a partner. Big girls with little girls. You have to hold someone's hand."

They jump to attention, looking up to her with wide eyes.

"Don't let your partner go for any reason. We don't want to lose anyone. Araby will lead us."

One small girl has no partner, so I hold her hand, showing them to the mouth of the tunnel, which we left open. April takes up the rear, and the courier, holding tightly to his daughter's hand, is somewhere near the center. Mina stays close to April.

One of the girls trips down the stairs, and they all squeal.

"Be careful and quiet," I admonish.

The tunnel is narrow, which is good for keeping them all within arm's length, but every time we get to a cross tunnel I hold my breath, worried that one of the little girls will disappear into it.

We have no light but what filters through the cracks in the paving stones above. Those tiny trickles of illumination only serve to make the darkness seem more oppressive.

One of the younger girls stubs her toe and begins to cry quietly.

We pass through a series of brick arches, and I hear rushing water.

And then I feel water seeping into the toe of my boot. The tunnels ahead may be flooded. "We need to find a way up," I say. "Look for stairs or a ladder."

We've passed a dozen ladders, but now I don't see any, and the water is flowing over my feet. This feels all too familiar. My ribs throb, the wound on my back burns, and panic is setting in. Just when I'm about to tell everyone to turn back and search for one of the ladders that we passed before, one of the side passages opens to a stairway. I stumble up the steps, holding tight to the squirming girl in my arms.

April herds everyone into an open square, and though I don't know how many we had to begin with, I keep trying to count them because it seems the right thing to do.

A cry startles all of us, and a woman runs toward us. The soles of her shoes seem to echo each time her feet hit the street. She grabs one little girl and embraces her.

Soon we are surrounded by a crowd, all talking at once.

We are in the Debauchery District, near the club, so it shouldn't surprise me that Elliott finds us, drawn by all the noise. He pulls me up, so that the two of us are standing on the base of a statue beside a stone horse.

People are shouting and crying, and I hear the words "hero" and "rescue." Elliott raises my hand, clasped in his own, above our heads, and the crowd cheers. I look around at all the faces. After the devastation of the city, it's just nice to see people smiling, to see that they have something to be happy about. The little girls are finding their families, being reunited.

Will is standing in a doorway, outside the adoring crowd. Elise must have found him. He has his hand on her shoulder, though his eyes are trained on me. Henry is holding Elise's hand.

He is the only person who isn't clapping. His tattoos stand out starkly on the pale skin of his neck. He must realize I took Henry into danger. He must be furious. But his face is completely blank. I pull away from Elliott.

But he doesn't let me get far, pressing his palm

against the stone wall behind us, nearly pinning me to the building. He leans in, as if to kiss me. The crowd cheers wildly. The way that he's claiming me makes me feel claustrophobic, and I put my hand to my ribs, gasping for breath.

Elliott says something about me being shy. He doesn't yell it for everyone to hear, but he says it loudly enough that the ones in the front will repeat it for the others. The crowd is exhilarated.

I don't like his possessiveness, but if he wasn't holding me, I might collapse from exhaustion and pain.

"Slip away with me," he whispers, and I think he means something suggestive, that he wants to be alone with me, and I do not want that.

"You should stay," I say. "You love being the center of attention."

"I believe they are clapping for you," he responds. "But that doesn't matter. We have to get away from all of this. I've found your father."

And he has to catch me because my knees give out. My father or my father's body?

"We have to get to my steam carriage," he says. "Come." He waves to the crowd and leads me away. Inside the stables, he hands me a pair of goggles. "We're going to go fast," he says, smiling.

We pass an entire city block that has been gutted by fire. Charred bed frames stand within neat brick squares. A chair. A chimney standing all alone, the wall that surrounded it gone. We pick up speed, and the wind blows through my hair. It rushes against my face, as if it's blowing away all the disease and decay.

Soon the top of the Akkadian Towers comes into view, far above the other buildings in this part of town. It seems impossible that we once had the ability to build such things. That I ever lived there.

"The tower is still standing," I marvel. "It was burning when we left the city."

"The rain doused the fire, so it's mostly intact. People still live on the lower levels. Most of the richest occupants moved to less damaged premises, of course." Elliott pulls the carriage into a building that once housed a smithy. The carefully lettered sign outside says the business services steam carriages.

"It's as good a place to hide this as I can think of," he explains. He secures the carriage, taking a few small parts from the engine and pocketing them.

The street-level windows of the buildings here are mostly shattered. Can we still make glass? Are any glassmakers still alive?

No blacksmiths, no new windows. Elliott's plan should be to start a school so that people can relearn these arts.

A potted flower sits on a balcony above us. A red geranium that has somehow survived all the death and destruction.

We're standing in the shadow of the Akkadian

Towers. For a year, I pulled up to the imposing double doors with April in her ostentatious steam carriage. Did the doorman survive the fire? What happened to our cook? Before the Red Death, couriers would have been in and out, going about their business, but the streets are deserted.

We enter the alley behind the unfinished tower. The last time I walked here was with Will, and we saw a dead boy with his well-crafted leather boots and his immaculate white mask. Elliott pulls open a door with broken hinges and ushers me into a dark corridor.

"Is this building attached to the other?" I ask.

"The two buildings share a basement."

If we had moved here when I was younger, when Finn was alive, the two of us might have explored the building more. Instead, I stood on the roof and thought about jumping.

Elliott leads me through the empty echoing cellar that connects the unfinished tower to the half-ruined one where I used to live. He takes a match from his pocket and strikes it, using the fleeting light to determine our path. When it burns down to his fingertips, he drops it to the floor.

"I need to start carrying candles," I say, mostly to myself. I follow Elliott to a stairway that leads up and connects to the stairs for the main tower. I suppose the elevator will never be repaired, now.

We are, perhaps, four stories up when we hear a sound

from the corridor. Elliott puts his hand on my arm, and then, slowly, one finger to his lips. We tread lightly, trying not to draw attention, as we climb the next set of stairs. Luckily, stairways in the Akkadian Towers don't creak, even after a fire. When we stop to catch our breath, I raise my eyebrows.

"Squatters," he whispers.

I frown, glancing upward. I hate the idea of anyone living in our old apartment. "They'll avoid the highest levels," Elliott reassures me. "The building is unstable, so they'll want a quick escape route."

"Is it safe?"

"Probably not." Elliott smiles. I tread more carefully and avoid any spots that look damaged.

Finally we reach the top floor. The door to my family's apartment stands partially open. I stop on the threshold. Elliott takes my hand, and with his other he pulls out a small gun, almost exactly like the one he gave me.

Our footsteps echo against the tile floor. If anyone is here, they will hear us.

Elliott leads me down the hall but does not stop at Father's study; he makes no move toward it. I break away from him and slide the door open. The room has been ransacked. The paneling is torn from the wall, the desk is crushed into splinters.

"There is nothing to see in there," Elliott says, except he hasn't entered the room.

"You did this," I say, stepping farther into the

destruction, away from him. "You came here without me."

"There wasn't enough information in his journal. I thought maybe I'd find more here."

I turn. He's leaning against the doorframe, his face inscrutable. I've been waiting for him to bring me here, hoping . . .

My eyes burn.

At the back of the study, nothing remains but wooden beams. It used to be covered with a handsome wood paneling that hid shelves upon shelves of glass jars. In the jars are rats, floating in liquid. Several have fallen to the floor and broken, spilling limp dead rats and noxious liquid, which is perhaps what is making my eyes sting.

"This is where he did it," I whisper. "This is where he created the Red Death."

CHAPTER
FIFTEEN

"Come away, Araby," Elliott says softly. And then, more urgently, "I didn't break those jars. The building must have shifted, or someone else has been here. We should get out of this room."

On the floor, I see a brooch in the glass. I bend down—it must have belonged to Mother—but Elliott grabs me.

"I don't think you should touch that."

He's right. We step back into the hallway and slam the door behind us. But as ever, it makes no sound.

We creep through the empty rooms. In the kitchen, Elliott's boots crush the shards of bone china that have fallen from the cabinet. Through the arched doorway that leads to the dining room, I see that the vase at the center of the table is still filled with roses—all dead.

I leave Elliott in the kitchen and slip into my bedroom.

Crossing the floor in three quick steps, I throw open the door of my closet. No one has pillaged this wealth of whalebone and silk, so I grab a favorite dress, a lovely muted red. In a quick movement I discard the one I've been wearing, which is stained and soiled with tunnel debris.

"Much better," Elliott says from the doorway.

I blush deeply and pull the red dress over my head. He steps into the room as I adjust the skirts, pretending that I was not just undressed in front of him. Mother would be mortified.

A glance in the mirror to adjust my hair reminds me how terrible my mask looks, cracked and stained with grime. In my bureau, my spares are packed in cotton. I drop the cracked mask into the drawer, where it lands with a hollow thud.

"Here." Before I choose a new one, Elliott hands me a tube of red lipstick. "I think you were wearing this the first time I saw you."

"The first time you saw me, you thought I was dead." But I glide the lipstick on anyway, because it reminds me of the days before, and April. Then I cover it with a new white mask.

Elliott raises an arm to escort me out, but I remove one more mask from the bureau. This one covers the whole face, and it glitters.

"This was for one of your uncle's infamous parties."

Elliott takes it from my hands, drops it back into the bureau, and slams the drawer.

"As long as I have anything to do with it, you'll never attend one of his parties."

He stalks from the room, but I hesitate. Should I tear the gemstones from the mask? In our little band, Elliott controls all the gold. And money often equals power.

I rip off a few gemstones and pocket them, then grab Mother's favorite scarf and wrap it around my shoulders.

"Your father won't come if he thinks anyone is here. Let's go to the other apartment."

And so we enter Penthouse A, April's old home. This apartment appears untouched, with chairs upholstered in gold silk still arranged around low glass tables.

"Where did your mother go?" I ask.

"As soon as the city became frightening, she ran to Prospero's protection."

The doors to the bedrooms are wide open, and Elliott collects a blanket from his mother's bed and two bottles of wine from the kitchen before he opens the door to a closet, steps inside, and gestures for me to follow.

"I'm not sure I want to crawl into a cupboard," I start to say, but then he pushes the back wall and light filters in. I follow as he walks into the garden where he first recruited me to join his rebellion. This humid, lush, abandoned place is where he and I began.

"It certainly was easier for you to get into the garden last time than it was for me," I say, remembering the utility closet on the floor below and the hatch I had to climb through.

"I was testing your ingenuity. I couldn't use a party girl who didn't have the initiative to find and climb a ladder. You know, my uncle murdered the architects who built the Akkadian Towers. He didn't want anyone to know the building the way he does."

"How well do you know it?"

Elliott's eyebrows draw together. "Not as well as Prospero. Not as well as I'd like to. The garden is far from the only secret in the Akkadian Towers."

I looked into this garden every day from Mother's comfortable sitting room, but I've only been inside that one time in the dark. There are stunted trees lining the fake stream. I recognize the bulbs of spring flowers. This place is ready to bloom.

But the earth is disturbed in some areas as well. As if by an earthquake.

Elliott takes a tentative step forward, as if expecting the floor beneath us to move. Vines cover some of the trees, strangling them in this sea of green. After a few steps, he seems confident that the garden is stable enough for the two of us. At least, he makes no move to leave.

He places the wine and blanket on the low wall, where he was sitting weeks ago when he asked me to join his cause.

"We might as well be comfortable while we wait for your father."

But I'm nervous. On edge after the excitement of

rescuing those girls and the discovery that Father may be alive.

"Walk with me," Elliott says, and takes my hand. "This was always one of my favorite places. No matter what villainous things he created, Prospero also engineered luxury."

He leads me through the garden, past arbors of flowers to a low swing attached to the bough of a weeping willow. "Prospero had to have extra water piped in to keep this old tree alive." Elliott pats the trunk. "But it still looks healthy."

"The tree gets clean water, but the people of the city are dying." I laugh a little, and then choke.

Elliott turns his head. There is something about him here, something calm and thoughtful. As if I am seeing a different Elliott. An Elliott who could have been a poet instead of a revolutionary.

He gestures to the swing, and I sit. The wooden seat is cracked and lined with fungus. All the piped-in water is now trapped in the air, making it heavy and muggy.

Elliott wraps his hands around my waist and pulls me toward him. Then he slides one hand to my back, while still holding me against him with the other, like he knows what he is supposed to do—push me away from him so the swing can ascend—but he doesn't want me to glide away from him.

Eventually he lets go, and the movement of the swing feels unnaturally slow, as if this moment might last forever. The moisture in the air settles on my skin, but instead of seeming clammy, it feels like fine silk.

When I swing back to him, he catches my shoulders, his hands trailing over the bare skin, delicately tracing my still-healing wound.

"Elliott." I shift, and he wraps his arms around me and pulls me off the swing. We tumble to the ground, laughing. I reach out and brush the tiny blue flowers in the grass.

"The same color as your hair," he says. "What was April thinking?"

But I don't want to think about April, not now. I don't want to think of anything that's happening outside these glass walls. No matter what, when we leave this place, people will die. We will find Father, or I will go with Malcontent. Elliott will overthrow Prospero, or not. So I lead Elliott back over to the wall where we left our things.

He spreads the blanket beneath a bower of leaves and opens the bottle of wine.

"I don't have glasses." He is not apologetic. "We'll have to drink from the bottle." He takes a long drink and then passes the bottle to me. It's better wine than what we've been able to buy from the market.

"This is—" I begin.

"Magical." Elliott finishes my sentence. I'm not sure it's what I would have said, but I don't correct him. "Will you will wear this?" He holds out his hand, and the diamond ring, the one that I traded yesterday, lies in the palm of his hand. It still sparkles, even after all it has been through.

I don't ask how he retrieved it. We are the children of murderers, abandoned by our fathers. We do things others wouldn't dream of. But here in this garden, we can forget.

So I take off my mask and kiss him.

And he kisses me back. All of his intensity and all of my own yearning seem to twine between us.

The ring falls from my hand to the earth.

"I love you," Elliott whispers into my neck, and I don't know what to say, but then I don't have to say anything, because he kisses me again. When I open my eyes a moment later, I think there's a slow anger burning in his. Yet he's still kissing me.

And then, abruptly, he stops. A shadow falls over us.

"Araby?" Father's voice is hoarse.

I jolt up immediately, readjusting my dress.

Father presses his lips together. He looks tired but the same as ever. His hair is mussed, and there are ink stains on his hands. A wave of love for him overwhelms me, and I throw my arms around him. He smells of cedar wood and tobacco.

Though he might've been shocked at finding me tangled up with Elliott, he pulls me close. Perhaps he didn't think he'd ever see me, ever embrace me, again, either.

"Dr. Worth." Elliott is standing now too, and his

voice is cold but unsurprised. He is perfectly composed. He knew Father would come here, to the garden. That he would find us.

He set it—me—up.

Like today after April and I rescued those children, Elliott is staking some sort of claim. The diamond ring is still lying in the dirt, and I leave it there.

Father ignores him and brushes my hair from my face. His eyes are filled with tears.

"I was afraid that you were in the explosion, but then I saw your messages."

The explosion—oh, God. He told me to leave on the steamship with Elliott, but I never boarded because Will gave me to Malcontent.

"I want you to pretend you never met me. Become someone else," Father continues. His eyes are more haunted than I've ever seen. He knows that I know, about the disease, everything. He's ashamed.

"I wouldn't do that," I respond slowly. There is no doubt, now, that he's guilty. "I couldn't, but you have to explain. I need to hear it from you."

He doesn't answer. Some childish part of me still hoped that he would proclaim his innocence, and somehow I would find it in me to believe him.

The silence stretches out. I've come all this way, and he answers me with silence.

But I didn't come back to the city just to ask him this. I came to save April.

"April is dying from the Weeping Sickness. Will you help her? Can you?"

Father's brow furrows. "You know there is nothing that can be done." His tone is completely without hope.

And this is somehow worse than everything that came before. Because if he can help April, he can undo a little of the evil he has done. In his journal, I saw a man twisted by remorse, but also a man willing to make excuses for his own deeds. A weak man. I want my father to be strong. To save the day.

I grip Father's sleeve. "But the rumors. You had something that you threw away when Finn died. April is dying because of me. We have to help her!"

"If there had been a way, would Finn have died?" The way he says my brother's name is just one more stab in my heart.

"So that's it?" I say in a low voice. "After Finn died, you stopped working on cures and just created ways to kill more people?"

Father stumbles back, away from me, his face completely white.

"It's all the prince let me do," he says, with the same lost look I've seen him wear for years. I turn away so he can't see how it infuriates me. Elliott doesn't need to see how weak my father is. Elliott is an expert at exploiting weakness.

As if to make some sort of amends, Father puts his hand on my shoulder. He takes a tiny vial from an inside pocket. "You did drink yours?"

I nod. "It protects against the Red Death?" I ask.

"Yes."

"Give some to Elliott," I say. And then, because he's still my father, I add, "Please."

Father squares his shoulders. He told me to go with Elliott, but he's never approved of our friendship. Elliott crosses his arms over his chest and smirks.

"You don't love her," Father says.

But Elliott said he did. Just moments ago. And I never responded. That's not the sort of thing he's likely to ignore.

Father rolls the vial back and forth between his thumb and forefinger, as if considering.

"Give him the vial," I say. "Whether you like him or not, Elliott is doing some good for the city."

Father hands Elliott the vial. "Drink half."

He does so without a word. I take it out of his hand and cork the vial before tucking it into my pocket. "I'll need another, too," I tell Father. That will be enough for Henry, Elise, and Will.

Father takes a second vial from his vest pocket, and I snatch it. Elliott keeps that slight mocking smile on his face, but I see the anger in his eyes. He knows that this vial is for Will. The gesture may be innocent, an attempt to protect a friend, the children. But it's too soon after ignoring his declaration of love. I care for him. But I don't love him.

His eyes narrow, and something between us changes.

We can't stay here. If Father can't help April, then my course has been chosen for me. I press my mask to my face and hold out Elliott's, for him to put on. In return, he holds out the diamond ring.

I take it, but I won't wear it. I drop it into my pocket.

Elliott gives a sharp, ugly laugh, as if my gesture confirms everything he's been thinking. I look into his eyes, trying to understand, but he's closed off to me now.

"I'll come with you to your friend," Father says. "If nothing else, I have an ointment that will soothe her—"

"That's what we wanted," Elliott cuts in. "To soothe my sister. As she dies." Elliott lights a cigarette as Father retrieves his small doctor bag.

"I'm sorry that she caught the disease," Father says. "There are ways to prevent the spread. A white powder." We're making our way back through the garden as he speaks. "Prospero wouldn't let us manufacture enough of the vaccine, but it exists. But after you catch either of them . . . there isn't much you can do."

"I need to know everything about the powder," Elliott says. "How to make it, how to distribute it. You'll help me?"

Father sighs. "It's better than watching the world fall to ruin, I suppose. Something to occupy our time while people destroy what's left of the city."

I hate his disillusionment. Father's face has become so lined in the last few weeks. Despite my anger and disappointment, I want to smooth the concern from his face.

He is about to say something else when the metal hatch nearby shudders. Someone is trying to enter the garden through the maintenance closet below.

Father hurries to it and twists a lever, locking them out and sealing us in. He doesn't know about the door leading in from Penthouse A. "Come quickly," he says. "It must be Malcontent. His men have been searching for me. We can break a window and escape through one of the apartments."

"There is still only one stairway leading down." Elliott paces back and forth. "All they have to do is block it. We're going to fight our way out. Araby, do you have your gun? Your knife?"

"I'm staying here." I step in front of Elliott, forcing him to look at me. Malcontent is on the other side of that door. As terrified as I am of him, he's April's last chance. And as much as they despise each other, Father and Elliott can work together. They can save some of the people. "Go through Penthouse A," I tell Elliott. "Take my father with you."

"Don't be ridiculous," Father says. "I've only just found you."

Elliott doesn't say anything.

"If anyone stays, it will be me. I'll tell them that I've been hiding here, alone," Father says.

"Malcontent will kill you," I say. "He wants you, and he wants Elliott."

"Do you think he wants you any less?"

I don't. Malcontent will kill me. Publicly, to show his power. But of the three of us, I am the most expendable.

Elliott's silence is unnerving. I know he's angry, and hurt. But we were trying to accomplish something together. Before I sacrifice myself, I want him to acknowledge that. He doesn't even look at me.

Whatever was between us, it seems to have slipped away.

"Araby . . ." Father's voice is anguished. "I've already lost your brother, your mother is imprisoned. I can't—"

What he says next is lost in the sound of hammering at the metal door. Malcontent's men have realized that it is locked from within. They know someone is up here.

"Go." I push him, and he doesn't budge. Elliott may be ready to leave me, but Father is stubborn. I steel myself to hurt him. "You might be able to save me later. If not . . . well, there isn't much for me to live for in this ugly, decaying world, is there?" Father blanches. And I shove him away from me.

But as I go to the metal door and begin twisting back the lock, I'm thinking of Will. He was the one who showed me that living was better. He knows that the suicidal girl is gone. But if I think of the things I'll never be able to say to Will, I won't have the strength to do what has to be done.

"If you're still here when I open this," I say over my shoulder, "Malcontent will take all of us. And everything will be lost."

"He'll search," Elliott says. "He isn't stupid."

"Then be quick and find a place to hide."

I hear their footsteps—the one who hesitates must surely be Father—but I can't look away from my task. I give the lever one last twist and steel myself. The hinges make a terrible sound as the great metal door slides back. I don't let myself look in the direction Father and Elliott have gone. I won't give them away.

"Miss Araby Worth." A chillingly cold voice calls from the bottom of the metal ladder. "What a pleasure. Now I can hand deliver your invitation."

CHAPTER
SIXTEEN

INSTEAD OF MALCONTENT WITH HIS CLOAKED henchmen, Prospero stands at the bottom of the ladder, a red rose in the pocket of a heavy, well-made jacket. He's wearing both a mask and protective gloves.

He sees my surprise and laughs. "Were you expecting someone else?"

"You never come into the city. Especially not with the Red Death . . ." I'm frozen at the hatch, staring down.

"I wanted to see it one last time," he says softly. "Come, join me."

I'm caught. I can't flee, or he will find Elliott and Father. I'll have to find some way to escape him before he leaves the city.

"Good, good," Prospero says as I climb down. "This is so fortunate, because I've already retrieved my niece from the Debauchery Club. I know she won't want to attend the ball without you."

"April . . ." My voice gives out. I have to swallow before I can finish. "You have April?"

"Of course," he says. "Have you ever known her to miss a party?"

"How wonderful that you found us," I whisper. "We've longed for a party." But how will we keep April's illness a secret so that he doesn't kill her on the spot?

It feels much farther going down the stairs than it did following Elliott up. We don't stop until we reach the lobby. Though the room is still ornate, it seems tarnished now. A doorman I don't recognize bows to the prince. Outside, the moon is rising.

Black carriages line the street, and two of Prospero's soldiers load crates and barrels into the steam carriage directly in front of the Akkadian Towers. The windows up and down the street are dark. Even here, in the wealthiest section of the city, all but one of the streetlamps have gone dark. Several young girls stand in the last flickering pool of light. They wear ornate dresses, their masks decorated with sequins. One clutches her gold invitation between gloved fingers. A young man carrying a violin case walks up. He's also holding his invitation. They all climb into a carriage, prepared to be shipped away.

I search the line of carriages. Prospero could be lying about April. But then something flutters out of a carriage window. A glossy black feather. And there's a flash of blond hair before the curtain falls back into place. *April.* Prospero puts his hand on my shoulder, and I jump.

As I watch, the carriages begin to move, carrying her farther away from safety and the hope that we'll find her father and get a cure.

Only Prospero, me, and a handful of his guards are left on the street. They are wearing black cloaks of the sort that Malcontent's men usually wear. Prospero waves, and one of the guards brings me a similar one. "All the better to blend in at night," he says. "My brother may be crazy, but he has a few good ideas." His eyes flash once, and then he turns away.

Three wizened guards join us. They all have silver hair. At least most of the young men seem to have defected to Elliott's side. One guard has a jagged scar from his ear to his chin. He is thin, and he wears a sword. The other two guards are stocky. One has eyes that are set too close together. The other holds a musket and gives me a look so cold that he must know who I am. And hate me for it.

I'd swear I've never seen any of them before, but the man with the sword reaches out to touch my hair. "I liked the purple better," he says.

"We must move quickly," Prospero says. "We'll pay our respects to the dead, give my brother these "—he holds up the keys I remember from the throne room, the ones to the pumping station that could help save the city—"and then we'll be on our way."

"So you have given up on the city." I try to put all the scorn I can into my voice.

"It's never been what I wanted," he says. "I tried, but your father ruined everything." This man has always been at the center of the web. He is even more to blame for all of the death and despair than my father. I slip my hand into my pocket to feel the cold solidity of the gun. I have one bullet left. If I get the chance, I'll kill him.

As Prospero leads us across two wide avenues, the tip of my boot crushes part of a shattered mask. We stop in front of the great cathedral. It is miraculously intact, spared from fire and vandalism. The stone is a costly white marble, and in the dim moonlight, it glows a little. It isn't tall, not compared to the skyscrapers that surround it. But it has a soaring quality, especially from where we are standing, under the great stained-glass window.

Gargoyles peer down at us from the ornate window ledges.

"Our mother was to be buried here," Prospero remarks. "Our father offered a very generous donation. But the priests said that the crypt was full. Father increased his offer, until the greedy priests agreed. But they never did it. They took the money and discarded her body because they were afraid to pry up any of the stones, terrified to open the vaults. The warnings are carved throughout the building, in Latin. 'Beware of the vault.' Inside were heaps of unidentified bones, the victims of a plague. The priests believed that a terrible illness would be unleashed on the city if they opened the tomb."

Prospero steps across the threshold, touching the scrollwork beside the door with one gloved finger.

I follow him, searching the scrollwork for any such warning. Could the plague have originated in this cathedral, instead of in my father's lab?

Prospero keeps talking. He's always loved the sound of his own voice, especially here, where even a whisper carries and echoes.

"Those priests were fools. My brother and I tunneled into the vaults. We found rings, jewels, and even a locket with a snippet of hair. Years later, I gave that locket to your father when I asked him to find a solution to our rat problem. He was excited to study an ancient plague."

My heart sinks. I should stop trying to find ways for Father to escape the guilt. It always comes back to him.

"Come inside." Prince Prospero beckons from the cavernous darkness. Without meaning to, I have stopped on the threshold. His cold eyes glint from the shadows, chilling me, though the night is unseasonably warm.

Names are engraved in each of the flagstones beneath our feet. Stepping-stones, burial stones, there is no difference in an ancient church like this. Some are engraved with images too worn to decipher. Pieces of an enormous pipe organ lie abandoned and decaying. A patch of night sky is visible where the roof has collapsed.

The prince murmurs something, and as I strain to make out his words, I hear something else. The soft rustling of thousands of wings, shifting restlessly in the darkness of the eaves. The cathedral is filled with bats. Enormous, bloated, disease-carrying bats.

Prospero freezes, and his eyes move upward, ever so slowly. Is it possible that he did not know bats have taken up residence in abandoned churches throughout the city? Even the smallest children know this.

By now the sky is fully dark. The slightest sound could wake the bats. I'm afraid even to breathe.

But Prospero walks to the front of the nave, easily a hundred paces from where I am standing, and kneels. His men stand in the doorway, watching me, their weapons ready. Prospero puts both hands to the altar and presses until some sort of panel pops out—a wooden drawer. He takes the keys from inside his vest, but before he places them inside, stone grates on stone, and one in the floor rises. A figure in dark robes ascends silently from beneath it. "You weren't supposed to be here until tomorrow," Prospero rasps.

The keys jingle, once, as he holds them above the secret compartment, as if unsure what to do with them. And then all I hear is the whisper of restless wings.

CHAPTER
SEVENTEEN

A SINGLE BAT LEAVES THE SAFETY OF THE ROOF and swoops downward, and then everything is silent again.

Malcontent lets his hood drop. His hair is shot with white, and his eyes are bloodshot.

While Prospero is cold, Malcontent burns. And yet . . . there is a little of Elliott in each of them.

"How appropriate to meet you here," Malcontent says, "where your crimes began." He steps away from the slab of limestone that must conceal a tunnel rather than a tomb. Two of his men follow.

"Elliott could do much to improve the city," Prospero says to his brother. "I trust you will stop him."

In this moment, my loathing for both of these men eclipses all other feelings. They are bent on destroying what's left of the city, sabotaging everything Elliott is trying to do.

"It was good of you to agree to meet me tomorrow, here at Mother's empty tomb." Malcontent gives a quick laugh. "But my men said that you were obviously leaving tonight, and I wanted to see you once again." He steps forward. Prospero's men are still in the cathedral but haven't left the doorway. They can still run if things continue to go poorly for the prince.

"Take him," Malcontent says.

Two of Malcontent's diseased men flank the prince. The prince flails as one of the cloaked men reaches up and grabs his mask. Prospero freezes.

In the silence, the crunch as the mask hits the floor is shocking. The other man, whose face is dripping with open sores, lunges at the prince, smearing the foul pus from his wounds onto Prospero's face. The movements are practiced. He's done this before.

Prospero's scream echoes through the church. The bats flap above us. Malcontent's man lets him go, laughing, and Prospero scuttles backward like a frightened crab. He's so close now that I could almost touch him. The keys fall to the floor.

I measure the distance to the door while keeping an eye on the diseased man. I don't want to draw his attention, but if he makes the slightest move in my direction, I'm ready to run.

Malcontent sees me and gestures for me to join him. Just hours ago I'd planned to give myself to him, but now April is on her way to the palace. I have to stay with Prospero, whether I like it or not.

A knife shines in the near-darkness. From his undignified crouch on the floor, Prospero throws the blade. It nicks Malcontent's ear, but he keeps his chin high, even as blood drips down. The knife hits a statue behind him and clatters to the ground.

Above us, thousands of wings flutter.

"Is this . . . the same knife?" Malcontent asks, retrieving the blade. Anger contorts his face. He stares up, not at the bat-covered ceiling, but at the statues around the church, chanting something under his breath. As he toys with the knife that Prospero threw at him, I hear footsteps. Even more men are ascending from the tunnels.

Our only hope is to get back to the waiting steam carriage.

Prospero and Malcontent are eyeing each other from across the room. "Find the keys," Malcontent says to his soldiers. No one is paying any attention to me.

I reach into my pocket, so slowly that none of them notices. The ivory handle of the gun is heavy in my hand. I pull it from my pocket, aim toward the ceiling, close my eyes, and pull the trigger.

The sound explodes and, all at once, is joined by the screeching bats and the screams from the men as the crazed creatures descend.

I put up my other arm, to shield my hair as best I can, and run. Bats careen in every direction, swooping down and then back toward the ceiling. Someone knocks into me hard, and I fall. Something touches my hair, and I scream.

Tiny pebbles rain down from above, along with bits of mortar.

I crawl across the floor, and my fingers find something cool and metallic. The gold key ring. Everyone in the cathedral is fending off the swarm. I've lost track of Prospero, and I don't see Malcontent. I clutch the keys and crawl into a small chapel.

I can't hide the keys on my body—now that I've revealed my gun, when one of them catches me, they'll surely search me. Above, a gargoyle looks down from a ledge. I aim and throw the key ring up. It falls over the statue's snout, then slides to lodge between it and the rough gray stone. It will have to do.

And I got rid of the keys just in time, because Prospero grabs me from behind and drags me out of the chapel and through a door that is so perfectly concealed in the stonework that I didn't see it before. Once we're outside, he shoves me ahead of him toward the covered steam carriage that is waiting.

One of the large, gruff men heaves me into the carriage, and then Prospero grabs my wrist and twists, hard, forcing me to drop the tiny gun and locking my right wrist into a restraint attached to the seat.

He kicks my ivory-handled pistol aside. It doesn't matter; both bullets are gone.

"Give me your mask," he says. He's scrubbing at his

face with a handkerchief, and his eyes water as he wets the cloth with wine from a bottle beside his seat and scrubs again.

"But masks can't protect anyone except their original owners," I say, holding tight to my mask.

He yanks it from my face. It's too small on him, and he looks ludicrous, and as crazed as his brother.

He coughs, and even though it's much too early for any signs of the Weeping Sickness to manifest, his eyes go wide with horror and he scrubs at his hands once again. Then he kicks at the empty gun again, mocking me and the weapon, though I saved his life with it.

"Elliott gave that to me," I say, wanting to see his response to his nephew's name.

He scowls behind the mask, and then, in a voice filled with childish spite, he says, "Your mother doesn't approve of him."

"No," I agree. "She doesn't."

"She used to cry over Elliott. She didn't understand that torture is an art. That I had to train him."

I shake my head, willing him to stop talking, but he doesn't.

"Do you know how I convinced your mother to stop coddling him? I told her that it might be entertaining to replace him with a pair of twins. Everyone loves twins. She never let Elliott hide in her room after that."

Not only is this his first smile since that diseased man rubbed infection into his face, this is the first time that I've ever seen Prospero's smile reach his eyes They crinkle up in the corners. I feel my hand balling into a fist.

I shift in my seat, as if trying to pull my knees into my body for comfort. But my knife is in my boot. If I can get it, I might be able to hurt him.

Elliott warned me that it would be difficult to put a knife into someone, but I don't think it will be so hard if that person is Prospero. And I did shoot a man for the first time today.

"You killed my brother," I say.

He raises his eyebrows in mock hurt.

"I sent the men who killed your brother, it's true. I didn't know Finn was among the ill. I would have preferred to have him alive."

He pours the wine left in the bottle into a goblet and drinks without offering me anything. Not that I would have accepted. Last time he gave me wine, it was laced with poison.

"You must realize that I wanted both you and your brother," he goes on, as if he is trying to convince me of something. "But your spineless father said that if I touched either of you, I would die, bleeding from my pores. Your brother died while your father was eating at my table. I don't believe he has ever recovered from it. And he's never known the truth, has he? The way your brother suffered, as he died?"

Father doesn't know. But I do. I try to put all of my

loathing into my eyes, but he won't really know how much I hate him until my blade meets his throat.

I listen for sounds of fighting or screams. For an ambush. Surely Elliott will send his men to try to stop the prince and all of these steam carriages.

But nothing happens; no one attacks. It's just me and him, alone.

With my left hand I push the window covering aside, fully expecting him to reprimand me, but he is silent. We've left the lights of the city behind.

"So this is the end, for you and the city," I say.

"Yes." He watches me stare out the window. "It's a shame your father ruined my plans by creating a disease that killed everyone, rich and poor, indiscriminately. But at least I have saved a thousand of its shining citizens. They'll have the experience of a lifetime and be safe from the dying masses."

I have nothing left to say to this man, so we ride on in silence.

At some point he realizes that he's lost the gold key ring. I watch him searching his pockets, but he doesn't mention what he's looking for.

"I thought you were giving them to Malcontent," I say.

"Not after he tried to ambush me. Not after—" He stops talking to wipe his face once again. He can't speak of what that diseased man did to him.

He deserved it. But he won't live long enough to die of the contagion.

"So the keys go to something . . . a device that can save the city from the swamp?" I ask.

He shrugs. "My scientists claimed it would work. I never tried it."

"Where is it?"

He smiles a toothy grin.

"Does Malcontent know?"

"My brother is too busy whipping his disease cult into a frenzy. But he would know if he was paying attention. I'm surprised he and his acolytes haven't tripped over it."

The swamp. The device is *in* the swamp. The doctor who escaped from the dungeon said the other scientists were heading there. But where?

If only I had paid more attention, the times I'd flown over or skirted around the swamp. Where would someone who wanted to hold back the swamp build a device? And then . . . I think of the manor house. The horror the family must have felt as the swamp approached their home. And I remember how all the doors were locked. That had to be it. The device was hidden there. Now I know where the device is, and I know where the keys are. And I'm trapped in a carriage, headed to Prospero's stronghold.

When we pass out of the forest, the sun is rising. A figure is standing on the bluff, looking down at Prospero's fortress. I hope it's someone who has come to fight, but neither Will nor Elliott could have gotten there before us. Could they?

Prospero's eyes mock me.

"You aren't the first prisoner in this carriage who wanted to kill me," he says. "None of the others have succeeded either."

"Why would I want to kill you?" I ask, trying to emulate April's sarcastic tone. He ignores my words, but keeps his eyes trained on my mouth, exposed without my mask.

"You know, I can cause you excruciating pain," he says conversationally.

"I've been through excruciating pain," I say.

He smiles, as if to suggest that he can prove me wrong. That he will.

As we approach the palace, it is evident that this is where all the smiths in the city have gone. Huge iron gates surround the palace, taller than before, forming rings around the other fences and ultimately the fortress itself.

"They sank the iron poles far into the ground, in case there are tunnels I don't know about," Prospero says. "And I flooded the dungeons. No one will be visiting my ball without an invitation."

"I hope you removed the prisoners." I wish I could take the words back the moment I say them. I keep giving him opportunities to show how frightening he is.

The fences and barricades are much too high to climb. Without the tunnels, how will I get April out of here?

The prince toys with his silver cufflinks, in the same way that Elliott does his. "I wonder which of your suitors will show up for my ball," he says. "Elliott hates being left out. And I gave William an invitation myself."

My heart misses a beat.

"When . . . did you see Will?"

"When I retrieved my niece from the Debauchery Club, of course. I almost thought he might try to stop me. He was prepared to fight, but he was outnumbered."

Will. I can't consider the possibility that he might come for us. I don't want Prospero to see the hope in my eyes.

"Elliott won't come," I say, to distract myself. And to distract Prospero. "He has to save the city."

"Against his own father? Do you really think he's strong enough for that?"

"Yes."

"I did try to teach him ruthlessness." He pauses, and when I don't respond, he continues. "Surely you are a better prize than a dying city."

I fold my hands in my lap, trying to keep them still. How difficult it would be to strangle a man with only one free hand?

We pass the first gate, and I see the open flame of a smithy.

"They are sealing it," he says, though I did not ask.

When the carriage pulls to a stop, it's near a dead

man hanging from the end of a noose, his body twisting against the inner fence.

"What did he do?" I ask.

The prince climbs out, smiling. "He was overwhelmed by one of my parties. Frenzied. He tried to leave."

Servants and courtiers rush out, and one comes to unlock the manacle. I can't help noting the clean and ornate clothing. Women wear floor-length silk dresses. Men wear brocade vests.

I search the crowd for April, though surely she is already in the palace. Her carriage left the city long before ours.

Rubbing at the welt that the manacle left on my wrist, I follow the prince inside. And that's where I spot her, standing in the shadows with a white bandage plastered to her forehead. So that's how she's hiding the contagion. At least for now, by candlelight.

Several courtiers stand near April, watching her suspiciously.

"Did something happen?" I ask, gesturing to the bandage, hoping she has a story.

"I was attacked. You know how it is, in the city."

The listeners whisper to one another, seeming satisfied to be able to report that the prince's niece was attacked by ruffians. That the city is as violent as they've heard.

We follow the prince's entourage. When he takes his seat, the room goes silent for half a second. Just long enough for me to hear a familiar tune. Somewhere in this great echoing fortress, my mother is playing piano.

And yet the piano in this room is empty.

I look around, at a loss, but April summons a servant who ushers me through the castle, past the rows of rusty old cannons, to the tower. At the top I push past the servant into the room with the piano.

Mother is wearing a light-blue dress with a lace collar. She turns, and I watch the emotions cross her face. Relief. Shame. She doesn't stand, and we don't embrace.

"You're alive," she says, and for a moment I think she's going to fall from the piano bench. "Thank God. I hoped . . . but the prince told me that the ship exploded. I didn't know what to think." So both of my parents believed that I was dead.

I look around the room at the textured wallpaper, the doilies that stand under oil lamps. It is warm and inviting, until you see the bars on the window. The piano dominates the room. It's how I knew this was her prison, when Elliott inadvertently brought me here.

"I missed your childhood and the last years of Finn's life in this room," she says. The tone of her voice is neutral. As if she is expecting me to judge her for being a captive here.

And I did for years. I thought she chose to spend time with her rich friends instead of in the basement with Finn and with me.

"I'm sorry," I say. "So sorry." I collapse onto the rug at her feet, and she runs her hand gently over my hair. She doesn't even say anything about the unnatural color of it. It's been weeks since I've seen her and years since I let her comfort me. I can't remember when I last slept. I know that I must find a way for April to escape and carry information to Elliott. And I must destroy this man who has ruined my family. But for now I let her lead me to her bed and tuck me in. As I drift off, her cool hand pushes the hair back from my forehead, and then she kisses my cheek.

A cacophony of hammering wakes me sometime later. When I walk over to the window, it's impossible not to remember how Elliott put his hands on my shoulders last time I stood here, gently drawing my attention to various escape routes. All of which now might be gone.

"I'm glad you're awake," Mother says from behind me. "You need to be fitted for your ball gown." A woman is already in the sitting room, waiting with measuring tapes and pins.

The seamstress measures Mother first, clicking her tongue and remarking that Mother has lost weight. And then she measures me, writing numbers in a small book.

"The gowns will be ready tomorrow afternoon," the woman says, and then she's gone and Mother and I are alone, awkward and silent.

She hasn't asked me about Father yet. Doesn't she want to know if he's alive? Does she care? Or has the

Red Death finally given her too much to forgive?

"I usually play in the afternoons," she tells me.

"Is that why he keeps you here, to play piano?" I'm not really sure what I'm asking her, what I want to know. But I feel the need to put her relationship with Prospero in some perspective. How did it happen? "How did you meet him?"

"I've known him since we were children. He likes having someone from that part of his life. Even then, he was driven, though not like . . . now."

Driven? Is that the way to describe a megalomaniac? "Father is also driven," I suggest, trying to determine how she is defining the word.

"Yes. Both of the men in my life have been consumed by a higher purpose."

A higher purpose? They worked together to destroy the world. She sees the disgust on my face, and for once she stands up for herself.

"I didn't choose to be his hostage. I've tried to be his friend because it's the only way I could help. I kept him from hurting people when I could. I stood beside him in the throne room and begged him to stop. Occasionally he listens."

"I don't blame you," I say. "It must have been terrible."

"It doesn't matter. You're alive. And we have to keep you that way."

I give her a quick hug. "I'm sorry," I whisper again.

"Come with me," she says. "I play for the young ladies

who like to practice their dancing in the afternoons. I don't want to let you out of my sight."

I've rejected her every time she's acted motherly toward me since Finn died. I may not have many chances to make up for my cruelty. So I follow her downstairs to a ballroom with a gilded ceiling, hoping that April will find me there. Dozens of girls glide about the room, not waiting for the music to begin.

Mother sits at the piano, arranges her skirts, and begins to play. Beautiful dresses swirl this way and that. I settle in a corner to watch.

One after another, the girls approach me to ask breathless questions.

Have I come from the city? Was it frightening? Did I see anyone dying? Did I see anyone with the Red Death?

I answer honestly. I have seen people dying, and it was terrifying.

One of the girls puts her hand on my shoulder. "At least you are here now," she says.

"Don't even think about the outside world. I pretend it doesn't exist," says another.

"It's safe here. We're safe." They grasp hands and start a dance that takes them in a circle.

What silly, deluded girls.

One of them glances out the window, then breaks away from the circle. At her squeal, everyone else follows. I join them warily. What horror is the prince constructing now?

"A new arrival." The girls are pressed against the glass.

"He has to be the last," another girl says. "My mother told me there are already one thousand. Someone must have died."

"Or someone is going to die," another girl suggests.

The girls laugh nervously, but they don't turn away from the window.

"How are you safe, if this is what happens here?" I can't help asking.

A blond girl frowns at me. "We're safe as long as we don't anger the prince," she says, as if I might be stupid. "Or draw his attention."

And then they are peering down at the guest once more.

"He is very handsome." The wistfulness of the girl's voice makes me think of how April and I used to admire Will.

Could he have come?

I push my way through to the window. The figure is on foot. Could Will have walked all the way from the city? Dark hair spills over the collar of the man's coat. But that's all I can see.

Mother has stopped playing. She watches me from across the room.

"He's tall," one of the girls observes. And then they are all talking at once. I will him to look up and show his face, but he never does.

"I'd give anything to dance with a young man," the girl continues. The others agree.

"All the men our age have gone to the city," another tells me.

Nervous excitement stirs in the pit of my stomach as the girls press in around me. I was sure that I would know Will anywhere, but now I'm afraid that I'm indulging in wishful thinking. I shouldn't hope that it's him. I shouldn't want to see him as badly as I do. I must be strong for Mother and April. I don't need Will to come and save me.

CHAPTER
EIGHTEEN

THE GIRLS EVENTUALLY GO BACK TO DANCING, with Mother playing the piano and smiling indulgently at them. They swirl around the small ballroom, and April finds me in the corner. Her bandage is smaller today, a white square affixed to her forehead. She's arranged her hair to mostly hide it.

"Do you have a plan?" she asks immediately. "An escape plan? They say that no one has left. Not since Prospero put up the new gates and fences."

"We have to find a way for you to leave," I say. I glance around to see if anyone is listening, but all the girls are caught up in their dance, so I finish in a rush. "And you have to take a message to Elliott for me. You have to tell him that the pump is in the manor house. He'll know what you mean."

April blinks her blue eyes several times. "Wait, aren't

you coming with me? I need you, Araby."

Her voice quavers. She's been so brave. But I can't go with her. I put my hand on her arm.

"We can't let the prince continue," I explain. "And if someone were to kill him, all the supplies stockpiled here would be free for Elliott."

"What makes you think you can kill the prince?" April studies my face, frowning.

"I'm the one who has to do it. We can't wait for Elliott or Will to rescue us," I tell her. "Elliott is saving the city, and Will . . ." I'm not sure about Will, so I don't say anything more about him.

A clock strikes, and the courtiers flock through assorted doorways toward the throne room.

"Time for dinner," April says. "Someone will die before the night is over, but unfortunately, I doubt it will be the prince."

A line of performers stands near the doorway of the dining room, juggling the porcelain heads of china dolls. The stuffing hangs from some of them. The performers do their juggling emotionlessly, not looking to the left or the right.

"Don't distract them, Araby." April pulls me along. "If one of them drops a head, the prince puts the juggler's head in a vise. It's . . . terrible."

And that is what Prospero wanted to do to Elise. He wanted to make her one of his performers. In a little swan costume.

April and I sit across the room from the prince's table, trying not to call attention to ourselves. I search the faces at each table, looking for Will. I don't see him or anyone who looks like him, but the room is crowded and I can't see everyone.

"The masked ball is tomorrow night," April says. "They've been holding nightly parties for weeks. Decadent, horrible parties. But the real fun begins tomorrow." She slumps for a moment, closing her eyes. She should be in bed.

Servants lead my mother across the room to the prince's table. She seats herself calmly.

"You'd think he would've replaced her by now," April murmurs. I'm not sure how to respond to such an observation. It never occurred to me before that if Elliott knew my mother, then April must have too.

"Why did you never tell me?" I ask. She raises her eyebrows. "That my mother was a hostage here?"

"Everyone is a hostage here. I just knew that the lady who played the piano, and who my uncle occasionally smiled upon, turned out to be our neighbor. I was pleased to learn that she had a daughter my age."

A group of entertainers are escorted into the dining room, and I notice how they cower when Prospero turns his gaze their way. He shakes his head, and they slink back to the shadows.

"Trained in the orphanages?" I ask.

"Yes. And even here, people have heard that we saved those girls."

"News carries fast." I'm surprised that anyone here knows what we did in the city.

The prince turns to my mother, and she goes to the piano.

The song she plays is like nothing I've ever heard before. Haunting and sad, but also defiant. I feel like she's speaking to me, like she's trying to express everything that we've never been able to say to each other. The crowd is mesmerized.

Finally she raises her hands and pushes back. The prince stands, signaling that dinner is over.

While Mother's song still echoes in my head, he leads us to the throne room. Each beam that stretches across the ceiling of the hall is in the likeness of a reptile—mostly dragons, but some are snakes or even crocodiles. I hadn't noticed that during my previous visit. The stained-glass windows are familiar, and the odd artifacts and objects of torture that lie on tables beneath. Prospero has gaslights throughout his palace, but for this room he's chosen open flames, which give the chamber a primitive, frightening look. The shadows are deeper and darker than ever.

April grabs my arm. "We should stay out of sight," she says. "Elliott and I had hiding places when we used to live here."

"Show me." But we're in the tide of hundreds of

bodies moving in the same direction. We couldn't turn and leave the room *without* drawing attention. A lady in an enormous dress pushes between us, and April is gone.

My mother stands by Prospero's throne. Her face is white. She makes a quick gesture at me, as if shooing me away. Beside Mother, Prospero is smiling. I go cold all over. But even as I turn, more people surge into the room, and the enormous wooden doors swing shut. I'm trapped.

Everyone follows Prospero's gaze to me. I back up until I'm against the great wooden doors, but they grab me, herding me forward to a red X painted on the floor. The crowd pulls back as a noose drops soundlessly from the ceiling. Before I can react, someone loops it over my head, cinching it around my throat.

I stand very still, trying to draw calm breaths, but can't quite fill my lungs. My knife is still in my boot, but how can I get to it?

And then the noose begins to rise.

"I had some lovely children who could have danced for us tonight, but the scientist's daughter robbed us of that pleasure," Prospero says. "We shall see what sort of entertainment she can provide."

Mother cries out. I'm on my toes, gagging, grasping at the rope. I can't turn my head, but my eyes find her. Servants hold her back as she tries to run to me. Then she holds out her hand, offering it to the prince. "Not her."

Around me, the couriers murmur expectantly.

"Your maternal affection does you credit." The prince smiles, and the servants release her. Tears course down her face.

A boy with a hammer is pushed onto the dais. Mother tousles his hair with her left hand. Her right rests on the arm of Prospero's throne. And I know instantly what's about to happen. No! I can't get my fingers between the coarse rope and my throat, but I keep clawing at it.

"Mrs. Worth has made her decision. Her daughter is more important than entertaining my guests. She no longer needs the use of her hands."

The courtiers press forward. Mother considers them with cool disdain. The boy raises the hammer and then looks to the prince, who nods. I scream as the hammer slams down on Mother's hand, but it comes out more like a croak.

When the boy raises the hammer again, it is shaking so hard that I think he might drop it.

"He's new," someone whispers.

The boy brings the hammer down again. I scream again, but my throat burns.

Suddenly the noose slackens, and I fall to my knees. A walking stick hits the floor beside me. In the silence, the sound reverberates through the room. Elliott. He came. To save me. Gasping, I look up, tearing the rope away from my throat. And it isn't Elliott. Will stands among the courtiers, holding the thin, sharp blade that was hidden within the stick.

"Is this what passes for entertainment in your court?" he asks. His voice is calm, reasonable.

He holds out a hand for me, never taking his eyes off Prospero. I take it and stumble to my feet. Prospero smiles. Anyone with any sense would run. But Will isn't budging, and I doubt we would make it far anyway.

"I've heard so many stories about this wonderful place, filled with marvels," Will says. "Is this what impresses you, seeing a woman's hand smashed with a hammer?"

The prince shakes his head slowly, as if we've disappointed him in some way. I stand so close to Will, he must feel how violently I am trembling.

Will finally looks over at me, and I see that he is as terrified I am. In one smooth motion, he has us running toward a small door at the side of the room. But we aren't fast enough. Someone hits Will from behind, and he drops to one knee.

Blood dribbles down the side of his face.

"Come on," I rasp, helping him back to his feet.

He pulls me close and swings out with his blade to clear our way. But we only get a few more steps before someone hits him again. I feel the impact this time too. Will wavers, but he raises Elliott's sword. I pull the knife from my boot.

"Take him," the prince commands, and the crowd surges forward.

Will thrusts and stabs a man in a purple velvet waistcoat. Blood pours out, splashing onto the floor tiles. But the blade is stuck, and in these close quarters Will can't yank it free. I keep my knife low, slashing at anyone who gets too close, but then the guards are upon us, and they have guns.

Prospero's men ignore me as they throw Will to the ground, chaining his hands behind his back. Our eyes meet for a moment. I reach out, and then drop my hand to my side.

And then the guards drag him away.

The throne room is completely silent, and as I look into the faces of the courtiers, I see pity on a few. I glare back. Some of these people purposely blocked our escape. Prospero shouts something about dancing, and then Mother is beside me. The crowd parts. They are letting us go. A servant leads us past the expressionless jugglers, out of the throne room. Once outside, the servant puts an arm around my mother and helps her up the spiral staircase to her tower room. Without saying a word to us, he locks us inside.

We stare at each other. Mother's face is ashen, and I'm still holding my knife. Prospero will pay for that oversight.

"Let me see your hand," I say, putting the knife down.

"It will heal."

She hides her face. As always, she won't let me see her pain.

"Mother . . ." I think it's my broken voice that makes her turn back to me and place her hand in mine. It's soft, from hours of soaking in scented oils. I probe it quickly, wincing when she does. It isn't a formless mass, not like the clockmaker's hand. Only one of the fingers is obviously broken, swollen over the others.

"See if you can move it," I say, because that's what Father would ask when Finn or I came to him with some injury. She can't.

Both Mother and I jump at the sound of a key in the door. It swings open, and a servant enters with a tea tray. Followed by April. Wordlessly, the servant puts down the tray and leaves. I grab a delicate silver fork and one of Mother's silk scarves and use them to make a clumsy splint for Mother's finger. Father used to do this for neighborhood children. Before sending them off for a real doctor.

If Will were here, he could help me.

If Will were here . . . I blink back tears. Who knows what Prospero has done with him? The remains of Mother's silk scarf fall to the floor.

"Fix her mask, too," April says in a low voice. Mother's mask has fallen askew. I reach up, but she adjusts it with her left hand.

Her eyes are dry, yet the way she sits, with defeat in every line of her body—I can't help imagining this is what it would have been like if she'd been with me while I waited for Finn to die.

"I'm sorry," April says. "I heard someone whispering. They could tell that I was diseased. I had to get out of there before they realized who I am. Then everyone would know." She drops into an armchair and looks up at me from under her lashes. It's a common pose for her, but her expression is not. "I think I may be dying."

"No," I say, as if my denial can change anything. "But you need to lie down." I reach out to her, unsure what to do. Frustrated that we're trapped here. I pick up the tea set and lead her into the bedroom.

"Have you come up with an escape plan?" I ask, crumbling a tiny cake beneath my fingers. The texture is so dry, I couldn't possibly swallow it. "You have to get out of here."

"Perhaps someone will rescue us." April smiles weakly.

"Will tried," I say. "And look how that turned out."

"You and your mother got out of that room alive because of Will."

"Do you think he's alive?"

"Yes." She says it too quickly, and I think she must be lying to make me feel better until she adds, "My uncle can keep people alive for a very long time."

I discard the rag I was using for her face, and wet another one for her shoulders and neck.

"Why?" I ask. "He's always stayed in the shadows before, keeping himself and the children alive."

"Araby," April says, "why do you think he's done any of it? Why do you think he went to the city? Because he loves to walk around stinking piles of dead bodies and listen to Elliott's snide remarks? He loves you."

I squeeze the cloth hard, and water drips down onto the floor.

"Isn't it wonderful, being in love?" she asks.

"No." It feels like the rope is back around my throat, cutting off my air supply. And yet, to finally be sure, to know my feelings, even if they are desperate, even if I may never see him again—it's terrible and wonderful at the same time.

"I love him," I whisper.

"Love." April spits the word out. "Even if I live and by some miracle I'm not hideous, all Kent really wants is to take his airship and explore, to see what's left of the rest of the world. That's why he built it."

"Kent?" I ask.

"Don't ask. I can't explain it. And it will never work. I could never go with him," April continues. "Even if we find a way to stop my illness, no one with the contagion can go exploring."

I take her hands. "We'll find a way."

"I'm pretty sure that everything doesn't always work out in the end," April says. "Not for everyone. You've just figured out that you love Will. So you're going to break my brother's heart."

A few weeks ago I might have argued that Elliott doesn't have a heart to break. Now we just sit in silence, waiting for the night to be over.

April drifts off, and I go check on Mother.

She is sitting in her chair, with her eyes closed. I'm

not sure if she has dozed off or not, but her mask is askew. I reach over and adjust it, not wanting to take any chances now that April is with us.

She reaches for my hand. Despite the makeshift splint on her crushed finger, her hand feels like it always has. Cool. Loving. Hands that tucked me into bed at night and felt my brow when I was sick.

"I'm sorry," I whisper.

She opens her eyes. "You don't need to apologize, Araby."

I kiss her forehead and then tiptoe back to the bedroom, where I stare at the ceiling as the gruesome images of the night replay in my head. April lies beside me, and though she is quiet, I know she isn't sleeping either. Tomorrow is the masked ball. Tomorrow it all ends, one way or the other.

Sometime in the earliest hours of morning, we hear screams. The nights' festivities are coming to an end.

CHAPTER
NINETEEN

FOR HOURS ONCE THE SUN IS FULLY RISEN, THE castle is silent. Guests are sleeping, or hiding, terrified by the revelries last night. We're given no breakfast, but taciturn servants deliver an afternoon meal. April asks if she can visit her mother, but the request is ignored.

She shoves back from the table and stalks over to the barred window.

My bag was brought to the tower, along with the mask that Prospero borrowed, so I pull out the little poetry book that Father gave me. Tucked inside is the flyer accusing Father of creating the contagion. I hand the pamphlet to Mother and watch as she reads. Her cheeks turn pink.

"Did he know—" I start, but I can't bring myself to finish. Did he know it would kill people? Would kill almost everyone?

"He had nightmares. So many nightmares. Afterward . . ." She crumples the pamphlet in her fist, rips it, and lets the pieces fall to the floor. "There was a time when he actually hung a noose in our bedroom. I begged him to stop, reminded him that you were still alive."

I dreaded hearing this from him, but it's worse hearing it from her.

"The guilt was crushing him," she whispers. "He never meant to hurt anyone. That's why he was so driven to create the masks. And then Finn—"

She stops at the sound of a key rasping in the lock. I leap to my feet, but Mother is seemingly frozen, and April remains at the window. A troupe of maids sweep into the room with bundles of satin and bows.

I bend closer to Mother's ear. "What will they do to Will? The one who saved me, last night," I ask in a low voice.

"He didn't save you, Araby," Mother says. "There are two plagues raging through the city. We're trapped in this palace, and Prospero has decided to use you for his entertainment. He never changes his mind about such things. None of us have been saved." It isn't an answer. She can't tell me that she thinks Will must be injured or dead. I refuse to believe that he's dead.

The maids draw us apart and shake out the dresses.

April's dress is silver, soft and flowing. It reminds me of the one I wore from Elliott's closet, though this is satin rather than silk.

BETHANY GRIFFIN

"You are going to be beautiful," a tiny maid says to her. Even in this terrible place, there are kind people.

"I already am, though this dress is nice." April smiles. But she is leaning against the wall and doesn't move to touch or truly admire the dress. I'm afraid to show too much concern for her in front of the audience of maids. Still, I keep my eye trained on her when I can. She is very pale.

Next the girls unwrap a dress the same shade of blue as the strands of my hair. It's lovely. I reach out to touch it, but they pull it away and usher us from our tower prison, down a hall and two sets of twisting stairways, to a series of interconnected rooms with bathing alcoves.

I look for a chance to break away, but guards flank us the entire time.

The room fills with steam and condensation builds up behind my mask, but I don't take it off. The maids begin to untangle my hair. If they brush April's, they will see that she's been hiding the contagion.

Even as I try to come up with a plan, they gather around her, exclaiming over the waves in her long blond hair. One brings out curling tongs and begins piling her hair on top of her head.

"No——" I start to say.

"Leave it down." April keeps her voice casual, throwing me a look.

I study their faces. These girls are young; they may have come from Prospero's orphanages. And so they

264

might be sympathetic to us. Even, possibly, to Will. I'm not averse to using his striking looks to help get us out of danger.

"You know what happened to me and my friend in the throne room last night," I begin.

They don't answer, but they all look sidelong at me, and then at one another.

"Is he alive?" I ask. "Do you know where he is?"

One girl glances at the red marks around my throat. As she rubs some sort of lotion into my hair, she leans close and whispers, "He is in the cell under the prince's private chambers. It's where he keeps the dangerous criminals."

One of the girls working on April's hair gasps and drops the curling tongs. She's seen the contagion. It was inevitable. The girl adjusts her mask nervously.

"If anyone sees this," she says fearfully, "things will get ugly. Even if you are Prospero's niece."

"We need to get her out," I say. "Back to the city. My friend, Will—he could help."

"There might be a way," the tiny maid who admired April's dress says. The other girls try to quiet her, but she waves them off. "What does it matter?" she asks. "If the prince kills them, then they're dead, like everyone else. But if not, they can take us all back to the city. They can save us."

The other maids have all stepped away from April. Her hair shines. It's the shadows under her eyes that worry me. And the oozing contagion.

"Tell me," the tiny one says to me. "Did you really attack the orphanage and rescue all of the girls?"

"Yes," I say.

"We were all trained there. We know what it's like. You saved those girls, even though you didn't have to. Even though you are the richest girls in the city."

"It was the right thing to do." I meet each girl's eyes. How far can this heroism take me?

"So can your father cure her?" The small one gestures to the sore that mars April's neck. "What about the Red Death?" They are as frightened of the city and what's outside the castle as everyone here. But they may be more frightened by what is inside. Enough to trust me, the scientist's daughter. I can't explain to them that it isn't my father who has promised to help April. That I have to get her to her own father.

"If we get her away in time, yes, I think she can be cured. And my father is working with April's brother to find a cure for everyone. I want to get her out tonight. She and Will must return to the city."

"Araby?" April says in a whisper. "I don't know if I can make it."

"You have to," I say. "Just a few more hours."

The maids help me into my dress. Mother reenters the room, followed by her own maids. She eyes the scandalous way the dress clings to me. The maids pull my hair back from my face and curl it, arranging a few strands to spill down my back.

One of the girls opens a box and presents a mask. At first I think it's the ornate one Elliott shoved back into the drawer in my bedroom. But then I realize that though it reaches over the eyes, disguising the wearer, it leaves the mouth terribly, dangerously, exposed. The girls have painted my lips a shocking red.

The mask is adorned with sequins and feathers. When I put it on, it complements my cheekbones, the contours of my face, while making my eyes look enormous and mysterious.

"Peacock feathers are unlucky, aren't they?" Mother asks. I used to say that I was the lucky one, because I lived and Finn died. The rest of this night will prove whether that was true.

April dusts powder over my shoulders, making my skin glow. "It isn't so different from all the nights when we went to the Debauchery Club," she says, her voice falsely bright. We both know how different this is. We controlled our visits to the Debauchery Club, deciding when to arrive and when to leave. Our lives were never at stake.

The maids dress Mother in a gown that is the opposite of mine, black with blue accents. Her mask also has peacock feathers. She considers it with distaste.

The small maid leans close to me, applying eye makeup.

"We can hide the prince's niece," she whispers. "She must act like she is going to the ball, and we'll take her to a hidden room. Couples sometimes use them, but not until much later. What about your handsome friend?"

"Can you take me to him before the ball?" I ask. I know it is too much to ask, and her eyes go wide, but then she smiles.

"Do you have something to bribe the guards with?"

"I have a diamond," I say. "But only one. They will have to find some way to split the wealth."

Elliott would be furious. But I have nothing else to give.

She grips the seam of my beautiful dress and pulls. The fabric separates, leaving a gaping hole.

"Her dress is ripped," she announces. "The seamstresses are all at work downstairs. I'll take her to see if one of them can mend it." And then she's pulling me through the corridor, down three flights of stairs, conferring with two more maids, and finally I'm handing Elliott's ring to a guard. The diamond flashes, and the men are suitably impressed.

"Through here," the guard says. "You'll have to speak to him through the door."

The last time Will and I spoke through bars, I was on the inside, and he was walking away from me. This door is heavy oak, and the bars are so high that I can barely stand tall enough to see through them.

"Will?" I ask.

"Araby?" His voice is full of disbelief. All I can see in the darkness is the impression of his shape, his dark hair. I sink to the floor and press my face against the door.

Chains scrape across stone as he moves closer too.

"We don't have much time," I say. "When the ball begins, if someone lets you go, can you take April back to the city?"

"I will take you anywhere."

"Not me, just April." Before he can ask questions or argue, I rush on. "I have . . . unfinished business. But I will join you later if I can."

"Don't ask me to leave you." His voice sounds harsh. What if I can't talk him into going?

"April is dying. You have to get her to Malcontent. I know it seems wrong, but he is the only one who can help her. And then you have to tell Elliott that the pump is in the manor house in the swamp. Please."

He doesn't say anything for a long time.

"You owe me," I say finally.

"I've been trying to repay—I'm no Elliott—"

"I don't want you to be Elliott. One of those is enough."

He laughs. The sound of it makes me stronger.

"And I don't want Elliott," I whisper.

Again, he doesn't say anything. Did he hear me? "Will?"

The tiny maid gestures that it is time to go.

BETHANY GRIFFIN

"Will, please," I say.

I stand and press the half-empty vial from Father through the bars. "Drink this."

And then the girl is pulling me away. "The guard changes just after the ball begins," she whispers. "We can get him out then."

We leave the corridor to find a seamstress, who frowns at the rip in my dress but sews it up deftly and sends us on our way.

"Do you love him?" the maid asks once we are alone.

"Yes." And if I survive the night, I will tell him so.

Before I reach Mother's suite I pass an enormous mirror. The back of my dress plunges indecently low and my wound is only partially healed, still red and puckered. The rope burns from last night are red and inflamed, all around my throat. There is no way to hide either.

Somewhere in the house, a clock marks the hour.

The ball will begin soon.

The moment I enter Mother's sitting room, I know that something is wrong. Neither she nor April is there. Worried that the prince swept them away while I was gone, I hurry to check the bedchamber.

Mother sits by the bed, holding April's hand. She looks up as I enter, but April doesn't move. She's sprawled across the bed in her ball gown, all silver and gold, and the purple of her bruises.

Mother holds my gaze. "I'm sorry," she says.

April is so still. She isn't going to escape with Will.

My father can't make her better, and neither can her own. Not now.

I shudder and, though Mother reaches for me, I collapse to the floor and hide my face in the blankets.

"Araby," Mother says in a broken whisper. "You don't have your mask. Not the one to stop the contagion."

In my grief I don't care, but she pulls me back.

I catch sight of myself in the mirror, my eyes wide and wild. The wound pulses red around my throat. I look back to April's lifeless body.

"She put on more eye makeup."

"Apparently what the maids did wasn't . . . dramatic enough." Mother takes a silk coverlet and pulls it over April. "The prince is planning to escort us to the ball." The sadness in her voice has been replaced by fear.

Everything crashes down on me. The prince is coming. But I won't let him have her, let him throw her away with the other victims of this terrible plague.

I'll get through tonight, somehow. I'll manage to get April back to Elliott, in her ball gown. He'll have her buried in some ornate grave. He'll commission a statue, something garish with weeping angels. Tears start at the corners of my eyes, but I don't let myself cry.

"We'll tell him that April went to her mother, to show off her dress," Mother says, and she guides me to the door.

"Wait." I hurry to the bureau. My hands are shaking as I open the drawer for my ivory-handled knife. I realize, too late, that I have no boot to place it in. My shoes are elegant slippers. But I need it, so I take two of Mother's silk scarves and tie it, with shaking hands, to my thigh.

Then I give one last look to April, hidden, shapeless beneath the blanket, before joining Mother in the other room.

She shuts the door to the bedroom gently.

Finally I'm able to ask, "Did she suffer?"

"No. She said she wanted to lie down for a moment, she made a great show of arranging her hair so she wouldn't muss it. And then it seemed she fell asleep. I went to sit beside her, and realized she wasn't breathing. She just—"

"I wish I had been here," I whisper. Mother, cradling her injured hand, looks away from me. "And I wish I had been there with you when Finn died."

I have a feeling that at this moment, she will answer anything I ask. "Why did Father release the Red Death?" I watch the emotions cross her face. She drops her hands, and for a brief moment I think that I was wrong, that Mother is going to treat me like a child. Lie. Suggest that Father didn't do it. But she doesn't.

"Do you remember the night you and April went to the club . . . you were wearing a long black dress, with a corset you had just dyed?"

I remember everything about that night. Will testing me, saying I should wear the silver eye makeup. Elliott

~ 272 ~

following me through the women's powder room, offering me his silver syringe.

"April brought you home. She had one of her servants carry you in. For a moment, we thought that you were sick, or dead. He'd been trying so hard to protect you from the prince. But he couldn't protect you from yourself. And he couldn't stand that. He couldn't stand the world we lived in, and he blamed himself for everything. Including your misery and your pain."

"He released the Red Death that night?"

"That was when he began to talk of it again. Then, when you were gone, when everything went to hell, I think Prospero called his bluff. But he wasn't bluffing."

My face feels stiff and frozen. "He asked me, after I returned, if I could be happy in this world."

"And what did you say?" She's whispering now.

"I didn't answer."

Mother looks away from me, and I'm ashamed. Why couldn't I offer Father something more?

But no, I won't hold myself responsible for my father's actions. Prospero was the one who used Father to start the first contagion. Who killed my brother. And then, instead of finding a cure, my gentle, loving father gave up on people. On humanity. On everything.

The door to our room is slightly ajar. The maid didn't lock it when she brought me back from visiting Will.

I could make a run for it now, could race down the corridor holding my gown up to my knees so that I don't fall. I could go back to Will. But Mother is holding tight to my hand, and she is the only one who understands, at least a little. She found me, holding Finn's hand. And tonight she held April's, even though April meant nothing to her. I have to succeed tonight. I saved those little girls. I refuse to give up, to make the same horrible mistake my father did. Instead, I will change the course of our world.

"Maybe you can escape," I whisper. I could send her to Will, even without April.

"It's too late," Mother says. And she is right.

A shadow falls over the threshold, and there's the prince. He notices the open door, and his eyebrows go up.

"I come bearing gifts," he says. As if he never tried to hang me, or to crush my mother's hand.

He's carrying three boxes. From one he extracts a circlet of glistening stones. Diamonds for my mother. A fortune in one velvet-lined box. I can't watch him fasten them at her throat. I don't want to see him touching her.

"Come here, Miss Araby Worth," he says to me. Sapphires flash as he takes them from the box. Ostentatious oversized blue stones, surrounded by tiny, sharp diamonds that reflect every light in the room. The prince seems to take pleasure in placing the gemstone collar directly over the rope burns at my throat. I don't give him the additional pleasure of seeing how it hurts.

His gift does not hide my injury. If anything, the necklace accentuates it. I want to tear it off and throw it away, but of course I don't dare.

The prince knows how I feel. He's smiling, and I hate him.

He holds the third box for a moment. I wait for him to ask where April is, but instead he says, "It's almost time." And taps his fingers together in a gesture that is, perhaps, supposed to indicate glee. "My most lavish party," he adds. "I've been planning this for years. I hope you enjoy yourselves."

He reaches out to kiss my mother's hand, lingering over her maimed finger. My stomach lurches as his lips touch her skin, and he looks up to meet my eyes.

Then two of his guards enter the room. Each of them takes one of Mother's arms, and they lead her away. She gives me a reassuring smile as they practically drag her out.

"When you locate my niece, bring her to me," he tells them as they are leaving. And then his attention is focused completely on me.

"I'd like you to walk with me," he says. "Because you and I are going to have a little fun. Do you like to play games?"

"No."

But of course it doesn't matter. He hands me a black satin bag lined with velvet. It is held shut with a heavy silk cord that I can wrap around my wrist to hold.

"The ball is held in seven interconnected rooms," he tells me. "In each room, I have hidden something that has a special significance to you. If you can find what I have hidden, and place the items in this bag before the clock counts down the hours, then you win."

"What do I win?" My voice has never sounded so cold and uncaring. Not even in the moments when I tried to punish Mother for all of the slights I imagined. For leaving me alone, for Finn's death.

"My prizes are always worth winning." He puts one hand under my chin and raises it so my eyes meet his cold, dead ones. I've made a terrible mistake. "At the end of the game, if you've succeeded, I'll let you choose. Your mother, or your beau. Don't worry. If you leave her with me, I'll take good care of her. I won't promise the same for the boy."

My hatred for him chokes me. Did he know my plan? Have the maids gotten Will out, or could he still be a prisoner?

"I'll play your game," I say through gritted teeth. But I won't choose. I won't have to, because somehow, before this night is over, I will kill him.

He puts out his arm, and reluctantly I take it, waiting for his answer. As we glide through the corridor, courtiers move out of our way. We pass mirror after mirror. I refuse to look into any of them. He smirks. He never doubted that I would play. I don't want to see his gloating face, and I don't want to see myself, not in this costume he created for me. Not when April will never wear a beautiful dress again.

Instead I study the other guests in their finery. How odd to see their mouths but not the expression around their eyes. It's the very opposite of everything I'm used to, and I can't read anyone. I am completely isolated in this throng of revelers.

And I'm going to have to accomplish this task, his so-called game, alone.

"How do you know seven things that are important to me?" I ask. "You barely know me."

He laughs. "But I know your mother *very* well, and she loves you. I've been collecting information about you for some time."

"Then you should know that I don't like games." I didn't think, when I tied the knife to my leg, how impossible it would be to retrieve. If I could get it, I would stab him right here. I would slip the blade up under his ribs or into his gut like Elliott showed me.

"And you should know that I don't care in the least what you like or don't like," the prince answers, his eyes gleaming.

CHAPTER
TWENTY

WE FOLLOW SATIN DRESSES AND JEWELED MASKS
to carved wooden doors standing open at the top of a
staircase. I hesitate only for a moment before I step over
the threshold.

"Have fun," Prospero says, and gestures for me to
descend before disappearing into the crowd.

This place is dark and deep. Perhaps what Elliott said
about his uncle importing this castle stone by stone is
true. The walls are a blue deeper than my dress. They
feel like they might close in and crush me. Though the
ceilings are high, my impression of the room is subterranean, as if we are in one of the dungeons, if Prospero
hadn't flooded them.

A thumping drum passes for music, and people press
in from every side. One thousand guests were invited
to this ball, and it seems like all of them are in this

room. Dancers wear primitive masks and costumes. I'm not sure if they are guests or were just placed here to entertain.

I force a smile because, in this mask, everyone can see my mouth. The sapphires at my throat are cool, but not cold enough to soothe the throb of the rope burns. At least, in this room lit only by torches, the welts won't be so noticeable.

The doors at the top of the stairway slam shut. No one else can enter. Drums throb. Faces are obscured. A girl steps on my foot. The pain is sharp, as if her slippers are adorned with spikes. Torch smoke burns my eyes.

I wish I understood Prospero's game. What kinds of objects am I looking for? What might Mother have told him about me?

Across the room, there's a deep shadow between two torches. Since the room is mostly an open floor, those shadows are one of the only places that Prospero could have hidden anything. I force myself to move, following the light of the torches.

But the shadow is only a bare, rough wall.

I feel my way along the walls, bits of blue paint flaking off under my fingers. This room is dark. How am I supposed to find—

The wall ends. Turning a corner, I come upon an alcove where dainty feet dangle before my eyes.

The maids who did my hair, who offered to help me, swing from nooses, limp. I swallow hard. They can't have been dead long. About the same amount of time as April.

I whip around. Surely the prince is watching me, gloating at the horror he orchestrated, showing me that he learned my plan to free April and Will. He can't hurt April, but what might he have done to Will?

Scanning the room for some evidence that he is watching, all I see around me are scantily dressed dancers, some writhing together on a raised dais while others whirl about the dance floor.

I force myself to look back. I killed these girls. I asked them for help, and somehow he found out. The little one is in the center, her serviceable boots a bit higher than the rest. I take two steps forward. Then a third. A deep-blue ribbon is tied around her ankle. Something hangs from it. Two more steps, and I recognize it. Elliott's silver syringe.

Special significance.

Mother didn't tell Prospero about this. She doesn't know.

But there is no doubt that it's meant for me.

And to take it, I am going to have to touch this poor dead girl. I brace myself and stand on my toes, reaching up, fumbling, ashamed that I am allowing Prospero to force me into this horrible game.

The syringe is cool in my hand. I stare down at it, realizing that I have never held it before. Elliott always handled it as he injected oblivion into my veins.

The music stops.

As horrible as the pounding drum was, hearing the whisper of the dead girls' petticoats in the sudden silence is worse.

I back out of the alcove and slip the syringe into the bag.

From someplace deep in the castle, a clock bell tolls. The dancers blink. Someone bumps into me, and one of the sapphires on my choker tears into my throat. Hot droplets of blood fall down onto my dress, but instead of soaking into the heavy satin, they roll off, disappearing to the floor.

The clock thunders seven times.

Then the drums pound, and the primal rhythm begins again.

I study the position of the torches. Another set, barely visible across the room, gives the same impression that the ones I'm standing beneath did. They've been placed at intervals to create the illusion that something lies between them.

So perhaps the real door is not marked at all. I look to where the shadows are the deepest, and after turning nearly in a complete circle and running my hands over the dark blue of the walls, I finally spot the doorway and pass through to the next room.

This room is lit by glowing gaslight bulbs in a huge chandelier that dangles low over the dancers' heads. The floor is mosaic tile, cool and elegant. The walls are purple, trimmed with gold, adorned with antique portraits, ladies and gentlemen in tall wigs posing with unnaturally thin dogs. Some feature gentlemen riding horses. In the corners of the room, ladies sip tea from china cups. Some have exposed legs; others wear skirts that touch the floor, like those from before the contagion.

The doors here are not hidden; in fact, there are too many. Dozens of white columns line the wall, and between each pair is another door. All are propped halfway open. I look for mirrors or some other sort of illusion; this chamber cannot be as large as it seems.

Across the room, I see April's mother. I hadn't expected to meet her here, and she's the last person I want to see.

As I try to decipher where the prince might have hidden an object of significance, she spots me and comes forward. The gold hair that both of her children have inherited is artfully arranged to hide the streaks of gray.

My breathing becomes quick and shallow. I have to tell her. I'm going to have to look in her face and tell her.

But she doesn't ask about April.

"Come." She sweeps me across the room, out of the way of the revelers. Throughout the room, the guests are dancing, their ball gowns swirling around them.

"We need to talk, you and I," she says, in a tone that suggests we have spoken more than a few words before tonight. Her tone is crisp. When I would visit April, her mother always sounded overly friendly, as if she couldn't believe anyone wanted to spend time with her daughter.

But she sounds different tonight. It hits me that she's speaking to me not as April's friend, but as Elliott's . . . whatever she believes I am to her son.

I need to get away from her, but she's holding my arm tightly, and I don't think it's in my best interest to cause a scene.

She's led me to the ladies with their china teacups and feathered fans. They wear lacy white masks and pastel dresses, in contrast to my dark, bold one.

"You have to help Elliott," April's mother says. Sharp blue eyes peer at me through her mask. Pink feathers caress her cheek. "He won't be able to kill his uncle," she says. "The man has power over him. You have to find someone who can actually kill the prince."

"Elliott hates his uncle," I tell her. I've run my hands over the network of scars on his back. I know a little of what Prospero put him through.

"He does. But that doesn't mean he can do what needs to be done. When you were here before, the prince poisoned you, yes?"

When I nod, the sapphires at my throat jab again into the delicate skin.

"You were alone in a carriage with Prospero. Elliott was planning a rebellion. Did you never wonder why Elliott didn't kill him then?"

I stare at her. What is she suggesting?

"Do you think that he didn't have a weapon, hidden somewhere? Or did you doubt that Elliott could kill a man with his bare hands? His uncle trained him very, very well."

"I don't doubt it," I whisper.

Around us, ladies sip their tea to the sounds of stringed instruments from some hidden alcove. Everything in this place is hidden under layers of deception. Like this woman's motives.

"Every day Prince Prospero is alive is a day that he will cause suffering."

"I understand," I say. And I agree with her.

"Elliott chose wisely in you. Share a drink with me before you got to the next room." She heads for a table covered with silver goblets.

I haven't found whatever's hidden in this room, but I can't stand to share a drink with this woman, when I know her daughter is dead and she does not. I can return to this room after I've found the other items.

People come and go. But I realize that they aren't really leaving. They waltz through one door and then back in through the next. It's a series of closed-in arches rather than passages to another room. But to the left is a wall draped with purple hangings. I'm guessing that, as in the last room, the main door is obscured. Edging forward, I'm about to brush one of the curtains aside when a guard blocks my way. He smiles and pulls a vicious-looking knife from a sheath at his side. So this is what happens if I try to move on without succeeding in my search. I take a step, as if to challenge him, but the extent of his smile unnerves me, and finally I step back. It's Prospero's palace, after all. He makes the rules.

April's mother is watching me. She raises her goblet in a mock toast. It's silver, like the one the prince used to poison me. What does she know? As April's mother sets her cup on the table, I see that a purple ribbon has been tied around the heavy stem of one of the goblets, and I lunge forward to take it.

Inside is Henry's toy airship.

I spill it into my hand. Is this supposed to tell me that Henry is in danger, that somehow the prince has found not only the treasured toy, but the child? I deny the sudden crippling fear. Henry and Elise are safe. It's Will I need to worry about. As I drop the toy into the bag, April's mother melts into the crowd. And the gong of the clock sounds once again, clear, loud, and deep.

Does it mark the hours, or my progress? It doesn't seem long enough for an hour to have passed.

I square my shoulders and move on, ignoring the dozens of open doors. Instead I go back to the wall covered with purple silk curtains. I push the first aside only to see bare stone, but the second one reveals a narrow passage. It leads to a room that is completely green, from the tapestries on the walls to the ornaments on tables.

A woman steps into my path and says, "At your age, you should be married." When I dodge her, I end up on the dance floor, nearly colliding with a pair of revelers. I stumble out of their way and look up to see a figure approaching me from across the room. He looks no different than the other revelers in his dark suit and vest. But the black mask accentuates his fair hair.

The first time I came to this terrible place, Prince Prospero said that at a masked ball, I might not even recognize his nephew.

But I know Elliott. He is all subtle grace and elegant menace.

Elliott's on my side. He can help me through this maze. Help me find and kill Prospero.

The green-tiled floor is filled with dancers.

But someone, somewhere, is watching me, recording my progress, and even as I allow Elliott to take me into his arms, as one hand moves to my shoulder and the other to my waist, I know that whether Elliott realizes it or not, this meeting is on Prospero's terms. That I can't let myself be swept up in the relief of not being alone. Even in Elliott's arms, it's still me against Prospero.

We glide across the floor without speaking.

Finally he says, "If you see Will, tell him I want that walking stick back. It once belonged to the mayor of the city, and as such, was precious to me for a long time. I thought it was all I had left of my fath—"

"Prospero has Will and my mother." I cut him off, his teasing tone not sitting well with me.

"Where's April?"

I hate telling him like this, in the middle of all these people. I reach up, putting my hand to the front of his well-cut coat. And that's when I see that a slender green ribbon has been affixed right above the pocket of his vest. Somehow Prospero has pulled Elliott in, hopefully unwittingly, and made him a part of his game. At least now I don't have to search this room. What I need is right in front of me. But first I have to tell him about his sister.

"Elliott, April is dead."

He misses a step. And then another. A pair of dancers collides with us, hard, and I'm knocked out of Elliott's arms. He stands there stunned, and guilty, and altogether too young for the amount of responsibility he has taken on.

The couple who crashed into us find their rhythm and glide past. Elliott closes his eyes briefly. When he opens them, they are bright with unshed tears. He doesn't ask for details, and for that I am thankful.

"Why are you here?" I ask.

"I came for food," he says. "And weapons. Thousands of people sought out my protection. With what Prospero has here, I can care for them."

Despite everything, he could make a good ruler.

"And to look for you," he says, but he says it dispassionately. As if I am something he misplaced. "After you rescued those girls, the city was abuzz with rumors about the scientist's daughter. I need you, at least until I've shored up my support."

Now the emotion is in his voice. A sort of longing

that makes my heart ache. Because it isn't for me. Not anymore. Our feelings are so twisted and confused. We don't love each other, not in the way that begets complete trust and sacrifice. Not the way I need to be loved.

Elliott wants to use me. April once told me that Elliott liked poetry better than women. She should have said power. But I promised to be by his side.

"I will always help you, however I can," I whisper, inching my hand from where I was holding his forearm, toward the pocket and the green ribbon. "How did you get in?" I ask. "Did Prospero send men after you that night in the Tower?"

"No, your father and I escaped that night. I took the clockmaker's invitation."

Did he kill the clockmaker? The horrible suspicion makes me stumble, though Elliott catches me. I don't meet his eyes. He's ruthless. I am trying to be. In the end, maybe we will be the same, but I'm not there yet.

"I told you not to trust me," he says, and smiles. It doesn't reach his eyes. And I don't trust him. Whether he's telling the truth or not, he's not here without Prospero's knowledge. I thrust my hand into his pocket and pull out the ribbon.

Elliott jerks away, releasing his hold on my arms. I trip over my feet and fall to the floor, a heap of skirts, and stare at what is lying in the palm of my hand.

I've never seen it before in my life.

It's a small gold pocket watch. I press the release, and

it springs open. Inside, there's an inscription: TO FINN. HAPPY BIRTHDAY. LOVE, PAPA.

"Where did you get this?" I ask.

The distant clock tolls.

For a few moments everyone on the dance floor freezes. Listening? Waiting?

Elliott extends a hand to pull me to my feet, but I wave it away. On the floor, I finally have a chance to untie my dagger. Removing it from beneath the midnight-blue skirts, I slide it, along with the small gold watch, into the black satin bag.

Then I climb to my feet without his help.

"I am sorry," I say. Apologizing for having to tell him about April. For not loving him. For the death of whatever might have been between us.

He puts his hand under my chin and raises it.

"Don't be sorry," he says. "I can't afford distractions, not now. Not even pretty ones."

The music ends.

In a ripple of movement, people begin to bow. The prince has mounted a dais in the center of the room. The musicians stare at him in apparent surprise.

The clock strikes once, a different peal than the one I've heard before. Deafening. The lights flicker, and a woman screams. Even the prince is completely still.

And I am alone. Elliott is gone. While I was watching Prospero, Elliott abandoned me. Without telling me how Finn's watch ended up in his pocket.

CHAPTER
TWENTY-ONE

MY KNIFE IS WITHIN REACH, AND SO IS THE PRINCE.

I edge closer to the dais. Now that the shock of the clock striking has worn off, people are moving again. The prince claps his hands and tumblers flip into the room, pushing the guests back to the walls. My eyes are still trained on Prospero, but then a man grabs me, and holds me in place, just for a moment. It's long enough for the prince to disappear.

To force me to continue the game.

I find a door at the back of the room leading to two staircases. One goes up, and the other down. Which to choose? In the end, surely they will all lead me back to wherever Prospero wants me to go.

Holding the black bag, and my knife, close, I go up and through an arched entryway into a room that hurts my eyes. Everything burns orange.

Contortionists do tricks on a brightly lit stage, and servants in orange dresses circulate with drinks.

Guests kiss in the corners. And on low divans, and on the dance floor. My face burning, I thread my way though. A servant hands me a chilled beverage, but instead of drinking, I rub the cool glass across my forehead. This room is very hot.

Dozens of shiny objects have been suspended from the ceiling on nearly transparent strings, so they appear to be floating. A diamond catches the light and flashes. I can't escape from Elliott's ring. As many times as I've traded it or given it away, it always returns. This time with a finger inside. It hangs from the ceiling, shimmering. The nail bed of the severed finger is covered with dried blood. I try not to imagine how it got that way, whose finger it was.

I slide the ring from the finger and drop it into my black purse. And then, before the gong can sound, I stumble out of the room, into a long corridor. No one interferes or follows. My footsteps echo.

It's mostly empty and drab after the decadence of the room behind me. Could I have left the path I was meant to follow? But no, signs have been scrawled above each door of the corridor. Elliott's eye symbol. The red scythe. I stop before a door covered with mathematical equations. It reminds me of father's incessant scribbling, and of solid, dependable Kent. I have something that reminds me of Elliott, of Finn, of Will, and of the

Debauchery Club. Could the next be something of my father's?

I choose the equation door, but have no idea if it's the right decision. Behind it is a quiet room, not a lavish ball.

As I look around the room, I realize that it feels familiar. It is almost the same as our sitting room in the Akkadian Towers. I tiptoe closer to the white curtains. Behind them is a garden nearly identical to ours except for a stunted sycamore tree in the center.

Leaning against its trunk is a figure dressed in black robes. A mask streaked with red tears covers his entire face. He is holding a scythe.

If Prospero had captured Reverend Malcontent, why would he place him in this garden, instead of using him as part of his gruesome entertainment?

But then the figure reaches up to adjust his mask, and I know his hands. The same hands that held me during the parade, that soothed me, that gave me sleeping drafts night after endless night.

I fear death like everyone else, but this is only my father.

And then he sees me. He raises his hand, as if to ask me what I am doing here. Covered in dark robes, he picks his way to the glass door that separates us. On my side, it is in an alcove, mimicking the closet Elliott took me through in Penthouse A.

The door of the garden slides open.

"Araby," he says, putting a hand on my shoulder.

"Father." I throw my arms around him.

"Not too close," he says. But still, he pulls me into him, crushing me against his chest. "Find your mother and get out of here, as far away as you can."

I don't have to ask why he's here. With his disguise, with everything the prince has done to our family, Father is here for revenge.

And he deserves his vengeance. But I traded my safety for his.

"You need to go back to the city," I say. "The prince would love to kill you."

"My life isn't worth anything," he says.

"It is to me," I say, "and to Mother. Please. You go. I can kill the prince, but you're the only one who can help the people dying in the city."

"I'm so sorry," he says. "So very sorry." There is so much regret in his voice that I think he's apologizing for all the deaths, for Finn. The atrocities I've been waiting for him to atone for. "I can't let you do this. I should never have let you trade your safety for mine. If you die, then I have nothing to live for."

He pushes me into the garden and slams the door. I hear the deadbolt slide home.

"No!" I throw myself at the window. Father turns away, dramatic in his costume. I pound the glass with my fists and scream for him to let me out, but he doesn't even look back.

CHAPTER
TWENTY-TWO

I DON'T WASTE A MOMENT. IF THIS GARDEN IS A replica of the one in the Akkadian Towers, then there must be a trapdoor leading out. Father didn't cover his tracks; he didn't expect to be locking me inside. I can see where the earth is disturbed, and I feel something metallic beneath my heels. The trapdoor. As I kneel, frantic to clear it, I see something else in the dirt. Father's glasses, tied with a white ribbon. The ones the man in the alley gave me to convince me that Father was dead. Did Prospero go through my room at the Debauchery Club? And does Prospero know Father's here, or is this simply a twisted reminder of the hero I thought my father was?

Clearing the hatch is messy but not difficult. As I work, the clock strikes again. I pry the door open and peer into the smoky darkness. This opening has no ladder.

The room below does not seem to be a closet like the

one in the Akkadian Tower, but part of a larger chamber. Voices and laughter float up.

I swing down, wincing at the pain in my bad shoulder. My dress makes a horrible tearing sound as I fall to the floor with a thump. I'm in a long antechamber.

At the end of the room is an archway. People stand beneath it, their eyes pass over me, but none of them seem surprised that I've appeared through a hole in the ceiling. I take a deep breath but choke before I've fully inhaled. Directly in front of me, a man lights a pipe. The smoke that billows around him is more than any one pipe could produce.

The walls of this new room are covered with lavender silk. The lights are low and purplish, streaming through windows with leaded violet panes. Low couches line the walls, and people recline upon them, laughing quietly. The conversation here is intimate, sedate.

On a low table is an assortment of implements. Syringes, pipes. Gauzy curtains caress my face.

"This is the good stuff," a girl murmurs. "It's been in the prince's storehouse for years. They say it gets better with age."

A dark-haired boy leans close to me. His hair is tousled like Will's. I wish, fleetingly, I could go back to the time when I was merely a patron of the Debauchery Club, waiting breathlessly for Will to flirt with me. That April could be beside me, laughing at my awkwardness whenever he appeared.

"I have what you want," the boy says, trying to entice me. But it's not Will's voice, and it's easy to say no.

Among the pipes and the vials on the table is a small brush with a painted handle. It's beside a small jar of sparkly silver eye shadow. April's eye shadow. She used it just hours ago. I grab both and drop them into the bag, pulling the drawstring tight.

I leave behind these people, lost in oblivion, as the gong sounds once more.

Six objects. The game is nearly over. And then I'll have to choose. Not between Will's safety and my mother's. I won't accept that. I'll have to choose how to kill the prince. Unless my father gets to him first.

The room that I've stepped into is completely white.

The music is sedate, but after the silence of the last room, it seems loud. Musicians play sitars and violins. I imagine that the girl from the Debauchery Club might be here, singing about suicide. The dances in this room are informal, people swaying to the music, too close for propriety. Mother would not approve.

Will—the real Will—is standing across the room. My heart stops. And when it starts up again, it hurts. It beats wildly. He's wearing a formal jacket, velvet with brocade trim, but underneath, it's the same sort of thing he wore when he was examining us at the club—a fitted shirt, dark pants. No vest or other fashionable additions. He's scanning the room, the dancers. He's looking for me.

He sees me before I reach him, and I stop a few paces away, too overcome with relief. Too confused to speak. He's wearing the same dark mask as all the other men, but on him it is entrancing.

I look at his mouth, exposed as it is. And then it's impossible to focus on anything else.

We've only stood here for a moment, but it feels so long that I've begun to believe that he is never going to touch me again. Finally he puts his hands on my shoulders and draws me in. His thumb caresses the base of my throat, carefully avoiding the rope burns.

Our masks bump together, and one of the peacock feathers drifts slowly to the floor.

But the moment is interrupted as the horrible clock toll pulses through the room, shaking the walls and the floor with a peal that is louder and longer than any before.

The crowd surges, pushing us back toward the bare white walls.

"It's the prince," someone says. "A madman is chasing him."

I have to stand on tiptoes to see anything, but indeed, the prince is running through the room. His mask is askew, and his eyes dart this way and that.

A figure in dark robes and a mask that covers his face follows. He carries a scythe in his hand. He moves like he's stalking prey, slowly, methodically.

The revelers are crying, falling to the floor, scrambling

over one another to get away from Father and his blood-streaked mask.

"Who let him in?" I hear a man scream.

"The Red Death," a woman moans.

"Don't let them out of your sight," I tell Will.

Pushing myself away from the wall, I force my way through the hysteria, pulling Will along. We hold hands even while pursuing death. My hand fits so perfectly in his.

Before we reach Father, guards pour in from every direction. Everyone freezes, from the half-dressed revelers to the contortionists in their unnatural positions.

The guards surround the prince. But Father has disappeared. I eye the soldiers. Before Will and I can proceed, Elliott enters the room.

He halts just inside the doorway, but his jaw clenches below the line of his mask, and I know he sees me. With Will.

"Take the prince," he says to his men, without taking his eyes from me.

"Araby, Prospero is up to something." At Will's warning, I look to the prince, who raises his arms and then drops them dramatically. Debris begins to rain from the ceiling. At first it's simply confetti, but then orange marbles pour down. The sound is like raindrops, and when the marbles hit, they sting. Courtiers trip as they run for the door, trying to shield their faces. Some scream as sharp glass slivers begin to fall.

"I want him alive," Elliott calls, lunging into the crowd. His fair hair shines in the candlelight.

I put my hand on Will's arm, allowing Elliott to pass us. The doorway he's headed for is one that I explored earlier. And Prospero is long gone.

Like the first two rooms of the ball, the shadows behind the stage hold a less obvious door. We have to fight the crowd running the other way, but eventually I drag Will into a black corridor. Only steps from us, two guards are pushing Father, in his deathly black robes, against the wall.

"Dr. Phineas Worth, you are under arrest."

"No!" I hurl myself at them.

One of the guards shakes his head. "We have our orders. Step away, Miss Worth. Your father is a murderer." But neither one touches me. They probably still think that Elliott and I . . .

Will tries to break in, but the guard blocks him. While they are distracted, I throw my arms around Father.

He strips off the dark robes and mask and presses them to me. "Do what has to be done."

The guards pull us apart, but they don't take the robes away.

Cradling the bundle, I feel something in the pocket. My heart constricts.

I look to Father as the soldiers shove him toward the violet room. He nods. When they are gone, I reach into the pocket and pull out a glass vial. Holding it to the light, it looks empty, but I know something horrible lurks inside. Not only is there a cork stopper, but it has been sealed with wax. Will draws a sharp breath.

"Are you going to try to stop me?" I ask him. Because I know he has strong opinions about murder and death. About right and wrong.

"No," he says. "But I'm going with you."

I couldn't ask for anything more than that.

I drop the robes and the mask of the Red Death. Clenching the vial in my fist, I lead Will through another door. And now we have reached the center of Prospero's labyrinth.

The walls, the floors, the ceiling, all black. Everything except the windows—those are a horrible bloody crimson.

This room is smaller than the others, and already crowded with courtiers fleeing my father and Elliott's guards. We move through the press, pushing when we have to. Like the outer room, everything in this room is black, from the wood floor to the wall panels. Manacles line the walls. Instruments of torture. And the clock looms over everything, ebony, tall, menacing.

Prospero cowers in the shadow of the great clock. No one recognizes him, because these people have never seen him cower. They don't expect the pathetic, trembling man with tears streaming down his face to be their cruel, sardonic prince.

Elliott warned me how difficult it would be to kill

someone. Even this man who deserves it more than any-one. Prospero and I stare at each other.

"Elliott is coming." Will puts his hand on my wrist. The movement reminds me of the black velvet bag that is hanging there. Of Prospero's mockery of decency and love. His destruction of my own family, and so many others. I consider dumping the contents over the prince's head, but these items are too precious to me.

"Tell everyone to get out," I say to Will. "Clear the room."

Will doesn't hesitate. "Move!" he shouts. "Out of the room, get out, or face certain death."

Most flee, but some wait, expecting some sort of show. They've been at Prospero's court too long.

Taking the final steps across the room, I break the wax seal with my fingernail. I stop when the toe of my shoe touches Prospero's silk jacket. He pulls his arm away, still hunched in the shadow of the clock.

I scrape at the cork to coax it out of the vial, but it breaks off, too far down in the vial to get at.

"What is going on?" Elliott is behind me now. I look back for a moment, and our eyes meet across the black room. He won't forgive me for taking his revenge from him.

I throw the vial to the floor. It shatters at the prince's feet.

The clock begins its thunderous peals, and Prospero's mask hits the floor with a crack.

He climbs to his feet and stretches out to me, but I just shake my head. A single red tear rolls down his face.

Elliott's men flood the room even as he collapses. Prince Prospero is dead.

The sun rises, blazing through the red windows. The glass shards sparkling against the wood floor are far more beautiful than the diamonds Prospero fastened at my mother's throat.

And then someone knocks my feet out from under me, and I hear the word "Murderer!" leveled at me as I hit the floor.

CHAPTER
TWENTY-THREE

ELLIOTT'S SHADOW FALLS OVER ME, AND I LOOK up at him over his uncle's body. He's looking at Prospero, his face stricken.

Two guards take my arms, but even as I find my footing, one of the guards begins to convulse. Red tears streak his face.

"I told everyone to clear the room," Will says from somewhere behind me.

"She killed the prince," the other guard insists. "Elliott ordered that he be taken alive."

Elliott silences him. "Araby Worth has always worked for me. She killed the prince at my command." He pulls me up and leans in to my ear. "I still need my execution," he whispers. "But don't worry, I have a prisoner who will do."

Father. The shock hits me like a blow. I see the truth

written on his face, which is so close to mine that we could be about to kiss.

Elliott lets me go. Will catches me, giving me a moment to find my strength.

"We should get out of this room," I say, taking Will's hand so he knows I can stand now. "We don't know . . . how well protected we are." Will just emptied his vial this afternoon, and I'm unsure how long it takes for the antidote to enter his system.

"The party is over," Elliott calls. "Everyone should return to the city."

Our camaraderie, whatever held our small band together over the past weeks, is gone.

"You should find your mother," Elliott says.

I don't look back at him or at Prospero's corpse as I guide Will out of the room.

"It's over," he says.

I don't feel any triumph. April is dead. Elliott hates me. My father is a prisoner. I just killed Prince Prospero, and all I want to do is collapse to the floor and weep.

"What do we do now?" I ask.

"Pick up the pieces," Will says. "Right now we find your mother. Tomorrow we hire some sort of lawyer to defend your father."

"Are there any lawyers left?"

We step out into the corridor and come face-to-face with a group of revelers.

"The party is over," Wills tells them, echoing Elliott.

They stare at us, stunned, as we brush by.

"At least we got fancy new clothes from the experience." Will adjusts the lapel of his jacket. But, as usual, my dress is in tatters. I stop to rip off a bit of blue fabric that drags the floor.

Will leans close. "It looks good on you that way."

I look up at him. When he kisses me, every nerve in my body tingles. My toes curl up, and my heart pounds. Prospero is dead, and we are alive.

We find my mother sitting alone in the white room, staring at the wall. When I call to her, she stands.

"So it's over," she says. "And you killed him."

"Yes." I don't know what else to say.

Will puts his arm around me. "We need to get to the roof. If Elliott is here, then Kent must have brought him."

"Do you know the way?" I ask Mother. She leads us silently. We pass through two mostly empty rooms, up a flight of stairs.

As we go, she takes in Will's tattoos, our linked hands. But she says nothing, and her face remains expressionless. I think maybe she's in shock.

On the roof, the wind whips my hair back and forth. It's midmorning now, and the sun burns my eyes. Kent smiles when he sees us, but it fades when he notes that April isn't with us.

The ship is beautiful. The great balloon floats above the roof, and the wooden deck gleams under the feet of the two children who spill out of the cabin as soon as we appear, leaping onto Will, hugging him, hugging me.

"Who is this?" my mother asks. It's the first time she's spoken since we left the party. Henry turns to her and solemnly holds out his hand. My mother leans down and shakes it.

"I'm Henry," he says. "And that's Elise."

"Why are you wearing those masks?" Elise asks. "Are you in disguise?"

"Does it look silly?" I ask her.

I put my hand to my velvet mask. One last peacock feather remains. I pull the mask from my face, and she takes it from my hand and peers through the eyes, holding it over her white protective mask.

"No, you looked magical," Elise says.

"Where is April?" Kent comes across the deck of the ship. The girl Mina is behind him, her face filled with concern.

"She's dead," I say, because April would be annoyed if I dragged it out. She wouldn't want me to be coy. She would want shock and drama and weeping. "I had a plan to get her out, but the contagion . . ." When I reach out, Will is there to support me.

Kent's face goes completely colorless. Mina sniffles. We stand together, unable to say anything. At least I know they understand.

"Where is she?" Kent asks. "We should bring her . . . body . . . but we shouldn't have her on board with the children, and Elliott wanted me to find the pumping station as soon as possible."

"It's in the swamp," I say. Everyone turns to me. "In the old manor house. That's what all those locked doors were hiding. Prospero almost gave the keys to the machine to Malcontent, but I hid them in the cathedral."

Kent pushes his glasses up on top of his head and runs his hand through his hair.

"Kent, we'll come back for April's body, if Elliott doesn't bring her," I say. "But we should go now."

He nods and moves to the wheel. The ship begins to rise. The wind is brisk, and we move quickly.

"What's the plan?" Will asks.

"The keys," I say. "Then the swamp."

"Exactly," Kent says. He's tapping his foot against the deck, as if he can make the ship move faster just with the force of his nervous energy. "We need to set up a hero, someone the people can look up to besides Elliott, so his power won't be absolute," he says. "You already saved those little girls. You killed Prospero. Now you're going to find a way to bring fresh water to the city. To cleanse the swamp. And Will and I will be there to help you. And it's . . . probably best that Will isn't within stabbing distance when Elliott returns to the city."

Will pushes back his hair, his expression somewhere between guilty and embarrassed.

"What did you do?" I ask.

He pulls a pamphlet from his pocket and hands it to me.

In an effort to right the wrongs of my forebears, I plan to hold an official election in two weeks' time. All occupants of the city are invited to vote. Anyone who would like to claim office may run for it. I shall be running for the office of mayor of the city.

"It doesn't even sound like him," I say. But we all know that it will do exactly what Will intended. Elliott can't renege on this election without looking like he plans to be the newest tyrant. And maybe it will keep him from executing my father without a proper trial.

Elliott is not going to take this lightly.

"I knew the risk I was taking," Will says. "And I'll accept the consequences."

"Not alone," I say.

I watch Kent steer for a few moments, wondering if I should say anything more about April, but then Will pulls me away. We stand at the rail at the back of the ship, but instead of the breathtaking scenery below, we look at each other.

"I don't deserve—" he begins, but I put my hand up to stop him. It's too close to what I thought after Finn died. That I didn't deserve happiness.

Neither of us should be thinking that way any longer. Not when he was the one who convinced me that living is worth it.

"Don't apologize again," I tell him. "It's over. We've both done terrible things. And we'd do them again if we had to."

He starts to say something, but I stop him with a

quick, mostly innocent kiss. The wind ruffles his hair. He stares out over the landscape, and then he looks back to me, a hint of a smile on his lips.

"Let's go into the cabin," he says. And with that, the contrite Will is gone. He's the Will I first met, whose movements are smooth, and whose eyes promise excitement. He shuts the door behind us, and then, as if we have all the time in the world, he runs his thumb over my cheek, lifts my chin. My eyelids flutter closed. But he doesn't kiss me. His hands caress the line of my throat before sliding to my shoulders. Every movement sends sparks through me. And though I can't help appreciate the skillfulness of his touch, I don't let myself melt. Not yet.

"Be still," I say, grabbing his hands, and placing them at my waist. Even there, resting lightly at my sides, his fingertips makes me shiver.

Starting at his collar, I trace his tattoos, ever so slowly, up, up, up. My hands are in his hair, delighting in the feel of it slipping through my fingers, silky and coarse at the same time. I follow the tattoos back down. I could keep touching him forever, but his slow smile indicates that he's not going to just stand there while I do it.

He leans in, and his lips capture mine.

It's nothing like the times before. Not gentle, not questioning. Just passionate. I'm pinned against the door, and he's devouring me.

At some point, my knees give out—it's been a very

long day and night—and he guides me to the cot. We don't stop kissing, even when the springs protest loudly. I can't get enough of him.

"Araby!" my mother calls. We hear the door creaking open and we break apart, but it's not enough to hide what we've been doing. She stands on the threshold, scandalized, her hand covering her mouth. She steps back, as if she might faint, and though she's had a terrible night, I can't help smiling—even knowing that I should be embarrassed, because she has to see that though I'm still wearing what's left of my dress, I've halfway unbuttoned his shirt.

Even now, his face red, he has to pull his hand back to stop an inadvertent caress. If she hadn't interrupted, I'm not sure we would've been able to stop.

"It isn't proper for you to be alone in here," she says. I'm not sure what she thinks I was doing, all those nights at the Debauchery Club. I wasn't kissing boys, but I could have been. Still, she is my mother, so I don't argue. Will and I follow her back out to the deck.

Now that the passion has faded to a bearable level, I can't help thinking of April. She wanted this for me. Encouraged it.

But April will never kiss a boy again. Not the ephemeral boys she used to meet at the club, or Kent with his glasses and messy hair. I hug myself and look down, realizing with surprise that we're over the city. Approaching the cathedral.

"Ladder drop in just a few moments," Kent calls. "Araby, you know where the keys are. Mina will go with you. The two of you are lightest."

"And neither of them is afraid of heights," Will says bitterly. Kent ignores him.

The cathedral has lost none of its grandeur and very little of its dark menace, even in the daylight.

"Be careful," I tell Mina once we're on the ground. "I shot a gun up into the ceiling, so the structure may be damaged. And there are bats."

"Bats?" Her hand goes immediately to her hair. It reminds me too much of April, and I turn away for a moment.

Inside, the smell is horrifying. I forgot that several men were killed during Malcontent and Prospero's fight. Mina gags as we move past the bodies, to the chapel where I hid the keys.

At first I'm afraid they're gone, but then I see the glint of gold. I point them out to Mina.

"How're you going to get up there?" she asks. I study the wall below the gargoyle. The stonework in this building is ornate; maybe I can climb it.

"Give me a boost."

It's difficult to find firm places to hold, but I slowly feel my way upward, using fissures in the ancient stone.

The key ring is looped over the gargoyle's snout and ear. I grab it and slip it over my wrist like a bracelet. I'm bracing myself for the treacherous climb down when something crashes in the nave of the cathedral.

Below, Mina curses. The sound of hundreds of wings thunders above us.

"Get out," I call to Mina, but she shakes her head.

"Not without you."

I slide down, having trouble finding my handholds. I hit the stone floor hard. The key ring is around my wrist, and I have Mina's trembling arm, dragging her toward safety. The keys jingle loudly. Whatever caused the crash, I don't want to know.

Outside, the sky is dark with bats flying up and around the airship. Kent drops the rope ladder. We will have to climb up through them.

I steel myself and start up.

As I reach from one rung to the next, all the wounds I've accumulated begin to throb. Halfway up, a bat flies straight toward me and I shriek, ducking my head. Its wings brush my hair, but I keep going. And then I'm at the ship, and Will has me in his arms.

"With this wind we'll be over the swamp in an hour," Kent says after we pull up Mina. "Better bandage up whatever needs bandaging."

We stand at the prow of the ship, watching the terrain beneath us devolve into swampland.

"There it is!" Elise exclaims as the manor house comes into view.

At the edge of the swamp we see a few steam carriages,

but we have no way to know who they belong to. "We don't want Elliott here, playing the hero for the people," Kent says. "But I hope those are his men. There aren't enough of us to fight Malcontent's army."

The swamp is like the sea, huge and undulating, making the manor house look tiny. "We'll take the ship down and tie her to the chimneys again," Kent says. And he and Will do so, quickly, anchoring it to the roof like they did before.

As we approach the hole in the roof, a crocodile splashes below, but I ignore it. We have more to fear from Malcontent's fanatics than from hungry predators.

"Wait here," Kent tells Mother and the children. "Stay in the interior cabin." He's holding two lanterns and a gun for each of us. He hands one of each to me, along with the keys.

Once again I find myself clasping Will's hand. Kent pushes the first door open. The room is filled from floor to ceiling with clockwork. I've never seen so many gears, so many different types of metal; it covers every bit of the wall.

Each door on the north side of the house hides a similarly amazing array of fitted cogs. Kent opens all of them and examines the machines.

"Amazing," he says. "Simply amazing. But something is missing." He goes back down the corridor, taking a paper from his pocket and studying it.

"The controls must be on the floor below."

"Isn't that floor flooded?" Will asks.

"Only partially. I'll start the fire on this level to produce the necessary steam. You two go below and find two levers that look like this." He shows Will a diagram. "Make sure they are in this position. Then insert the keys." He looks to be sure I still have the key ring. "Turn them at the same time."

Muskets fire from outside the house.

But we can't stop or turn back now. We have to set this thing in motion.

The floor below is more than partially flooded. Will and I stop at a gently sloping grand staircase that twists and turns and disappears into the dirty water below. I hold up my lantern, only to see it reflected by dozens of glowing disks.

Crocodile eyes.

"Be careful," Will says quietly. "They may lay their eggs inside, which would make them especially aggressive."

We hear more shooting outside the house, and then a soft splash. One of the reptiles swims very slowly toward the staircase.

"The levers are over there," Will says, pointing. I tear my eyes away from the rippling water below.

The room was once dominated by the gracious staircase we are standing on. It's a tall room, and even with the water covering the floor, the ceiling is high. A metal beam stretches from about midway up the staircase to a decorative balcony across the room, where the levers and a great wheel are. It must be the remains of the scaffolding used by the scientists who built this device. The rest has fallen into the water below.

"We'll have to climb across and turn it on," Will says. "The scientists who built this thing must have had a platform suspended below the beam, but it's long gone."

I look at the beam and then, slowly, to the water below.

"We'll scoot across," Will says. "It won't be so hard."

But he's only saying that to make me feel better. It's going to be terrible. The light of one lantern is not enough in this place.

I hold tight to the lantern, and my palm is sweaty. A crocodile has climbed two steps up the grand staircase. I reach for my gun.

"Wait," Will says. "We don't want to disturb the rest of them."

"I want to shoot them all," I say.

"You could go upstairs and help Kent," Will suggests. "Give me a turn to play hero?"

I shake my head. "I'm not leaving you alone."

He kisses me quickly and then lifts me up onto the beam. I set the lantern before me and hesitate for a moment. It's too close to the ceiling to stand, and almost too narrow for crawling. We'll have to slide.

Halfway across the beam, the pistol that Kent gave Will falls out of his pocket and splashes into the water below.

The crocodiles dive after it from every direction, and the water churns. The splashing and gurgling are bad enough, but in the half light of the lantern I can also see the gleam of their teeth, the glow of their eyes.

I freeze, gripping the metal beam with all my might. Will wraps both arms around me. I feel his heart beating, and I borrow courage from him.

"Will?" Kent is standing at the top of the stairs, holding his lantern high. "The fire is going strong. Those levers must be pulled *now*."

The light of his lantern wavers, casting shadows, and I'm not sure at first that the shape I see is real. Until it's lunging toward Kent.

"Behind you!" I cry, but he must have sensed the movement. He throws himself to the side. The assailant raises something and brings it down, crashing, over Kent's head. At the sounds of the scuffle, the big crocodile lounging at the bottom of the stairway raises its head.

For a moment Kent seems to be getting the upper hand, but the attacker is pounding him over and over. It's Malcontent. He isn't wearing his dark robes, but the hulking shape and nearly graceful movements give him away.

"I'll pull the levers," I say. "Take the gun. Help him."

Kent pushes the reverend back, and his red scarf falls to the water, where a crocodile bites into it, shaking it back and forth in the water.

Will takes the gun as the big crocodile noses up the steps. I tear my eyes away from all of it. I have my job. I'll let them do theirs. I scramble to the end of the beam.

I hear a gunshot, and the crocodiles below me are moving. Afraid? Or angry? I lean toward the levers from the edge of the beam, as far as I can without falling into the water.

I grasp the first one and pull it up. The second is stuck, but I yank hard and it finally moves. I shove the keys in and use both hands to turn them. The great wheel begins to turn with a loud grinding sound, and the water ripples.

Craning to look over my shoulder, I see Will, nearly across the beam, holding the gun in front of him. The other two figures have disappeared, but the crocodiles seem very interested in the area they vacated. Will must have shot someone.

The water below us is rising, and with it the crocodiles that couldn't clamber onto the stairway before. I scoot quickly to where Will is waiting. Several crocodiles are just a few steps under where we'll have to step off.

"You go first," he says. "If they snap at you, I'll shoot."

"Then how will you get past them?"

"I'll figure something out."

The water is rising too quickly.

"Jump off and run! Now, Araby! You have to trust me." And I do, so I leap.

My feet hit marble, and I jump over a snapping

crocodile to a higher step, finding my footing and turning to see that Will is trapped. If he does the same thing
I did, the big crocodile will tear into him.

I scream for help, even though I don't know right
now if Kent is alive. Will still has our lantern, and with
the churning of the water wheel, I'm unable to tell if
anything is approaching me, if my screams are drawing
more predators.

Suddenly Elliott is beside me, lighting a match. He
rips something from the top of a vial with his teeth,
lights it, and tosses it into the water.

Fire blazes across the surface. The creatures in the
water dive away.

"It won't last long," Elliott says. "We don't want to
burn down the entire structure." As I pull away from
him, Will joins us, and we limp down the corridor, away
from the rising water and the crocodiles.

Through the open doors on the next floor, we see the
clockwork parts turning. Great wooden wheels move the
water. Smaller ones control its flow, sending it through
huge barrels.

Kent is alive. He's wearing his goggles and kneeling in
the corner of the room. We all rush to him.

"Where are you hurt?" Elliott asks over and over.

"I think a rib or two are broken," he says. "And one of
the crocodiles took a nip at my leg. It's lucky that Will
took that shot."

His eyes slide over, and we all turn to see Malcontent

sprawled on the floor. He's holding a blood-soaked pillowcase to his shoulder. He's bloodied and only half conscious. He opens his eyes as Elliott stares down at him.

"We're going to take you back to the city," Elliott says. "And you will answer for your crimes."

"I'd expect no less from you," Malcontent says, his inexplicable hatred for Elliott burning in his eyes. "But just try to leave this house alive."

Elliott raises his eyebrows but doesn't respond. Will walks over and ties up Malcontent, giving the wound a cursory glance. Then the rest of us turn to look at the machinery.

"Does this thing really work?" I ask Kent. "Can we cleanse the water? Can we save the city from the plague?"

"I don't know. The men who built it didn't even know. Prospero killed them before they could test it. It's tragic to build something so magnificent and never even discover if it worked."

Elliott lights a cigarette. "Almost as tragic as taking over a city and then having it pulled out from under you with an election." His face is impassive, but he says the word "election" like it is a curse.

Kent looks up. His face is badly bruised where Malcontent hit him.

"How did you get here so quickly?"

"You mean just in time? I didn't come to tarnish your attempt at heroism." It would be hard to miss Elliott's sarcasm. "But I didn't want to miss out on any fun."

With the machine running, we collect ourselves and limp back to the roof. When we emerge, there is an eerie silence, broken only by the splashing of the water and the grinding of machinery.

We take two steps, and then a gunshot rings out. "The Hunter," I breathe. Of course Malcontent would bring his most deadly soldier.

Elliott looks at his father, who smiles from his place in Will's grasp. "The Hunter never misses."

"He did once," Elliott murmurs. And he walks across the roof as if there is no danger.

"No!" I scream. But Elliott no longer cares what I say. He scans the swamp with one hand shading his eyes. Another shot rings out. I gasp, but Elliott is still standing.

A boy stands waist-deep in the water of the swamp, holding a gun.

"Is that Thom?" I ask.

Will nods.

Thom points to a man who floats facedown. "Please send someone to fetch the body, and me, before the crocodiles come," Thom requests politely. "I hope you'll accept this as my apology for letting him go the last time we were all here."

Luckily the crocodiles are wary, avoiding the churning water around the house. Elliott's men hoist Thom into their boat.

He climbs up the side of the house where the interior stairway was once exposed, easily scaling the sections that Kent tried to make impassable with his ax.

"Thank you," Elliott says. "You've done a great service—"

"I did it for Will," the boy says. "He saved my life. Took the blame for me. And for Miss April, because she was kind to me."

"Fair enough," Elliott says, ignoring the fact that *he* was the one who posed a threat to Thom.

Below us, windows shatter and crocodiles swarm out of the lower levels of the house. The manor seems likely to fall to ruin, destroyed by the machine within. We are falling to ruin as well—gashed, tattered, burned. Will wraps his arms around me.

Elliott looks over at us. "I'll be a good leader, Araby. Better than the others."

"A benevolent one?" I ask.

"Doubtful," Elliott says. "One who gets things done."

"I hope so." Kent heads to the ship. "Would you like to go back to the city in style?"

For a moment Elliott seems ready to take us up on it, but he shakes his head. "I'll stay with my men. We'll need to organize patrols. Clear out the bodies of the dead crocodiles before they block the water wheel. And I'm going back to the palace for April. I won't leave her body in that place."

"We can take him," I gesture to Malcontent.

"Oh, I think he'll stay with me," Elliott says. He prods his father with his boot. "The reverend will answer for his crimes. As will your father."

Will goes with Kent toward the airship, but I'm unable to walk away from Elliott yet. I want to scream at him. I want to hurt him. More than I already have. He's going to punish me for what I've done to him. I can see it in the tilt of his head, the coldness of his eyes.

"Let's not forget that we still need each other," I say.

He slumps against the chimney, and though he kicks at his father again, the movement is desultory. I turn away and climb the steps onto the deck of the airship.

Kent lifts off, and it seems that everyone needs Will. First he's being attacked and kissed and hugged by Elise and Henry. Then he's applying salve to the slash across Kent's face.

"A physician is a respectable profession, with some training," my mother says to no one in particular as she watches Will patch everyone up. The seams of Will's shirt come apart a little more as he dabs at Kent's forehead.

"Araby." Mina's eyes are huge. "I . . . think there are more tattoos."

So much for respectability.

My mother seems ready to say something else, but my attention is on Will. The way he moves. The way he scans the deck, making sure Henry and Elise are safe. The way it feels when his eyes catch mine and his attention is focused completely, for a few moments at least, on me.

"You were amazing—"

"What about you, with the heights?" My voice is teasing, and his mouth turns up in the corners.

"We make a good team."

CHAPTER
TWENTY-FOUR

I**T IS RAINING AGAIN, AND THE CITY SMELLS OF** dead leaves. Will holds a black umbrella over me. Henry and Elise stand close to my mother to avoid the downpour.

In front of us stand three statues, weeping angels holding out their hands in supplication.

"She will be missed," Elliott intones, and he shuts the book that he was reading from, pushing wet blond hair from his eyes.

The cemetery is filled with black dresses beneath white masks. It's the first time I've been to a funeral in years. The first time we've had the luxury to bury our dead.

Cold water washes over the ankles of my boots. It is a fitting day to bury April. I waver a bit, too miserable to cry, and Will holds me tight. Thom, our newest hero, rearranges flowers and then settles beside the grave, his head bowed.

But the rainwater running through the streets is clean. Already the swamp has receded a few feet.

Elliott postponed the election, but he's going to have it—even though he's unopposed. Will now prints a newspaper, reporting on Elliott's every move. Kent is making plans to leave the city, though at the moment Elliott has requisitioned the airship to bring food to the populace. It's a daunting task.

Father is still in Elliott's custody, and when he goes outside escorted by his guards, people yell obscenities. But he's alive. My father is a murderer. But so am I. The magnitude of what he's done hits me sometimes. And then I think that maybe Elliott is right to seek retribution.

At least I've had a chance to tell Father that I love him, and soon I may be able to tell him that I forgive him. He's helping to produce the white-powder vaccine and mixing it with the water supply. New cases of the Weeping Sickness are almost unheard of. No one has died of the Red Death in days. People still wear masks, but eventually we may not have to.

I go to the Debauchery Club every day, to beg Elliott to release my father. Most days he won't see me. Sometimes he speaks as if we are friends, but on those days, when I finally bring myself to mention Father, his eyes go frosty.

Perhaps it would be different if April were alive. I don't know.

By the time we leave the cemetery, the rain has stopped. Everything is still wet, but the sun is shining now.

We pass over a low bridge, and I rest my hands on the stone rail, listening to the unfamiliar sound of childish laughter. In the green space between two buildings, a group of boys is kicking a ball back and forth. Laughing. Henry watches them with interest.

"You can cry," Will says. "She . . . would want you to wail. Loudly and dramatically."

And something opens up inside me, because he's right. She would want dramatics.

"I wish she could see this." I gesture past the children playing, to a new hat store that has opened down the street. Imagine a store that sells only hats. With sequins and feathers.

I cry for a long time, and Will holds me.

The children are with us, silent and still. I know this must be hard for them, and yet I draw comfort from them being here. Elise takes one of my hands and Henry takes the other.

"I miss her," I say into Will's shirt.

"I know."

I wipe my eyes. The river runs bluish gray through the center of the city, and even though the rain just cleared, crews are already hammering at burned-out buildings.

Perhaps tomorrow Elliott will listen when I beg him for my father's freedom.

"Could we go talk to them?" Henry asks. "To play for a little while?"

Will grumbles a little as Henry pulls him toward the boys.

Henry is glowing with anticipation, but when one of the boys kicks the ball too far, it's Elise who retrieves it. She hands it back to him, and he smiles at her shyly. Will's eyebrows go up.

Two of the boys wave at me. I helped their mother move their belongings to a new apartment last week. My status as hero has earned me some responsibility, helping to reunite families, particularly children who were lost.

"We shouldn't stay . . . ," Will begins. He's bothered by my mother's continuing disapproval of him, and it's getting late, but I shake my head. The children have been absorbed by the group. The boys gather around Elise to show her how to kick, but she's a natural and doesn't need much instruction. Henry is laughing with the younger children. A bit of parchment is half buried in the dirt at the edge of the field. I pick it up, half expecting an indictment of my father, but it's merely . . . an invitation to a party? Not a sumptuous masquerade ball. A child's birthday party.

When is Henry's birthday? I wonder. And Elise's? Perhaps this year I will even celebrate my own. And Finn's. April would approve.

I wipe away the last of my tears and settle into Will, watching the children play.

"Is your birthday coming up?" I ask him. "Maybe we could throw a party."